Weirdbook

VOL. 2, NO. 8 **ISSUE 38**

Features

From the Editor's Tower, by Doug Draa. 2

Stories

HARLOT ROAD, by Michael Bracken 3
WITH A POET'S EYES, by John C. Hocking 15
THE WISHING WELL, by Robert Graves 25
O KING OF PAIN AND SPLENDOR!, by Darrell Schweitzer. 28
YOU'D DO IT FOR DIAMONDS, by Adrian Cole 43
DREADFUL APPETITE, by Franklyn Searight 64
THE HANDMAID OF THE KEY, by R.C. Mulhare 80
BLUE MOON, by Allen Mark Price 88
SHE WHO GIVES LIFE, by C. I. Kemp 96
AN IMPLEMENT OF ICE, by W. H. Pugmire 98
NIGHT OF THE CIRCUS, by Sharon Cullars 104
WOLVERS HILL, by Tim Jeffreys 111
RAFTS, by Lorenzo Crescentini. 121
CLEAN SWEEP, by Edward Ahern 124
LEAVING MALAGA, by Cynthia Ward 133
CATTLE CALL, by Gregg Chamberlain 142
ABOMINATION IS HER NAME, by J.N. Cameron 145
KACHINA, by Kenneth Bykerk. 152
FLAT IS FLAT AND THAT IS THAT, by David J. Gibbs 168
DEATH IS NOT MY MASTER, by Scott Harper. 179

Poetry

THE OLD ROCK, by Russ Parkhurst. 87
SLEEPING WITH MAD SHADOWS, by Frederick J. Mayer 130
THE LIQUID PROFESSOR, by Jeff Barnes 144
THE TOAD STOOL PEOPLE, by Chad Hensley. 177
THE PROMISE OF A POLIDORI SORE THROAT, by Clay F. Johnson . . 186
THIS HUNGRY EARTH, by S.L. Edwards. 188

Artwork

Alexandra Petruk . . . . Front Cover
Allen Koszowski. . . . . Interior Artwork

From the Editor's Tower

It's a new year, and that means a new issue of *Weirdbook*!

I truly hope that 2018 has started out as well for all of you as it has for *Weirdbook*.

I'm very excited about this issue. Darrell Schweitzer returns us to the world of *Mask of the Sorcerer* with new Sekenre story. Adrian Cole gives us another thrilling adverture starring his British Fantasy Award-winning private detective, Nick Nightmare. We also have a brand spanking new (Derlethian) Mythos tale from the esteemed Wilum H. Pugmire! Another *Weirdbook* first is a wonderful fantasy adventure from none other than Mr. John C. Hocking himself! I could go on and on. Cynthia Ward, Sharon Cullars, and R. C. Mulhare are along with stories of the weird that will leave lasting impressions on the readers.

And never forget, *Weirdbook* isn't always about stories with good taste. Weirdbook is *always* about stories that taste good!

Enjoy!

—Doug Draa

Staff

**PUBLISHER &
EXECUTIVE EDITOR**

*John Gregory
Betancourt*

EDITOR

Doug Draa

**CONSULTING
EDITOR**

W. Paul Ganley

**WILDSIDE PRESS
SUBSCRIPTION
SERVICES**

Carla Coupe

PRODUCTION TEAM

*Steve Coupe
Sam Cooper
Shawn Garrett
Helen McGee
Karl Würf*

HARLOT ROAD
by Michael Bracken

The King's Guard came before dawn, rousting us from our beds and not allowing us to gather our belongings or even to change from our sleep-wear before driving us into the cobblestone street of Harlot Road. A quarter moon hung low in the night sky, mostly hidden behind fast-moving storm clouds headed south, and the only real light came from lanterns carried by the soldiers.

"We need thirty for the mining camp in Dragon's Maw," the commandant shouted. "Volunteer or be chosen."

A few women stepped forward—young girls who had never worked the mining camps, old women who had no other options—but not enough of us. The commandant pointed his sword and shouted. "You. You. And you."

I huddled in the middle of the pack next to Gwyneth, an amply en-dowed woman from one of the communal shacks at the end of the street near the privy house who charged less and serviced more men in an eve-ning than ever I did. Hunched over so that my height would not draw the commandant's attention, I waited until Gwyneth and twenty-nine other women had been chosen and herded into a trio of ox-drawn carts for the daylong trip to Dragon's Maw.

Then I returned to my bedroom and sat in the dark with my arms wrapped around my knees until the blazing morning sun replaced the night's quarter moon and my room glowed from the light filtering through the parchment covering the full-length opening in the outer wall where each evening I displayed my wares to passersby.

A light tapping on my door, barely loud enough to be heard above the street sounds on the other side of the parchment, caught my attention. I swung my legs off the bed and faced the door.

"Enter."

The door scraped open and Zelle pushed her oval face through the widening gap. She held a tray containing my breakfast—herbal tea, warm biscuits with jam, and a single hardboiled egg. Less than a month earlier her parents, dirt farmers from north of the city, had apprenticed her to me, presenting me with the meager dowry they would have given her husband had she married before first blood. She was pretty enough, though beauty alone would never compensate for a lack of marketable skills, and she was smart enough, though uneducated and with limited social grace. She slept in the attic and had not been discovered by the soldiers.

After she served my breakfast, Zelle asked about the early morning activity in the street, and I told her the King's Guard had recruited women to service the conscripted miners at Dragon's Maw.

"Recruited?" my apprentice asked. "That's not what it looked like from my window."

"You should not have gone near your window," I chided. "Had the soldiers seen you, they would have come for you."

The young woman's eyes widened and her hand flew to her chest. Though she had yet to know a man, she understood how I provided for the two of us. "But I've not—"

"Thirty for three hundred and only one night to serve them all before the long journey home," I said. The women would spend the day in the ox-drawn carts climbing the mountain to the mining camp at Dragon's Maw, a night and a day bedding the miners, and another night returning. "Some will service more than their share and all will be far too tired upon return to service even the impotent vicar who merely wishes to clasp hands and pray for our souls."

"Two evenings without income?" my apprentice asked.

"They'll be paid scale for their services at the mining camp—the guild will see to that—but I've no desire to work so hard for so little." Had I been willing to work for scale, I would not have been able to take an apprentice. "Tonight we shall take advantage of the situation."

We cleaned my room and changed the bedclothes that morning. Late that afternoon I bathed and slipped into my most seductive gown before opening the parchment so that I could flirt with passersby. During the course of the evening, I entertained several men despite charging a premium for my services, and I fell into a deep slumber after my last visitor decamped.

* * * *

I awoke sometime later to the sound of heavy breathing, and I slowly scanned the darkness of my room until I saw the shape of a man silhouetted against the moonlit parchment covering the wall opening. I kept a dagger on my nightstand to ensure that no man would ever take from me what I had the power to sell, and I quietly took it into my fist.

I whispered harshly, "Who are you and why are you here?"

The silhouette jerked with surprise. Came the whispered response, "Forgive me."

Somewhere in the distance, men shouted.

"The King's Guard is after me and your door was unlatched."

For that oversight I would reprimand my new apprentice.

I dared not burn a candle, so I led him though my darkened row house with little more than the moonlight shining through the parchment window covers to guide us. Once in the kitchen, I slid aside a hidden panel and hustled my nocturnal visitor up a narrow staircase into the attic with my apprentice. I admonished Zelle to maintain her silence and returned to the kitchen.

I had just pressed the hidden panel into place when soldiers pounded on my door, forced their way into my row house with their lanterns held high, and searched the three rooms of my home.

"What do you seek at such an hour?" I demanded.

"A sneak thief," one of the soldiers spat.

"What's he taken?"

"The King's jewels!"

The soldiers moved on to the next residence having never discovered the man they sought nor the staircase that led up to where he hid. When the soldiers finished with my neighbors and the sounds of shouts died down as the men moved on to the next block, I slid open the panel and ascended the stairs to Zelle's attic room. She sat alone on her straw-stuffed mattress.

"Where is he?"

"Gone." She pointed to the parchment covering the small window at the rear, which had been peeled aside and not properly reaffixed.

I crossed the attic, pushed back the parchment, and looked down upon the small courtyard behind the kitchen. A daring man could have dropped from the window to the courtyard and escaped into the alley behind the row houses of Harlot Road. Then I looked up. An acrobatic man could have swung out, grabbed the eave, levered himself onto the roof, and run along the rooftops to the end of the block. Either way, the sneak thief had escaped the soldiers and was no longer a matter of my concern. I pulled my head inside and fastened the parchment into place.

When I turned back, Zelle held out her hand and said, "He gave me this and said it was for you."

A silver sovereign lay upon her upraised palm.

* * * *

The following morning Harlot Road was empty save for Abigail and Hazel, two elderly women in tattered clothing who kept the cobblestone street swept in exchange for scraps from the residents. For a half-sovereign each fortnight, they also attended to my stoop. Because they knew all the gossip along Harlot Road, I asked about the previous night's disturbance. They told me what I already knew—that the King's jewels had been stolen—so I asked, "And what of the thief?"

"He disappeared into the night," said Hazel.

"Good for him, I say," added Abigail, who had no love for the crown following her husband's death during a brief peasants' uprising several years before my birth that had led to the establishment of the guilds.

As my neighbors awoke—those who remained after thirty had been dragooned into servicing the miners at Dragon's Maw—the talk was of little else but the night's excitement.

When I realized I would learn nothing I did not already know, I set Zelle to work laundering my bedclothes in preparation for another busy evening.

* * * *

The next several days passed without incident. The thirty women returned from Dragon's Maw, exhausted from both the trip and their mandatory service. The younger women swore they would never again volunteer for such duty, but many of the older women carried purses fatter than they would have been had the women remained home. Still, they complained. They had serviced more soldiers than miners and had been short-paid because of it.

These things I discussed with Zelle, teaching her the value of supply and demand, but more importantly, teaching her how the crown could manipulate the value of anything by conscripting workers for cheap labor, by taxing goods and services, by driving prices up, by hoarding supplies or driving prices down, by flooding the market with supplies previously hoarded, and by taking for the crown any goods or services for which they did not wish to pay. Her lessons continued each market day as we haggled for our meat, eggs, vegetables, soaps, perfumes, and other necessary household and business supplies.

Rumors spread throughout the city about events beyond our ken, the information brought to the marketplace by farmers and merchants from outlying villages and spread in hushed tones by the housewives and harlots who frequented their stalls. Soldiers were becoming more aggressive, paying for goods with promissory notes that were worth less than the parchment upon which they were written, when they bothered to pay at all. Those who protested were quickly dissuaded by threats of injury or worse.

The presence of soldiers in the marketplace increased as well, as if we needed policing, and my neighbors reported nocturnal visits from soldiers who offered no compensation for their services.

The unfamiliar faces of the men in uniform encouraged me to keep Zelle close to my side at all times, especially so after I spotted a trio of drunken soldiers eyeing her from a table outside the mead merchant's stall.

In the market several days after the King's Guard had rousted the residents of Harlot Road on two consecutive nights, a well-dressed gentleman stopped me and said, "You dropped this."

He pressed a silver sovereign into my palm and my fingers closed around it even though I surely had dropped no such thing.

I said, "You are mistaken."

"I've made no mistake," he said, and then he leaned forward. When he whispered in my ear so softly even Zelle standing on the other side of me could not hear him speak, I recognized the voice of my nocturnal visitor from a fortnight earlier. "I owe you far more than this."

My eyes must have widened in surprise but I did my best to keep my voice level. I was no actress, but I often acted as if the men who visited me were the greatest lovers on earth when even the best of them were no better than rutting dogs. If I could so easily simulate pleasure, I could just as easily mask surprise.

"Perhaps," I said thoughtfully, "perhaps you are correct." I opened my purse and dropped the sovereign in with the other coins. "I thank you for your honesty."

He continued, "Might I enjoy a few additional minutes of your time?"

"You know what I am and where to find me," I said, certain that neither of us meant what those around us thought they were hearing.

"This evening, then," he said, "and I will expect your undivided attention."

"That you shall have, kind sir," I promised with a salacious wink. "Each of my visitors does."

As the sneak thief disappeared into the crowd of shoppers, Zelle said, "You did not drop that coin."

She had not heard what the man whispered in my ear and I dared not tell her who he was with so many of the crown's ears surrounding us.

"Hush," I commanded. "Who are we to cast aspersions upon such a gentleman's honesty?"

My apprentice stared at me wide-eyed but said nothing further about the incident until we returned to the privacy of my home. As she unloaded our shopping basket, Zelle asked, "Why would that man give you a sovereign that clearly was not yours?"

"Did you not recognize the gentleman who pressed a similar sovereign into your palm a fortnight ago?"

"I fear not, mistress," she said. "In the dark I saw not his face, and his whisper as he presented the sovereign sounded nothing like the voice of the man in the market."

* * * *

That evening, following sunset and two visitors who fattened my coin purse appropriately for the special services I provided, the sneak thief appeared at my front step. When Zelle opened the door upon his knock, he strode in as an invited guest and settled himself at the kitchen table. Zelle served him a tankard of dark brown ale, and he waited while I rinsed my mouth and doused myself with perfume to mask the sweaty stench of my previous visitor.

I knew the man had not come to sample my wares, so I joined him at the kitchen table and had Zelle prepare a tankard of ale for my pleasure. Then I sent her to the attic room so my guest and I might speak in private.

Once we were alone, Corliss introduced himself.

"If you stole the King's jewels," I asked, "why have you not put a thousand leagues behind you?"

Corliss laughed. "The King has no jewels to steal," he explained. "And were I to thrust my hand deep into his codpiece, I fear I still would find no jewels."

Surprised, I asked, "How can that be?"

"The crown has neither the economic power nor the will to govern. The king's half-brother controls the military and with it commands the fate of the kingdom. That's something we intend to change."

"We?"

My tablemate described a cadre of men determined to overthrow the crown and place the power of governance in the hands of the people. The last time the oppressed had attempted to wrest power from the crown, the reigning king had placated the rebellion's financial backers with the creation of the guilds—loose confederations of like-minded business people who set minimum prices for goods and services but held no real power.

"Men?" I questioned. "Oh, they'll wave their trouser swords at one another for a bit and then they'll grow limp and nothing will change."

"That may well be true," he admitted, "but I think not."

We had spoken of many things, but not the reason for his visit. "So, why have you come to me?"

"I need to send a message to the miners at Dragon's Maw, but there's no way past the soldiers who guard the camp." He paused. "Except—"

Corliss let his sentence hang in the air but I refused to complete it for him.

He took a long drink from his tankard and wiped his mouth with the back of his hand before continuing. "A fortnight from now soldiers will conscript another thirty harlots to service the miners at Dragon's Maw," he said. "I need to send a message with one of them."

"Why bring this to me?"

"You could have turned me out when you found me in your bedchambers, but you did not. Why not?"

"I've no love for the crown," I said. I kept a dagger at my beside to prevent men from taking from me that which I did not wish to give, but I had no such power against the crown. "What the crown takes I do not provide willingly."

"Many share your views," he said. "We've no voice, and the guilds have proven of little value."

"And what difference is it to me?"

"When the people make the decisions, all will benefit."

"Promises are like smoke, blown away by a strong breeze of change."

"If you'll not do this for the good of the people, then what will convince you?"

I named my price.

"I can assure you of payment after the revolution," he assured me. "The mine at Dragon's Maw is the source of the military's wealth. We will control the mine, and by controlling the mine we will control the money."

"And if the revolution fails?"

"It will not fail."

"So, you are telling me your purse is as empty as the king's codpiece."

Corliss smiled and sipped from his tankard of ale, perhaps expecting his masculine charm to convince me to aid the revolutionaries.

Instead, I said nothing.

Finally, he said, "Half in advance. Half upon your safe return from the mining camp."

"Agreed," I said. "Now, what is it you expect of me?"

* * * *

The next day, Corliss delivered a purse fat with silver sovereigns, which I hid behind a loose stone in the hearth when next I found myself alone. He spent that afternoon and many subsequent afternoons facing me over the table in my kitchen, ensuring that I memorized a complicated plan for the pending revolution that he refused to commit to writing. The more Corliss explained, the less likely I thought the plan capable of success. He seemed a boy playing at war with other boys rather than a man destined to lead his people to freedom. There were passwords and secret codes and battle strategy that made sense only if the miners were able to surprise and overthrow the garrison incarcerating them at Dragon's Maw. What they needed and did not have was a diversion.

I continued serving my clients each evening as if my decision to aid Corliss had not altered my life, and I continued providing Zelle with lessons in harlotry. I had been teaching her to dress and to speak properly, but lessons about how to use her body remained in the future.

I also made plans for my trip. Knowing that Zelle would be alone for three days while I was away at the mine, I ensured that my apprentice had all that she needed. I gave her explicit instructions not to leave the house during my absence and to never answer the door, not even for my regulars. I also showed her the dagger I kept on my nightstand, certain that she knew how to wield it after having watched her butcher a piglet the way her dirt-farming father had taught her.

* * * *

When next the soldiers rousted the residents of Harlot Road seeking volunteers to service the miners at Dragon's Maw, I was prepared.

Once herded into the street with the others, I dared not volunteer, lest I appear too eager. However, after few volunteers stepped forward, I straightened to my full height. Half a head taller than the surrounding women, I was not easy to miss, and when the commandant pointed his sword and shouted, "You. You. And you." I was one of those selected for the trip.

Then soldiers herded us into a trio of oxcarts, and I was lucky to find myself in the first, eating the dust our oxen kicked up but not the dust of all three oxen teams as the women in the last cart would. I settled into one corner, a small bit of hay beneath my bottom serving as a cushion against the cart's rough journey over the cobblestones of Harlot Road, the rutted path beyond town, and the uneven terrain up the mountainside.

"I'm surprised you were selected."

I turned to find myself facing Gwyneth.

"Always acting superior," she said. "You think you're special, but you're no better than the rest of us."

I said, "We each serve at our appointed time."

Gwyneth stared at me for a moment, unsure what I meant. Then she turned her back and we did not speak again for the entire journey. Some of us watched the road ahead, but I watched the road behind. As we ascended the mountain and the sun rose, I saw the capital city in a way that I could not from within the confines of its narrow streets. The castle dominated the north end and the city spread out to the south of it. The open ground of the marketplace filled a rise near the city center nearly as visible from most anywhere in the city as was the royal family's abode to the north, and it was surrounded by permanent mercantile establishments. Beyond them were stone row houses, and further from the center, clinging to the edge of the city, were wooden hovels barely fit for livestock but home to many of the less fortune.

When we reached the mining camp at Dragon's Maw early that evening, the camp commandant had his pick from among us. He chose amply endowed Gwyneth, taking her into his private quarters and leaving the rest of us for his men to escort to our temporary quarters—rooms barely large enough to contain a straw mattress, a chamber pot, and an oil lamp.

I serviced three soldiers upon my arrival, but did not even feign interest in their rutting. I also met with two miners who came to my temporary quarters. At first I had thought them eager to take advantage of the circumstances in order to perform an act that would have required a significant surcharge had they visited me on Harlot Road, but one of the miners identified himself as the man Corliss had sent me to meet.

"Drop your trousers," I instructed.

"But we're not—"

I repeated my instructions and then sat on the straw mattress between the two men, where I carefully recited the information Corliss had demanded I memorize, repeating myself whenever the attention of either of the miners wavered.

They listened for almost an hour before Gwyneth complained to the commandant that I was not servicing my share of men, and a horse-faced soldier pushed into my temporary quarters to find me with my fists wrapped around the two miners' drilling equipment.

The soldier smiled, ran the miners out of my quarters, and took a turn riding me before relinquishing me to the next man in line. And thus, the night and the following day passed.

* * * *

As we queued up for the ride home, expecting to receive our guild-mandated pay, we realized the paymaster was nowhere to be seen. We asked about his absence.

"Get in the carts!" the commandant shouted.

"We've not been paid."

"And you'll not be."

Perhaps because she had serviced the commandant first upon her arrival and thought that gave her special consideration, Gwyneth approached him to protest. "But the guild—"

"The guild?" The commandant spat. "There are no more guilds! The King has abolished them."

At the insistence of his half-brother, if one were to guess.

Gwyneth straightened her back and glared at his. "You can't—"

The commandant backhanded Gwyneth, sending her to her knees in the dirt. "Anyone else dare challenge me?"

None of us did.

Then the soldiers herded us into the oxcarts. I helped Gwyneth to her feet and used my sleeve to dab at the blood trickling from the corner of her mouth.

"How can they do this to us?"

I dared not tell her of the pending revolution, but I suggested that one day we would need to take matters into our own hands and refuse the crown's oppression.

* * * *

The sun had barely risen as the oxcarts wheeled onto Harlot Road. As tired and frustrated as my companions, I climbed down to the street and made my way home over the uneven cobblestones to find that the front door of my row house stood open, the evidence of forced entry only too apparent. I rushed inside, calling my apprentice's name and hearing no response. All three rooms were trashed, blood stained my bedclothes, and a slash of it painted my bedroom wall. A small pot containing only an un-broken egg graced the cold stove. The hidden panel remained in place and the attic room appeared untouched, but Zelle was not present.

I ran back down the stairs.

Abigail, one of the women who swept the streets each day, caught my arm as I rushed outside. Before I could speak, she whispered, "Zelle's with us."

She led me to their home, a hovel beyond the privy house, where Zelle lay upon a straw mattress, one eye swollen shut and the bruises covering much of her young body only too evident in the dim light when I drew back the tattered cover to examine her.

I demanded to know what had happened.

Zelle, barely able to speak, told of a trio of soldiers who kicked in the front door, caught her in the kitchen boiling an egg for dinner, and dragged her into my bedroom. She told how she had grabbed my dagger and slashed out at their ringleader, and she used the tip of her finger to draw a line from her left eye to the corner of her mouth to indicate where she had cut him. Then the three soldiers had beaten her, had taken turns with her, and had left her.

Not knowing what had already happened, the two street sweepers had seen smoke pouring from the chimney of my supposedly empty row house and had gone to my home to warn Zelle of the danger of announcing her presence within. Arriving too late, they had found my apprentice uncon-scious upon my bed. Abigail and Hazel had taken Zelle home and had tended to her ever since.

There were residents of Harlot Road who would accommodate the violent tastes of men, so there had been no need to violate an untrained young woman. Zelle's financial value had been greatly diminished by the soldiers' actions, but more importantly, they had stolen what should have been hers to sell.

By midday all the residents of Harlot Road knew what had happened to Zelle and knew as well that no justice would be forthcoming were we to report it to the magistrate. He would merely record the incident as a business disagreement, the solution to which was best left to the guilds— which, apparently, no long existed.

* * * *

Corliss arrived a few evenings later. Though she had returned home, Zelle had not yet recovered and remained in her attic room. So, I served him myself when we sat at my kitchen table. He handed me the second half of my payment.

I told him what had happened in my absence and told him I desired justice.

"You seek justice?" he asked. "For a harlot? We have more important concerns."

"Zelle is no harlot."

"As good as, if she's your apprentice," he said. "Besides, the revolution is bigger than one young girl."

If the revolutionaries found no value in one young girl, what hope did we have post-revolution? Corliss did not understand my concerns, and perhaps he never would. I sent him away from my house without further discussion, for I would never beg a man to do what I could do myself.

* * * *

At the market a few days later, after she had recovered enough to accompany me away from the house, Zelle cowered behind my skirts when a trio of the King's Guards passed by. I realized why when I examined the soldiers closely and saw that one had a thin scab bisecting his left cheek.

That afternoon I shared with my Harlot Road neighbors the sovereigns I had received from Corliss, though many refused my offer by insisting that justice would be payment enough for their assistance. During the next fortnight they monitored the activities of the three soldiers who had defiled Zelle, reporting to me through Abigail and Hazel whenever the trio visited Harlot Road or the nearby taverns. I waited and I watched, turning away paying customers on several occasions so that I could observe the soldiers from the parchment-covered windows at either end of Zelle's attic room.

I caught their ringleader alone one evening, drunkenly voiding his bladder in the alley behind my row house while his two companions slept off their debauchery at the communal shack where Gwyneth made her bed. With my dagger in hand, I slipped out the back, across the small courtyard, and through the rear gate into the alley. Boisterously singing a drinking song about maidens young and fair, he did not hear me creep up behind him.

I grabbed a fistful of his hair and jerked his head backward. Before he could mewl in protest, I thrust my dagger into his throat, severing his larynx, and then I dropped him to the cobblestones at our feet.

Zelle helped me drag the dead soldier to the marketplace, where she removed his family jewels before we hung his naked body from the crossbeam of an empty merchant stall at the crest of the rise. Abigail, Hazel, Gwyneth, and the other women from Gwyneth's communal shack sliced the throats of the remaining defilers, dragged their bodies to the marketplace, and dumped them at the feet of their ringleader. We doused the two bodies with lamp oil and set them ablaze to illuminate the dead soldier hanging above them, and then we drifted into the shadows while townspeople awoke to see what we had done.

In seeking justice for Zelle, our assassination of three of the King's Guards on Harlot Road had created the diversion Corliss and his compatriots sought. So, using the passwords and secret codes the sneak thief had made me memorize, I sent word to the men in the mining camp at Dragon's Maw.

Whether they were ready or not, the revolution had begun.

WITH A POET'S EYES
by John C. Hocking

The grounds of Lord Kelsh's mansion were enclosed by a tall, ivied wall. The single gate opened on the poet's lavish gardens, where he was said to take moonlit walks while musing over life's profundities and otherwise behaving as poets are wont to do.

Lucella was angry for a number of reasons. Primarily because although our employer, the Princess Eurythenia, had given me the key to the gate, I had forgotten it in my chambers, half the city away. But also because the garden gate was surrounded by several women, mostly young and mostly clad in black, loudly weeping and lamenting the disappearance, and widely supposed self-exile or even death, of Lord Kelsh.

The wall, while imposing, was not meant to repel a determined climber. Given that Lucella was wearing her Legion cuirass and I just my robes, and admittedly weighing in my forgetfulness where the key was concerned, I took on the task of climbing the wall. This was an embarrassing and sweaty job in the afternoon sun, and made considerably worse by the reaction of the mourning women in the street below, who hooted and wailed, threatened to call the city guard, and demanded to know who I was to violate the sanctum of their beloved poet hero.

The heavy ivy was sticky on my hands, but thick and sturdy enough to make the climb fairly easy once I began. I stopped at the top, straddling the wall, and took a breath. The complaints from below had ceased and I imagined that Lucella had stern words with the women, perhaps telling them we were emissaries of royalty or simply that she would commence kicking them if they didn't shut up, but probably a combination of both. I could see a distance over the rooftops. Lord Kelsh's home was on the fringe of The Tiers, where much of the nobility lived, so there were mansions great and small, many trees and elegant gardens. The sky was clear overhead, but I could see a rim of dark clouds on the horizon, blue-black as a bruise.

The door opened readily enough from the inside. Lucella stepped through quickly, tossed back her golden hair, turned and pushed the door closed in the faces of the women without. "If only his eyes had seen me…" one of them wailed. "She enchanted him!" cried another.

"Gods," gasped Lucella. "Are they all mad?" I'd seen her look less distressed after fighting a clutch of bandits.

I laughed, which she didn't like much. "Lord Kelsh is the most widely read poet of modern times," I said. "There hasn't been a poet in Frekore who made a living wage out of it in more than fifty years, and Kelsh earned so much off his poesy that he could afford all this..." I waved an arm at the gardens, verdant and magnificent, and the distinctive mansion that rose above them.

"He earned this by..." Lucella groped for words sufficient to express her astonishment, "...by making rhymes?"

"Well, yes, but the rhymes were primarily overwrought declarations of eternal love, generally beginning with something about the poet's eyes gazing upon the overwhelming beauty of whatever lovely damsel crossed his path that week. Lord Kelsh's eyes figure in most of his poems, and are well known to be very big, very blue and said to enchant every woman who gazes into them."

"Gods, what nonsense. What does Eurythenia care about this fellow?"

The cobblestone path did not head directly toward the house but wended down through a copse of manicured trees where we could hear a rushing sound as of distant wind. We came out of the trees at the base of small waterfall. The path continued around the broad pool that lay at its foot, rimmed with green reeds, and then turned toward the house. As we passed the waterfall it emitted a startlingly loud, gulping splash, throwing fine droplets of water over us, icy cold despite the bright sun.

"Well, Kelsh did write one poem in praise of the Princess. Quite out of his normal style. But honestly, I think our mistress met him at court and was as entranced with his blue eyes as those women at the gate."

"What's so grand about blue eyes? Aren't my eyes blue?" This was a mystery Lucella could not penetrate and it troubled her.

The house was of a somewhat eccentric design, said to be Lord Kelsh's own. It wasn't large in that each of its three floors didn't hold more than four or five rooms each, but it was tall, with lofty ceilings and an open roof with a low, crenellated wall around it like the fortifications of a castle. Kelsh was said to moon around up there, gazing out over the city and writing his fevered poems.

The city guard had been all through the house, of course, and some of the rooms showed their less than delicate attentions. Princess Eurythenia thought Lucella and I might bring a higher level of attention to the task of seeking some clue as to where Lord Kelsh might have gone. We scoured the place from the first floor up, but found nothing, of course.

The second floor was taken up mostly by his bedchambers, including an outsize closet. Lucella was surprised to discover a rack of perhaps a dozen feminine cloaks of the same identical design, lavish silk of a pure shimmering blue. She held one up to show me and, when I told her they were gifts he bestowed upon his lovers and said to be the same color as his eyes, she dropped it on the floor.

The third level was mostly devoted to writing space and a small library. I skirted the almost comically oversized desk, set in front of a broad window, it was scattered with elegant parchments and writing quills as long as your forearm. I scanned the volumes of poetry and was pleased to see a few collections by Laridoro. Lord Kelsh clearly had better taste in what he read than in what he wrote.

Outsized stairs to the roof dominated the floor and as I walked around them I became aware that the area had an odd, close feeling to it. We looked around but there was nothing to see, and finally went up onto the roof. The view was spectacular.

We lounged around for a while, leaning on the parapet, looking out over the treetops, drinking strong wine that Lucella had brought in a belt flask, and putting off searching the gardens. The dark clouds I'd noted earlier were drawing near, so we resolved to begin the task despite having no expectation of accomplishing anything beyond returning to our mistress able to truthfully tell her that we had performed our due diligence without result.

"Who's that?" Lucella pointed. I looked where she indicated and saw nothing.

"What?"

"A woman. There, by the waterfall." I didn't see anyone and said so.

"She's gone. I think she might have leapt into the pool."

"Are you sure?" I shouldn't have asked that and regretted it immediately.

"Yes," she said, biting the word off.

"Well, let's go ask her what she's doing here."

We made our way back down through the tower, and I felt a certain envy for the poet. The place really was a scholar's paradise, a comfortable retreat from the world. One could get a lot of work done in a place like that.

The gray rim of clouds moved ponderously overhead, dimming the sun, and a cool wind rushed over the gardens. I wished we had searched the grounds first as it was apparent there would soon be rain, and that it would be more than a brief shower.

When we got to the waterfall there was no one there. Lucella stepped off the scattered flagstones set around the rim of the pool, sinking her heavy legion-issue sandals in the mud and reeds, and scanning the ground. I saw that there were no tracks, no traces of the woman's footprints in the area where she had been seen. I looked questioningly at Lucella, but she would not meet my gaze.

"I saw someone," she insisted, frowning and stepping deeper into the shallows. The little waterfall seethed and threw sheets of chilly mist that the growing wind whipped away in glistening shrouds.

Perhaps goaded by my silence, Lucella moved waist deep into the pool, pushed through a stiff green wall of reeds, and suddenly lost her balance. Her feet slid from under her and she threw her arms up in the air before going under.

Her blonde head, hair plastered down, popped back up. I started to laugh and stopped before I could make a sound. Lucella moved swiftly forward, drawn into the pool, toward the waterfall. Her arms thrashed and she let out a gurgling cry that sent a physical shock through me.

I took three long lunging steps forward and threw myself headlong into the shallows. The frigid impact of the water was stunning and my face went under, but my outstretched hand caught Lucella's wrist. I heaved back, curling my body, seizing a handful of thick reeds with my free hand, and hauled both of us toward shore. For a vertiginous moment she seemed drawn away from me by a force stronger than I, by an impossible current, somehow rushing like a rapids beneath the surface of the little pond. I set my heels in soft mud and pulled. I heard her choke and curse, and then she came toward me violently, as if suddenly cut loose from a bond, thumping into me and driving me back off my feet.

Lucella helped me up and we staggered back out of the shallows, past the muddy shore and onto the well-tended grass, soaking wet, smeared with mud and spitting dirty water.

It started to rain gently, droplets dimpling the pool. The situation seemed at once so miserable and so absurd that I started to laugh and was about to make some doubtlessly poorly conceived joke, when I saw what Lucella held in her left hand.

She stared down at it wordlessly. Sodden, dripping and wrapped around her hand and wrist was a cloak of finest blue silk. One of Lord Kelsh's elegant gifts for his lovers.

A white flash dazzled my eyes, thunder cracked like a heavy bough splitting overhead, and it began to pour in earnest. We ran for the mansion through sheets of rain. The wind lifted, seething through the trees and hurling heavy droplets into us with stinging force. Soaked to the skin, we slammed the mansion's doors behind us.

There was a bath chamber toward the rear of the first floor where we found towels. Lucella tossed the twisted blue cloak into a corner without comment.

"What happened?" I asked. "You're usually a strong swimmer."

"I was being pulled under," Lucella responded flatly.

I looked down at the tiles, trying to conceal my skepticism. "You slipped, and I could tell there was a bit of a slope…"

Lucella's mouth twisted bitterly and she held out her left arm. There was an angry scarlet abrasion around the wrist, and the impression of twisted fabric was etched into her skin. I cursed under my breath.

"It was wound around my wrist like a damned noose."

We were silent for a time, drying ourselves off as best we could. Thunder rumbled outside and rain drove rhythmically against the windows.

A dark mood had fallen upon us, and it occurred to me that locating some lunch might go a way toward dispelling it. The small kitchen on the second floor gave up some sausage and crusty bread. There was a big beaker of water, and we used Lord Kelsh's outsized goblets to drink our fill, but Lucella lamented that we'd emptied her belt flask of wine. I found it hard to believe that a poet wouldn't have wine somewhere about his home and went off to see if I could find it.

My suspicions were confirmed on the third floor, where I found a goblet of exceptionally strong wine stashed in a drawer of Kelsh's huge desk. I had just taken it from the drawer, and was looking forward to Lucella's pleased reaction, when a tremendous clap of thunder seemed to jolt the entire building. It was loud and sudden enough to startle me into almost dropping the goblet, but it had hardly begun to fade when another sound, dimmer, more distant, yet infinitely more disturbing, followed in its wake.

A strangely muffled screaming. One cry, then another, masculine and almost mindless with terror and a quavering misery. My throat closed and a chill blew over me like a stern breeze off Lord Kelsh's waterfall. I listened intently but the cry faded and ceased.

"Lucella!" I called. My voice seemed smaller than it should have.

She came up the stairs at a trot and, when she saw my face, laid a hand on the hilt of her short sword.

"What is it?"

"Wait…" I said, lifting a palm. Rain pattered the window behind the desk, blurring an afternoon that had gone dark as twilight. Thunder rumbled and I tensed.

"What?" demanded Lucella.

I was about to tell her again to wait, when lightning cracked like the earth splitting open and thunder roared loud enough to make the floor shudder.

The scream rose again, muffled and muted as if sealed in a box, tapering into a chain of indistinguishable pleadings before falling silent. Lucella's eyes grew large.

"Gods and demons!"

"Someone is here," I said stupidly. "That is not a phantom or illusion."

"But where? Outside?" Lucella glanced around wildly. "We've looked everywhere!"

"No, it has to be someone inside the house. It sounds like it's coming from behind a wall."

"But every door is open," said Lucella, "even his closet."

I had an idea. There was a single area inside Lord Kelsh's mansion that had seemed odd to me. I walked quickly out of the poet's study and stood by the stairs that led to the roof. The space felt wrong, constricted. Frustrated, I stood there and waited.

"What?" Lucella began, "Do you…"

Thunder exploded overhead in a deafening avalanche of sound and, as it faded, rain roared anew, seemingly strengthened by the tumult. And the screaming came again. Even muffled as it was, there was such desperate, hopeless fear in that cry that the hair on my forearms stood up and my throat was pinched shut as if in the grip of a hostile hand.

"Right here!" I said. Between a rain-battered window and the base of the stairs the wall was set inward almost indiscernibly. The stonework was cunningly designed to camouflage it, but there was clearly a walled off space beneath the stairs. A secret room with no apparent door, from whence came those terrible cries.

A sense of awful urgency seized me and I drew my dagger from its sheath at the small of my back and hammered the pommel on the stone wall, desperate to aid whoever was suffering such torments. The screams came anew, and there was no doubt they came through the wall before us.

"We're here! Are you trapped? How can we help you?"

The screaming did not let up and no answer to my questions was apparent there.

"It doesn't sound like whoever that is wants to be let out," said Lucella.

I scanned the wall and thought I could make out a razor thin seam in the stonework. I wondered about wedging my blade into it, using the well-balanced throwing dagger as a chisel, or perhaps hunting for something in the house heavy enough to use as a makeshift battering ram, when the door abruptly gave a pop and creaked open a hand span.

I took a step back, and saw Lucella had gone to the baluster that formed the base of the stair's handrail. The baluster was topped with a decorative sphere of black marble, inlaid with silver astrological symbols. She had seized it and simply turned it like a doorknob. I looked at her, doubtless with amazement writ plainly on my face.

"It was made for a poet," she said by way of explanation, "how difficult could it be?"

The door stood open a mere notch but I thought I could see vague light within. There was a scrabbling sound, like feet hastening to the door. I recoiled involuntarily, clutching my dagger, but Lucella leapt in, seized the door's rim with both hands and threw it open.

A small room was revealed. Much of it was taken up by a circular table with a single chair. The table was strewn with scrolls, open books, lit candles, goblets, mugs, quills, and a broad tray covered with crumbs and, lying on its side, a big water beaker like the one Lucella and I had found in the kitchen. The walls were lined with shelves holding stacks of books, rolls of parchment, odd little statues, unlit candles and a great many less classifiable oddities. Black sigils of arcane design had been crudely drawn onto the walls, across the spines of books, on the floor and even the ceiling. They appeared to have been smeared on with fingertips.

Between the table and the far wall cowered a tall man in elegant but bedraggled robes of dark blue and ivory. He was crowned with a matted mane of splendid blond curls and his deeply set eyes were as wide and blue as a summer sky.

It was Lord Kelsh. He smelled terrible.

"Close the door!" he howled. "Go away!"

"Kelsh!" I shouted, as authoritatively as I could. "Control yourself! We were sent by the Princess Eurythenia and mean you no harm."

"I am exposed!" His voice lowered, hoarse and still thick with panic. "She'll get in."

"Who'll get in?" demanded Lucella. "There's no one here but us. Where is she?"

"In the rain, in the thunder, trying to crash her way in," stammered Kelsh, plucking at his robe. "I've taught myself the protective signs and she cannot reach me as long as this room remains sealed, but I must close the door!"

"Wait!" I said. "She isn't here, and even if she were she couldn't get past Lucella and I. How long have you been in there? I don't see any food or water. Aren't you hungry? Thirsty?"

That seemed to reach him. He closed his eyes and lifted a hand to his broad brow.

"Yes. I finished my supplies two days ago. Please, bring me food and water and wine from the kitchen below."

"Come out of there and down to the kitchen with us," said Lucella. "We'll all have wine and we can talk about why you locked yourself away in secret while the whole city's been wondering what became of you."

"I was missed," he said. "Of course, I was missed. I should have known the world would never leave me alone."

I rolled my eyes involuntarily, and thrust my dagger back into its sheath. "Yes, come out, get something to eat and drink, and tell us what troubles you. You might take a little bath while you're at it."

"I can't leave this room," he said stiffly. "Let me close the door now. I'll open it for you when you return with my food and drink."

"Why must you stay in this cramped little hole?" asked Lucella. "Who is this woman that she makes you hide away like a mole?"

"Adalla," he said softly. Thunder rumbled. "I wrote her my greatest poem."

"What?" Lucella gave me a look that indicated that she had no doubt we were dealing with an utter madman. Lord Kelsh did not notice.

"One of your paramours, right?" I said. "I recall hearing something about how you caused a bit of scandal by bringing a low born Southron woman to court a few months back."

Kelsh tossed his head. "The constraints of court society have no power over my heart. It knows no master save passion, and goes where it will."

"And now your heart has gone in a different direction and you're concerned that Adalla is sufficiently annoyed by the loss of your affections that she's seeking revenge?"

He looked at me soulfully but did not answer. His eyes really were impressive.

"Gods and demons," burst out Lucella. "Enough of this nonsense. Come out of there and tell us the whole story."

"Yes," I said, "come along, my lord." I stepped into the room, felt Lucella advancing close behind me, and reached out to take Kelsh's arm.

"Don't touch me!" Kelsh's long right arm shot up theatrically, and in his hand was a short, curved dagger. It was inlaid with enough decorative etching to darken the entire blade, but it came to a wicked point. "Stay back or I'll strike!"

I didn't have a chance to tell him not to be an idiot.

Lucella drew and lunged in a liquid flash of steel. The point of her blade was sunk a slim finger's width into his left shoulder so quickly he went on speaking for a moment as if he hadn't time to realize he'd been stabbed.

Those who cross blades with Lucella Esteriak are often prone to underestimate her strength, her ruthlessness, and most especially her speed. I could only be grateful she hadn't killed him outright.

He fell silent and took a faltering look at where her sword's tip was imbedded in the juncture of arm and shoulder. Lucella gave the blade the slightest twist. smiled coldly and withdrew. Her blade had a tiny spot of scarlet on its very tip.

"Drop the dagger or I put the next thrust through one of your pretty blue eyes."

Lord Kelsh fell to the floor in a dead faint.

He was too heavy to carry down to the kitchen, so we settled on pulling him out of his bolt hole and sitting him in the chair behind his oversized desk. Sprawled there, face pale and slack, a dribble of scarlet on his shoulder where Lucella had pricked him, he looked more like a student unused to wine than a tormented poet of great renown.

"I'll go get a little food and water. You'll watch over him?"

I nodded and she trotted off. The rain on the window slackened a bit, but a gust of wind pushed at the pane. Lord Kelsh moaned and his eyelids flickered.

"Why are you so worried about this Southron woman, milord?" I mused, blunt because I was reasonably certain he was unconscious. "She have dangerous friends?"

"Father was a shaman," he said thickly, not opening his eyes. "Demanded we marry."

"Oh my," I said, feeling what in retrospect seems a rather cruel pleasure. "The great poet of romance can't have that. Those eyes are not about to gaze on matrimony."

He sat up and looked at me imploringly, bleary but abruptly awake and desperately earnest.

"I loved Adalla! I wrote her my greatest masterpiece and gave it to her! But it was not enough. She had to keep me for herself."

Lucella entered the room, arms full of bread, sausage and a beaker of water.

"So," she said, "you sent her away in disgrace."

"No," said Lord Kelsh. "I drowned her."

Three thunderous hammer blows struck the front doors, one after another, the knock of some unguessable titan seeking entry.

"Gods preserve me!" Kelsh quailed.

Lucella dropped her load of foodstuffs to the floor. "Come on!" She drew her blade and we raced toward the stairs. I pulled my dagger as I followed, wondering exactly who or what we hastened to encounter. I heard Kelsh behind us.

"I'm going back to the room! I'm going…" There was the explosive sound of glass shattering and Lord Kelsh's voice rose in a terrible scream.

I came to a staggering stop on the stairs and Lucella, on the landing below, did the same. For an instant we goggled at one another, then I swiveled and ran back up the stairway.

Rain blew in the blasted window behind the desk, wet wind scattering parchments and casting a chill over me that seemed to sink without resistance to my very core. Lord Kelsh was gone.

Thunder roared. I went to the ragged edged gap that was the window and stared out into the rain. The wind was rising again and the trees tossed wildly. I thought I saw movement, a slivery flash, down by the pond. Lightning shot jaggedly across the darkened sky and I flinched away from the window.

I hurried down the stairs to where Lucella stood by the doors. They were closed and undisturbed. Whatever had knocked for entry to Lord Kelsh's mansion had left no sign of its presence. I pushed past Lucella, out the doors, and set off down the path to the pond at a run.

Rain pelted me, ran in my eyes, obscured the path. There was a silver shimmer of movement ahead of me and I thought I heard Lord Kelsh's cry in a peal of thunder. I gasped with effort, running to catch I knew not what with no thought as to what I might do should I catch it.

I couldn't hear the waterfall over the wind and rain. The surface of the pond leapt into mist under the impact of the downpour. I drew to a stop near the pond's edge and squinted, trying to see something in the water before me.

There was a woman standing in the pond. She was a silver phantom made of rain. She turned to me in a swirl of spray like a cloak of flying droplets, shining white in the blaze of lightning, then shining black in the thunder that followed.

"Adalla!" I cried. There was no face, just a sheen of water with glistening eyes. She spread arms of falling mist, then moved toward me with terrible speed.

I cried out as she hurtled upon me, blank silver visage filling my vision as she blew over and through my body like a gust of frigid storm wind. I staggered backward, breathless and gasping, almost losing my balance.

The rain stopped. I spun around but the phantom was gone. I heard Lucella calling my name and yelled something back so she would know I was well. The sky lightened and the world seemed immensely silent after the relentless thunder. I stood beside the pond, dripping wet and trying to settle myself. I bent, put my hands on my knees and drew a deep breath. It froze in my lungs.

On a flagstone that bordered the pond before me were two pale bulbs trailing tendrils like tattered bits of vine. They lay wet and exposed on the cold stone.

Two blue eyes.

I told Lucella everything and she believed me. I can't say as much for Princess Eurythenia, who held me in audience for two hours telling the story over and over. I believe she wondered if I was losing my mind. That changed a few days later when she had the gardens painstakingly searched and, finally, the pond drained. They found Adalla's body, sodden with rot, and in the arms of the corpse of his lover, the fresher, eyeless, body of Lord Kelsh.

⚡

THE WISHING WELL
by Robert Graves

About seven miles from the village of Castle Hill, in Maine, on the old road leading to Mapleton, stands an empty farmhouse most recently occupied by a family named Miller, and before that by a family called Deluse, about whom much more will be said. It was acquired and owned by Mr. Abel Miller in 1869, and he and his wife Martha passed a single winter there before the extraordinary events here recounted compelled them to quit the area, absconding to a town called Jackman in the western part of the state. By every account Mr. Abel had known of the disappearance of the Deluse family before purchasing the property, an event that had occurred only three years prior, but when pressed on the matter stated only that he "did not believe in haunted houses." To this point, an observer unfamiliar with the house's history would not suspect it to be evil in any way; its windows are intact, its doors wide and solid and without breach, and the gray paint is only recently beginning to fade. The house is well-treed on the northeast and its occupants hence protected during the harsh winter storms which are known to prevail from that direction, but to the southwest opens a broad field containing a particular feature important to this account—an ancient well familiar to locals of that area as the "wishing well," long in disuse, its circular wall high with old stones placed there by the area's first settlers.

It is at this point that the peculiar history of the Deluse family, and their disappearance, must be addressed.

The Deluses consisted of Jeb Deluse, his wife Catherine, his young daughter Matilda, and Miss Emilia Hunt, the younger sister of Catherine. Catherine Deluse was commonly described as a kind and pensive woman, if not sad-eyed and often aloof. Jeb Deluse was considered to be a quiet and obstinate man with few friends, even amongst his fellow workers at the nearby Frankfort Quarry in Westfield. He was about thirty-five years old, cantankerous, and by the reckoning of his neighbors, was seen too often in the company of his sister-in-law without his wife. As for Miss Emilia Hunt, perhaps ten years her sister's younger, she was considered by the town's matrons to possess a wild streak, though no further elaboration was offered. Of the child Matilda, believed to be six years old at the time of the disappearance, two qualities took predominance in describing her—that she was always silent, and that she had been born blind. Because of this latter trait, she walked with the aid of a small red-tipped cane. At the time of the events here discussed, the road that now runs adjacent to the Deluse property was a commonly traveled footpath, and so Catherine and Matilda were frequently seen sitting together at the wishing well. Wanderers on the trail rarely spoke to them, as the mother and daughter looked quite content, often-observed dropping coins into the well while cupping their ears to listen.

In the early winter of 1866 a severe storm swept over northern Maine, during which Castle Hill town records indicate almost three feet of snow fell. Three days passed before the first neighbor of the Deluses thought it odd that the deep snow surrounding the house remained pristine and undisturbed; no tracks led from any door. Indeed, when finally inspected several days after the storm, its four occupants were absent. More peculiar was the fact that almost all of the Deluse's personal effects remained undisturbed. Clothing, food, tools, dishware and furniture were all accounted for, and as one witness stated, "Their possessions rested in a peaceful and intact manner, with a half-eaten meal left on the table," leading the superstitious to claim that the family had simply vanished; more careful observers, however, noting the absence of any valuables, insisted that the family had been the victim of bandits. This too was an unsatisfying conclusion, as no evidence or suspects could be produced. In time, Androscoggin Savings & Trust reclaimed the property, and in its possession it remained until the fall months of 1869, when Abel Miller arrived and made his bid.

While Mr. Miller did not at any point discuss the disturbances (even long after they commenced), Martha Miller, a much more outgoing and personable woman than Catherine Deluse had been, began relating the odd accounts to her neighbors almost immediately. As she told it, upon the early eve of 1869's first snowfall, Abel, staring through the window toward the wishing well, called her over to stand with him.

"Who would be out there at this hour, and in this snow?" he exclaimed.

Martha peered out and witnessed the distinct shape of two figures, appearing to be "a woman and a child," who stood at the well, barely visible in the squall. The following morning dawned bright and pleasant, yet Martha recounted feeling a dark presence about the house as she woke and began her chores. Then, Abel, while outside gathering firewood from the shed, called for her. She joined him in the freshly fallen snow and quickly understood his reason for fetching her: Two sets of footprints led up to the wishing well, but none led away. Furthermore, a thin, jagged furrow ran beside the tracks, as though something had been trawled alongside.

Abel, assuming the two visitors had fallen into the well during the night, alerted Constable Elias Saylor, but, as no townsfolk had been reported missing, the constable took no action. The event was gradually forgotten over the days until the next snowfall, which began during the daylight hours of November 19th. On this occurrence it was Martha who first peered out and saw the two figures, now plainly visible to her as a woman and a young girl, the latter of whom walked with the aid of a probing cane. At the time of this second appearance, Martha had become quite familiar with the circumstances that had befallen the Deluse family, and by common description believed the figures to be Catherine and Matilda Deluse. At her pleas, Abel dressed and started toward the wishing well, but after a large gust of wind obscured the figures in a drifting flurry, the strange visitors were gone.

Throughout the winter, neighbors often gathered at the house during storms to witness the apparitions, and the phenomenon was well reported. However, each time the well was approached, the figures simply vanished. It was not until late in the winter of 1870, during a severe storm in March of that year, that Martha ventured to the well alone. She later told her neighbor, Mrs. Henrietta James, that on this occurrence the apparitions did not vanish, but remained in absolute stillness at her careful advance, until she at last reached the edge of the wishing well, opposite the two blanched figures. What she witnessed was a woman of sad countenance staring downward into the well, and a pretty young girl of six or seven looking up to her, unblinking, with clear, colorless eyes of an almost transparent hue. When Martha moved to speak to the girl, as she explained to Mrs. James, a most horrifying scream erupted from within the well's depths, the shock of it causing Martha to slip and fall in the snow. When she returned to her feet, the two figures were gone.

With the town in near hysterics, according to the report made by Constable Saylor, the wishing well was excavated by a posse of men from local towns, including Presque Isle, Easton, Caribou and even as far away as Houlton, with many of the volunteers being workmen at the same quarry of Jeb Deluse's former employ. After two days of rigging and failed attempts, foreman Henry Finch, from the township of Ashland, reached the bottom of the well. There, under the snow and a deep pile of rock, later identified as the same variety found in the quarry, Mr. Finch uncovered the remains of two bodies, a woman and a child. The subsequent discovery of a short, red-tipped cane left little doubt as to their identities.

Of Jeb Deluse and Miss Emilia Hunt nothing is known. Abel Miller, at the demand of his wife, promptly forfeited the property at a moderate loss and moved his family westward to Jackman, Maine. The Deluse house remains empty, and the wishing well is visited infrequently.

⚡

O KING OF PAIN AND SPLENDOR!

by Darrell Schweitzer

Vashru the Second, who reigned in Riverland during a decadent age, commanded that an immense barge should be built, a kingdom unto itself, wherein were represented all the lands of his dominion. So cunning were his artisans, and so terrified of any possibility of failure—for in this reign, as was famously remarked, only executioners never feared unemployment—that the vessel was indeed a wonder of the age, so vast that it seemed a floating continent. Indeed, no observer could make out the bow from the stern, nor one side from the other. A jungle grew amidships, where tribes of pygmies dwelt in palaces of human bone. Great pits belched forth flame, giving monstrous birth to giants of living metal with voices of thunder, and to golden birds leapt into the sky and shrieked Vashru's name in glory among the stars.

On a wide plain spread below the decks, beneath an artificial sun, armies contended and slew, for the amusement of the Great King.

Whole cities rose upon this barge, inhabited by courtiers and slaves, by the favored of the land and by the doomed. Among them walked creatures other than men, which nevertheless spoke the words of men and praised the king without cease.

Far below, amid the stinking bilges, augurs labored, assisted by the most skilled torturers, to divine secrets from the living entrails of screaming prisoners whose lives were sustained by such fiendish arts that they could not die until the King commanded so in his mercy (for which he was not noted.)

Scribes recorded results in a special script of the King's own devising, which only he could read, its secrecy reinforced as each scribe turned in his report, then was made to contribute to the ongoing endeavor in another, more painfully intimate manner.

Through the middle of the barge a winding channel flowed, a model of the Great River itself, a river that floated upon the River to confound nature itself; a stream thick with blood and foulness, yet perfumed with the rarest herbs and incense, and so wide you could sail a boat on it.

Truly this was a mighty king and terrible, the first in twenty generations to seize into his own hands all of Riverland and Reedland, all the broad plains and deserts and marshes, from the Delta to the Horns of the Mountains at the edge of the world. That he had murdered his own father and five half-brothers to reach the throne was no stain; it but affirmed his fearsome greatness. The story went that he'd entertained his stepmother with exquisite poetry of his own composition all throughout a languorous afternoon while her sons were being drowned in their bath.

Yet, too, he could lead an army of fifty thousand and make the earth and sky tremble.

He was fond of saying that what would be, in an ordinary man, megalomania beyond description, was in himself a mere attribute of his identity, like spots on a leopard.

He was fond of proving it, too.

So he set forth at night upon this fantastic, floating world, accompanied by his fleet of war-galleys, the dronthas, more numerous than had ever been seen before or any historian has recorded. Thus would he progress through all the lands he ruled, to instill awe in all the peoples of the Earth, to take his pleasure where he would, and to write his legend upon the face of the world for all time as a carver cuts words into stone.

And yet he kept his own council, and told no one his true, ultimate purpose.

When the highest of all his high officials, after much deference and ceremony dared to ask, the King said only, "The scripture of my deeds is to be deciphered for ten thousand lifetimes and still the wise man may not come to the end of it."

"Ah," said the official, understanding, or pretending to, even as the King struck his head off.

He was one of the lucky ones, who suffered little, though the King had his head reanimated by clever arts, and stuck upon a post, where it could say, "Ah, ah," endlessly and increase in wisdom.

So the barge began its journey, its countless oars churning the water, its sails billowing like golden clouds, its voice that of a thousand trumpets; then louder still came the King's own voice, cleverly magnified by speaking tubes, so that his words might seem to descend from the sky, to be recorded by priests and visionaries for the eternal amazement of mankind.

In darkness, he sailed, and the lanterns that dangled from his masts and from the trees of his floating forests, and the small, boat-shaped lamps which drifted along his own river-upon-the-River were more numerous than the stars.

He sat on his throne, high above all in his palace of rare stones, far aft, his beehive-shaped, double-crown of Riverland and Reedland upon his head, his flail and his sword (bloodied from the recent decapitation) before him as emblems of his office. Beneath him, arrayed on either side sat his Queen, Buran, and his seven sons, the Princes of Riverland and the Delta.

With his own hand he poured wine for each of them into blood-red, crystal goblets, and he did them the singular honor of rising from his seat to convey the cups to them on a little tray. Then he sat down again and raised his own goblet in a toast, and they had no choice but drink.

They drank, and all of them fell down, writhing in agony, smoke pouring from their mouths, rising from their very pores, as they burned and shrivelled and died, yet rose again. As smoking liches, they resumed their places. Such was the price of their ambition, which, the King knew, the Queen and her sons harbored in their hearts—all except the youngest son, Vakitares, who was only a child, and already mad, a babbling idiot.

It was a discerning wine. When the youngest son drank, it merely tasted sweet. He was allowed to live, because he had not inherited his father's greatness. For this, his father loved him in that small space in his heart reserved for such things.

* * * *

The King sat in silence for a long time, as the air swirled thick with smoke, as, somehow, the sun did not rise and the daylight never came, and winds not quite of earth stirred through the branches of his floating jungle and set the lanterns swaying.

Then he spoke aloud, "Spirit, have I done it well?"

Vakitares, the idiot, mewed softly. The liches sat where they were, staring out of empty, smoldering sockets, and such automatons as served the King stirred not; but cloth rustled by his right hand, and a soft voice said in little more than a whisper, "Impressive, Lord. I've seen nothing like it."

And the King said, "Spirit, say again your name."

"Sekenre, Lord." The voice was still soft, a little mumbled. There was a hint of a slurping sound.

"I read of a certain Sekenre once—"

"A sorcerer, Lord—

"In an ancient book—"

"Yes, very ancient. Centuries old. I wrote it."

"Show yourself, Spirit."

"If you want."

Already the King's eyes could discern a hint of a shape, silhouette of a slight figure, with thin shoulders that shrugged. Then a flame flickered from the palm of an outstretched, frail-looking hand, which touched a candle, and the other hand reached over and set the candle before the King.

"Better?"

Now Vashru could see, in the dimness, a pale, round face with dark eyes, and a mop of unruly hair, soft, beardless cheeks, a partially bare, bony chest, so sunken that the collarbone cast a shadow. What he saw before him, as his eyes adjusted, was a skinny, scruffy boy not much older than his own youngest, idiot son. This boy wore a beautifully embroidered court vestment obviously not his own and several sizes too large, beneath which was revealed, as he sat cross-legged with the vestment bunched in his lap, ragged, cut-off trousers and bare legs and feet, none too clean; but also his legs and such of his chest as was exposed, and his forearms, were criss-crossed with thin, faintly-glowing scars.

Sekenre was helping himself to a tray of sweets and fruits in his lap. He mumbled because he was talking with his mouth full.

By these signs the King knew that this was no beggar boy in a stolen robe, no ordinary mortal at all. For no one, not even a lunatic, would dare be so unconcerned, or so familiar in his presence, much less interrupt his speech. (Vashru the Dreadful, the Utterly Magnificent, Greater than Great—from officially-appointed Court Flatterers, who were all linguistic scholars of the highest order, the adjectives could go on for hours.)

"Spirit," said the King. "You are not as you seem."

The boy licked his fingers. "I'm not actually a spirit."

"You came to me in a dream like a spirit. It pleases me to call you thus."

"Then may it please you, Lord."

"I have read," said the King, "that no sorcerer truly dies, and that his physical body does not age, and if he is slain—as sorcerers often are, by other sorcerers—the dead one lives on inside the mind and body of the victor, and may even sometimes reverse the victory—"

"But Lord, you have read too in the same book that such persons serve the Titans, who are themselves shadows cast by the Gods in their darkest dreams; and that eyes like mine are incapable of apprehending the divine vision. You, who are greater than all men born, whose only worthy opponents are the very gods, must be able to see them. A sorcerer cannot. You'd be fighting blind. Therefore, you should not become a sorcerer yourself. It wouldn't be in your best interest."

Then the King felt the boy take his hand. The touch was warm and solid. Yet Vashru drew back with a grunt of surprise at the sheer impudence of the action.

"Spirit—?"

"Lord King," said Sekenre, "I am your guide, whether spirit or living flesh. Let us go then, and make a journey through your kingdom, and read its secrets like a book."

Now the boy's voice had changed. The tone was somehow a little different. Where before he spoke plain Riverlandish with a slightly uncouth accent, now he had the polished tones of a courtier of the Delta.

And again Vashru recognized that this was no ordinary child, however crazed, for this Sekenre seemed to know his very thoughts before he could voice them, as if he, the Great King, were a puppy trying to impress an infinitely learned philosopher with the few tricks he'd learned. The thought was absurd, humiliating. He wasn't sure how it got into his mind, but there it was. He raged. He would have his revenge.

"It would be inadvisable to kill me," said Sekenre. "Come."

The King rose from where he sat, took up his sword and his flail, and went with him.

Sekenre tossed his empty tray at the foot of the throne, where it landed with a clang.

* * * *

In the darkness, for the night went on and the sun did not rise, while through the high windows of the floating palace, the stars went gliding by—in this darkness, King Vashru floated upon the river-upon-the-River, in a small boat poled along by Sekenre.

They passed through vast chambers hung with gold, where fantastic lanterns burned, casting shapes like dragons and fierce birds upon the walls and ceiling; where thousands of courtiers sought desperate pleasure by every conceivable means and perversion of nature; but the King did not even pause to look.

It seemed they went on for many miles, upon this river of water and blood and ash and exquisitely perfumed foulness, through a dense forest, where lions fought with gryphons. Sometimes one or another splashed nearby in the darkness, splattering the boy and the king.

They came to a temple left deserted but for gigantic, brazen figures representing all the gods of Riverland, those with animal heads and those with heads like men. All of them had blank faces without eyes and groped about, slowly, blindly.

Yet the mass of them parted when Sekenre led the King from the boat. He led Vashru into the temple and consulted a book there, written in burning letters raised upon metal pages.

After Vashru had studied it for a long time, he looked up and sighed. "Lord King?"

"It says I should not fear the gods of earth and sky."

"But you are not yet satisfied then?"

The King looked up at the blind, golden figures all around him.

"I am not."

"Then let us continue our journey."

Somewhere, on one river or the other, a monster coughed.

The sun did not rise. The night went on. The King began to suspect that something was wrong with Time, as if all the sands had been spilled out and he were left with an empty glass, which measured nothing.

Either that, or, he prided himself to think, he, the Great King, had conquered Time and need not fear its passage any more than he feared the blind, faceless, ineffectual gods.

Sekenre poled the boat through another kind of forest, where thousands of the king's enemies, all dressed in gorgeous robes, crowned with tall crowns, bedecked with jewels, streaming fantastic ribbons and feathers and sashes, writhed impaled on tall stakes, all of them screaming with faint voices like a terrible, yet pathetic wind, each spewing pale white fire out of his mouth, burning from his eyes and his ears with a magical flame that would not let them ever die.

They burned like lanterns. They seemed more numerous than the stars.

Their blood filled the artificial river and the current increased.

And they prophesied, speaking to the king in the special language of the dead, which he understood as if he awakened into a dream of the understanding of that tongue. Sekenre spoke that language fluently, as sorcerers do; and the King recalled that Sekenre, when he had first appeared to him in dreams, had whispered to him in such words and such speech.

A while later, across ruins of towns, they could see the actual edge of the barge, and beyond that, far away, a burning city on the shore. Even at this distance, the King could discern faints blasts of war-horns.

"What place is this and who wages war there?"

"It does not concern you, Lord King," said the boy, "for it is merely of the living world."

Nearer at hand, corpses were trying to climb up out of the River onto the barge, but guards along the railings pushed them back in with poles.

"I dreamed," said the King, "that all my kingdom, nay, all the Earth was spread out like a map floating on the waters of the Great River, and I, with all my strength, hurled a great stone into the midst of it. The stone sank and the map wrapped itself around the stone and streamed with it into the darkness; and I knew that I myself was that stone and the map was indeed the world."

"At whom did you hurl the stone, Lord?"

* * * *

In the darkness that did not end, while winged, gigantic shapes circled among the stars and sang strange, wailing songs, the King turned to the boy who sat opposite him in the boat. The water was too deep for Sekenre's pole to be of any use. He held it across his lap.

"Sekenre, are you insane?"

"Lord King, a thousand years ago, when I truly was little more than a child, I journeyed into the land of the dead, and there I slew my father who contrived that I should do so, and I swallowed his soul into my own, and with it came all the souls of every sorcerer he had ever slain, and every one they had ever slain; and I knew the secrets of all of them, and, and a thousand thousand voices babbled in my dreams and became my voice, each of them, when I chose to call upon them. No, I am not insane."

"You are quite beyond madness, then?"

"Yes, Lord."

For once, King Vashru's heart was truly touched. He felt a stirring of such emotions as he had almost forgotten, like a phantom sensation from a severed limb; as if some courtier had angered him, but then softened his rage with an unexpected, sincere compliment, so that the King resolved to kill the fellow, not now, but later, and not quite as cruelly as he had otherwise intended. Such was his magnanimity, another sign of his greatness, another spot on the leopard.

* * * *

The sun did not rise. Now the stars overhead were few and far between, and very faint, not the stars of the Earth's sky at all.

The King realized that he was afraid of only one thing, that, in his hidden heart of hearts, he had forgotten his true object, that he did not know where Sekenre was leading him or why, that he'd read all the sigils and signs and secret scriptures, that he had worked all the secret magics to no purpose at all. He was afraid that he, the Great King, actually didn't know more than his own idiot son Vakitares, the one he had spared.

He was afraid that the real reason he kept his council so guarded was that he had no council, that he was an empty goblet.

But Sekenre, who seemed to sense all his thoughts before he could even form them, merely said, "Are you insane, King?"

"No."

"You are beyond all that then, even as the eagle that flies is beyond the concerns of the crawling insect."

"Ah…" said the King.

Somewhere in the back of his mind, in some memory, there was a severed head on a post that kept saying "Ah, ah, ah," as it increased in wisdom.

And, increasing in wisdom, the King knew that he must be like the stone, hurled with all his great strength.

He drifted on in darkness.

Vashru awoke in broad daylight, on a cool spring morning, in his room in a house made of wood and reeds and standing on stilts, at the edge of the Great River.

Outside, the sky was a brilliant blue. Far away across the water, a single boat with a white sail flapping limply drifted lazily downstream.

Nearby, long-legged birds, herons, waded in muddy water below his window.

He'd awakened from a strange and terrible dream, something he strove to put out of his mind but could not.

He had known this place all his life, this meager house in the swamp where Reedland borders upon Riverland. The boat that he saw, he knew, was headed downstream to the City of the Delta, where dwelt the Great King, although Vashru wondered how great he really was—he wondered because the village elders asked such questions, because no warship or army or official of the king had been seen this far south in generations.

It wasn't that Vashru cared about politics, or could even formulate the concept. He was, after all, a little more than a child, twelve perhaps, although he admitted sometimes that he wasn't sure, because neither he nor his mother nor his sister Ashaia could read or write, or even knew much about numbers.

All he knew was this place, where the bugs bothered you in the hottest month of the year, but then went away and it was otherwise pleasant and never very cold in the winter. He and his friends paddled small boats around between the houses, and played games of tossing balls between the boats. Sometimes they swam, but only in protected places, where the villagers had built a fence into the water to keep out the crocodiles when the women did washing. Most of the men worked at fishing, or, in season, gathering reeds, which they sold in huge bundles to men who came along the river in barges.

But the dream wouldn't fade. In it he was a grown man. He had already lived much of his life, had sired seven sons. Six had died hideously and the other was an idiot. He himself had turned into a monster of unimaginable cruelty. It had all started, in that dream, on a morning like this one, when a royal warship, a drontha, came to the village for the express purpose of fetching him, because his father, Big Vashru, who had left the family to go down river and seek his fortune in the Delta, had joined the army, worked his way up through the ranks, deposed the not-so-great king, and become king himself, which made Little Vashru and all his family royalty. Dazed, weeping, without words, they had all been fetched in the drontha, made to put on heavy robes and jeweled buskins—and he, Little Vashru, had never even worn shoes before—and things went from bad to worse, as they had at the other end of his dream, which circled around and around in his head, until a spirit in that dream whispered into his ear every evil thing imaginable.

That morning, he sat with his mother at breakfast, and she said, "You don't look well."

"Bad dream," he said.

She laughed gently. "Nothing to be afraid of."

But he knew better, even at his age. Some dreams are more than dreams. He'd never heard of oracles or prophets, but he had some idea.

That morning he took his boat far into the reed-swamp, through winding ways, past many islands, some of which had names, some mere tufts of reeds, until he came to a place where the water broadened out into a kind of lake, but was still and black with mud.

There he saw a ragged boy only a little older than himself walking barefoot toward him across the surface of the water. He had a long pole in one hand, which he used as a traveler would use a staff when walking on land. He wore a leather satchel at his side.

Vashru was afraid. But he hesitated. He sat there, while the boy approached him. The boy spoke to him of the contents of his—Vashru's—dreams, describing and commenting on them in detail even before he, Little Vashru, could quite call them back into memory.

In his dreams, his father Vashru the Elder became King Vashru the First, a great conqueror, who extended the power of the Delta as it had not been in a long time—for this was a decadent age—and he, Prince Vashru, had learned everything he possibly could about the art of kingship from his father, then murdered him, seized his throne, and become an even greater king, whose deeds were the stuff of legends—or nightmares.

In excruciating detail, the strange boy, who said his name was Sekenre and that he was a thousand years old, recounted every vile, wicked thing Vashru the Second had done, explicating every lust, every base desire, until Little Vashru wept and tried to paddle away, shouting, "No! No! It's not true!"

But Sekenre opened his leather bag and got out a book, and explained how all these things were in this book, which he had written, or would write in the future. He showed Vashru the very page, but it all looked like squiggles, because Vashru couldn't read, and didn't want to learn.

"No," he said.

"It's all right, then," said Sekenre. "It's just a story."

But Little Vashru turned to him and said, "Is it?"

"Does the great and terrible king dream that he is an innocent boy, or does the boy dream he is the terrible king? Which is it, do you think?"

"I don't know!"

Then Sekenre did something that only grownups do. Standing on the water by the side of the boat, he put his arms around Vashru and held his face to his chest, and comforted him until he stopped crying.

"Maybe you won't ever have to know," he said.

Vashru, distracted, had dropped his paddle.

Sekenre handed it back to him. "Go home now," Sekenre said.

* * * *

So Little Vashru went home, though the journey took him all day. He found his mother and sister weeping. His mother demanded to know where he'd been, but when he didn't answer, she didn't press him on it. Gradually he learned from the two of them that word had come up from the Delta on a trading ship that his father, Big Vashru, had indeed joined the army, but had caught a stray arrow through the eye during a training exercise and died. There would be no fortune coming, or any money at all beyond a handful of silver coins the trader had brought. He'd also brought Big Vashru's sword, which by custom was left to his son. But Little Vashru wouldn't touch it, any more than he would touch a poisonous serpent.

Life, nevertheless, levelled out after that. His mother had long silences, but she went on living. His sister Ashaia got old enough to start courting boys. Before long she teased him about courting girls, and this goading, or chance, or just the passage of time made him fall in love with a village girl called Neferket. For all his sister was a year older than him, he, very much to everyone's surprise, got married first, at seventeen. He continued to work with the village men, fishing and gathering reeds. He was old enough to wear shoes now, but nobody ever did, because they spent most of their time wading in mud.

Time and seasons passed. When he was eighteen, Neferket grew great with child. Because they were poor, he and his wife and his mother and his sister all lived together in the house he had grown up in.

Because the kings of the Delta were weak, the river now swarmed with pirates. One night in late summer pirates took the village entirely by surprise. They cut off Vashru's mother's head and stuck it on a post (where it gained no wisdom and said nothing). They raped Ashaia and left her bleeding in the street. They killed almost everyone. Vashru they would have killed too, save that he was beaten so badly they thought he was already dead, and when one of them laughed and kicked him off the porch into the water just before setting the house on fire, the shock of the water awakened him. But he was clever enough to pretend to be dead and float away with some logs.

Only much later did he return to the village. There were only a few survivors. He shouted and searched and wept. He found his sister, Ashaia, who was dead. He and some neighbors built a reed boat for her—little more than a bundle—and pushed her out into the River with such funeral rites as they could remember (not much), that she might go properly into the afterlife.

Later still he found his wife Neferket lying among the reeds at the water's edge. She was badly hurt. Although she lived, she lost her child, and her silences did not end. Vashru tried to go on, but it was no use. There was nothing he could do. He wished he'd kept his father's sword. He started to remember his dark and terrible dreams. At least in those, he figured, the Kingdom of the Delta was stronger than it had been in centuries, and all pirates had long since been impaled or crucified.

Then he looked one last time into his wife's vacant face. He kissed her and he wept. She did not know him.

So he borrowed a boat and paddled deep into the swamp, to the black lake where Sekenre was waiting for him.

"I am the king who dreamed he was someone else," he said. "Wake me up."

"You do not have to choose this," Sekenre said. He opened his book and showed some incomprehensible squiggles. "The story has more than one ending."

"I have hurled the stone."

* * * *

In the darkness, floating on one river or the other, King Vashru the Second awoke with a start.

The faint stars overhead were the stars of the deathlands.

"I know who the enemy is," he said. "If I am to be the greatest of all, I know who I must confront."

And Sekenre spoke to him and he spoke to Sekenre, and they recited together how the God of Death is called Surat-Kemad, who is the great crocodile who devours the world, whose mouth is the night sky, whose teeth are the numberless stars. Truly Surat-Kemad is the greatest of the gods, for in the end he devours all things, even what the other gods have made or raised up.

Only Vashru, in his greatness, could conquer Surat-Kemad.

Now they were already deep within the Crocodile's mouth. The Great River issues forth from Surat-Kemad, so that Death is the source of all life, yet all life flows again into Death. There is another current, called the black current which flows in the opposite direction from the Great River of the living world. A rich man's funeral boat catches that current seems to move, to the eyes of living men, against the flow of the water. Then it disappears and drifts back into the belly Surat-Kemad, even as does a pauper's bundle of reeds.

Now King Vashru the Second had drifted far on the black current, in his little boat, and Sekenre got out of that boat and walked barefoot on the water, pulling the boat with a rope over his shoulder. He used his pole as a land-traveler uses a staff.

Now the burnt-out liches which had been Vashru's family gathered around him in the boat, pressing upon him, stroking him lovingly, entreating him to commend them to the Lord of Death.

Angrily, Vashru tried to push them aside, but somehow, for all they could touch him, to his hand they were as insubstantial as smoke.

Now ghosts in the reeds by the water's edge implored him likewise. These were the spirits of those who had not been sent to the gods properly, or had met some catastrophe on the way there.

Vashru had no time for them.

He saw that the water was thick with reptilian faces with long snouts and small, cunning eyes. The water rippled slightly as they parted before Sekenre's steps. He understood then that everything Sekenre had told him, whether waking or in dreams, was entirely true. The boy was a sorcerer and very likely a thousand years old. Ordinary death could not touch him, for a sorcerer is infected with a kind of soul-cancer, which makes him unpalatable even to the Devouring God.

Those were not crocodiles. Though they had tails, scaled faces, and long, tooth-lined jaws, otherwise their bodies were those of men, pale, bloated, like corpses long drowned. These were the evatim, the messengers and minions of Surat-Kemad.

Truly now he was on the threshold of the Kingdom of Death.

Sekenre reached a shore and dragged the boat onto it. The evatim swarmed out of the water onto the beach, hissing. Some of them stood up and walked, clumsily, like men, their tails dragging. More of them crawled into the boat and devoured the hollow husks of Vashru's queen and princely sons.

But as long as Sekenre led King Vashru by the hand, the evatim did not molest him.

The King had his sword with him.

"Sekenre," he said, "speak to me again out of your great wisdom."

"If I've learned anything," the sorcerer said, "it is that the way to stop being evil is simply to stop. Simply do not commit the next crime. Let vengeance go by. You can never be pure again. You cannot undo your past deeds. But you can stop. Take up love and kindness again. Resume your good life where you left off. The choice is yours."

"I have learned," said the King, "that if a man were to kill a sorcerer, even as a boy called Sekenre killed his own father a thousand years ago—

how shocking, shocking, a depraved act, no excuses allowed—if that man were the mightiest of all, one who fears not even the gods—if that man were to gain not only the sorcerer's power but the sorcerer's deathlessness—who knows what he might not accomplish, like a hurled stone with the world wrapped around him?"

"Who indeed?" said Sekenre.

And King Vashru, placed his hand on the boy's shoulder, whirled him around, shoved his sword into his belly, and gutted him like a fish. The body collapsed surprisingly easily, like a husk, something brittle and crumbly. The head fell off, and Vashru was left holding nothing more than an elaborately embroidered robe.

Several fruits and sweets dropped out onto the sand.

The evatim hissed, loudly, almost at a roar. They closed in, their jaws gaping wide.

Vashru waited for something to happen. He expected to feel something, but there was nothing, no infusion of souls, no transformation.

He had not become a sorcerer. Not yet.

Then he felt a long, thin knife slide between his ribs from behind and probe upward toward his heart.

Sekenre, behind him, whispered, "Did you really believe that a thousand-year-old sorcerer, even if he's a boy, would be so stupid as to let you do that?"

Vashru could only say, "Ah, ah, ah ..."

Sekenre twisted the knife to keep his attention.

"I have been waiting for you on this shore, reading my book, to see how your tale comes out."

"Ah, ah, ah...."

"You could have chosen better."

"Ah—"

"But a sorcerer moves outside of time. I wrote it down, in the future, from memory, and I read it now. The conclusion disappoints, but it does not surprise. Sorcerers experience very few surprises."

Now with all his effort, Vashru managed to speak. "But I am mightier than a god. I have vast armies. My barge. My magicians. My monsters—"

Still pressing the knife into him, Sekenre turned him to see his great barge, like the whole world set afloat, ablaze with a million lights, its oars churning the waters like a rushing tide, suddenly stop and collapse inward onto itself, like a flimsy reed boat bitten in half by a crocodile.

"I see!" shouted the King. "I see my enemy! I see the god himself! Oh! I see the great jaws crashing down! How many teeth he has! More numerous than the stars!"

"I think even Surat-Kemad would agree," said Sekenre, "that you have delivered unto him a most impressive morsel."

"I spit on him!"

In that instant, as Sekenre's knife found his heart, Vashru did not see the crocodile jaws at all. He saw the stars overhead ripple, and then tear away as if they were sparkles on a filmy veil, and he saw, looking down on him, not the gods at all, but the faces of the Shadow Titans, vast and terrible; those Titans who are the nightmare-shadows of the gods, from whom sorcery flows, who are beyond life and death, who look down upon even Surat-Kemad with indifference.

Only sorcerers can see them. He knew that as he died.

* * * *

Sekenre was not able to explain to Vashru until well after Vashru was dead, until he had awakened inside the babble of voices within Sekenre's mind, that the corruption of the soul which is called sorcery may be acquired unwittingly by an innocent, or stolen by a villainous stroke; but then again it can also be achieved by relentless study, hard work, and sheer depravity, which is how Vashru had done it. Perhaps his final blasphemy of spitting on Surat-Kemad had pushed him over the edge. His great scheme had ended with the murder of a sorcerer, and with his becoming a sorcerer, but not quite in the order he had planned.

"You jerked me around like a puppet," Vashru wailed. "You determined everything."

"No," said Sekenre. "You hurled the stone. Again and again, you hurled it."

* * * *

Sekenre wrote these things in his book, earlier, later, outside of time. Meanwhile, back in the Delta, there was a sudden change of dynasty.

* * * *

It was Sekenre who struggled to control the storm raging inside himself. There, on the very shore of death, he staggered. He fell. He got up again and stumbled out on the water, to the wreck of the great barge. He reached down into the black water, caught one person by the hair and drew him up. It was Vakitares, the idiot son of the late king.

The boy-prince babbled. He rolled his eyes.

Sekenre touched his tongue with a finger and smoothed it, commanding him to go prophesy, and speak these mysteries to mankind.

Then it was Sekenre who fell down, choking, babbling, foaming at the mouth, for fresh within his mind was the divine vision, from the last instant of Vashru's mortal life. No sorcerer can ever see a god. Yet, in a way, stolen from King Vashru's memories, he had.

He beheld Surat-Kemad, and the god beheld him, and the god trembled, knowing that at the end of time the last sorcerer must confront the gods, and to have seen an enemy beforehand is to be strengthened against him.

They would meet again.

The evatim did not touch him.

* * * *

Much later, when Sekenre awoke by the water's edge, he wasn't in the underworld at all, but somewhere in Reedland. He was completely covered in mud, his clothing torn, but his book, which he still clung to, remained unharmed. It was, after all, magical.

He got up and walked and found himself by the shore of the black lake, where he wept for Little Vashru, even though some sources insist (contradicted by others) that a sorcerer cannot weep.

YOU'D DO IT FOR DIAMONDS

by Adrian Cole

From the files of Nick Nightmare

Not many people know about my private fortune. There's more than one good reason why I don't blab about it. If word got out, I'd be buried under enough guys hungry for a piece of the action to sink a battleship. Mostly undeserving causes. The Mob, hoods, crooks, you name it. So why don't I hang up my guns and buy someplace out there in the sun, off the beaten track, where I can sip malt whisky all day with my feet up and forget about the world?

Well, I'd get bored rigid in five minutes. I'd miss a certain, very tough business lady, and some bad stuff would go down that I could maybe have prevented. In my old age, maybe, if I reach it. For now, it's the business as usual.

But I'll tell you about my hoard.

Twelve years ago, I'd set myself up as a private dick, when I met a guy who was to have a big effect on my life. Sir Henry Riderman. The Big Apple is full of the weird and wonderful; you never know what kind of character you're going to bump into. One of the reasons I love the place. And Sir Henry is definitely weird and wonderful. Don't get me wrong, he's no crank. He's a genuine, grade A gentleman, something of a leftover from Victorian Britain. Not something you'd expect in modern day New York.

That long-gone night I was sitting in a cheap burger joint, Laughing Joe's, mechanically chewing one of the house specialities, swilled down with a gallon or two of a dark liquid Joe referred to, questionably, as coffee. I was scanning the evening paper, ready to call it a day and crash down early in my nearby two-bit apartment.

Then things got weird. First, a scrawny, rat-like punk, balled up in jeans and a jacket several sizes too big for him, scurried in like a cat with its tail on fire. He chose my table, which was squeezed up against a soup-stained wall, to flop down, hunched up, trying to make himself as invisible as possible.

I gave him the look that said, don't try and touch me for a dime, pal, and went back to my paper. The door to the joint swung open and two more guys came in. Did I say guys? They were the size of bull gorillas and far less handsome. They wore thick black coats you could have hidden a tank in, and they meant business. I knew because they were carrying sub machine guns.

The place emptied very quickly. Joe was behind the bar, his grin marginally less wide as he eyed the two thugs. My guess was he had a sawn-off something under the counter and he'd use it if they gave him any trouble. One of them stood in the middle of the narrow room, the other came along the rows of empty seats to my table. He stopped and favored the heap of clothes opposite me with a glare that would have stripped barnacles from a ship's keel.

"Hey, worm, stand up," he growled, levelling the gun. "No messing. You know what I want."

This guy had a boxer's face, beaten up and scarred, only it was a mottled, pasty gray color: the eyes were lidless and too wide. The mouth was a clumsy slash across his lower face, and when he spoke, a thick, scarlet tongue wriggled about in there like a snake in a pot. You don't want to know about the teeth.

The animate clothes shrank down even further. The punk wasn't coming out today. I realized the gunman wasn't blessed with much patience and his next move was going to be a radical one. He was going to turn the little guy into a heap of diced steak.

"I wouldn't use that, buddy," I said, keeping my eyes on the paper.

The thug favoured me with the smile that sank a thousand ships. He asked me who I was, only he used mostly words banned in even the dictionaries of slang.

The heap of clothes exploded as the punk's terror got the better of him and he dived under the table and got ready to bolt. Dumb move. The big guy fired off a burst, filling the place with noise and smoke. I'd been expecting something like this, which is why I'd already pulled out one of my Berettas and had it lined up out of sight under the table. I put three slugs into the big guy's chest and he went backwards like he'd been hit by a locomotive.

His buddy swore and was about to come barging over, presumably to rip me into pieces, but a loud blast from behind the counter confirmed my earlier thoughts. Joe did indeed have a sawn off something. Its twin barrels had discharged their payload and the second guy was torn near enough in half by the blast. Joe came forward, his grin wider than ever, and used the butt of his gun to make sure he'd terminated the two fallen thugs. Nice and efficient, like he was squashing bugs.

"Never can be too sure about these guys," he said. "You want to call the cops while I clean this mess up? Hell, I'm losing business here."

I put my gun away. "Sure." I saw no reason not to comply. The local cops would probably pin medals on us for flushing out these two monsters. After I'd rung the precinct, I checked over the little punk. His body was a mess, completely rearranged by the bullets he'd taken, and no longer remotely serviceable. Dead as it gets. I dug around inside his pockets for some kind of i.d. There was only one thing in there—a map. I shoved it into my own inner pocket while Joe was busily stacking the other two corpses against the counter, bawling for someone out back to get in here with a bucket of hot water and suds.

"Who was he?" I asked Joe.

"Little Jimmy Ratter. Thief. Good one, though he looks—looked— like he couldn't tie his own shoes, never mind pick a lock. Word was he could get anywhere and lift anything."

"Wonder what he stole," I said innocently. "These hoods wanted it bad. Know them?"

"Never seen them before. Look foreign to me. Once you've spoken to the cops, scram. Lie low for a week or two."

* * * *

I was still a mite green behind the ears in those days, when I got a message asking me to visit some guy name of Sir Henry Riderman. I didn't know him, and even less about his swanky address in Gramercy Park. As far as I knew it was a place where you took your shoes off when you walked the streets, never mind indoors. I got a taxi and we were like a cockroach crossing a Persian rug.

The house was something else. The very high-walled gardens, the perfectly pruned trees and manicured lawns, all the expected elements of modernity, wealth , as well as a high class security system, gardens out of a society magazine—they were all there in spades. But the house—that was another matter. For a start it looked like a half dozen architects had brainstormed their designs, argued over them, failed to agree on anything and built the damned thing anyway. Half of it was hidden under dense forests of ivy and other climbers, which was just as well, because if you'd stared for too long, you got giddy. I almost thought the place was shifting and reconstituting itself. My guess was, if you saw it at night, it would have given you the shudders.

To add to its mystique, the inside belonged in another world, a world of Victorian extravagance, gas lights, huge paintings of battles—Omdurman and Waterloo, giant potted plants, chandeliers—you get the picture. I didn't know it at the time, but that house did belong to another world, one which dovetailed into ours at certain points. Kind of like a dream realm, only solid. There are ways in, and a select few get the key. At the time, I didn't have access to one.

All that was about to change.

Riderman was a tall, bronzed guy of about sixty, who'd worn well and I guessed, lived well. He'd looked after himself. If you'd said, explorer, big game hunter, mountain climber, I'd have believed it. In fact, he'd been all that and more, although he didn't kill big game, he photographed it.

"Thank you for coming, Mr Stone," he said in his deep, rich accent, a true Brit. He stroked his bristling moustache, immediately putting me in mind of any number of monarchs of the early twentieth century—a whole bunch of Georges as I recalled. "You must be wondering what the deuce I asked you here for."

I had a good idea but I nodded and let him do the talking.

"I was reliably informed, if I wanted the best, I should come to you, Mr Stone."

I smiled my mysterious smile, which is a tad more convincing than my dumb one. "Not sure I'm the best at anything."

"You're an occult investigator. A psychic detective. A seeker after hidden truths."

Hell, I'd used all these connotations as a hook to keep me in work—after all, there were private dicks falling over each other in the city, all trying to earn a crust. I'd needed an angle. Okay, it had got me into a few very strange corners, and I'd met up with some very wacky people, so yeah, I was a sort of psychic investigator.

"I have an ear for these things," I said. Which was kind of ironic for a private eye.

"Something of mine has been stolen. The consequences are likely to be catastrophic. I know who has the items."

"Got any names?"

"There's a complication. They're not in the New York you know. What do you know about a place called—the Pulpworld? Around here that seems to be its commonest cognomen."

We were sitting in the household library, its walls of books towering over us up to the rafters. In this unique atmosphere it wasn't too hard to believe in some other annex to our world. And the truth was, I'd heard the name a few times, in certain very shadowy areas of my patch.

"Rumours," I said simply.

"It's a curious realm," he said, lighting up a pipe and sitting back very comfortably. It was the cue for a long and, I have to say, absorbing, dissertation on the Pulpworld and stuff related to it. Most guys listening would have figured Riderman for a nut, someone who'd been smoking the wrong weed for too long, or who'd maybe had his brains scrambled on one of his forays into the Dark Continent. Not me. I bought it. I knew the guy was on the level.

Whatever it is that links me to these other places, told me intuitively this was no bull. Something clicked into place in my mind. My guess is, he knew that, too. It's why he trusted me.

"An alternative world, to use the modern idiom." He poured two brandies and handed me one. "In 1903 my grandfather, Morton Riderman, undertook an expedition to an area of Africa known at the time as the Congo Free State. Morton was searching for the lost cousin of his friend, David Claywood. Lavender Claywood had been shipwrecked on the east coast of Africa in 1888 with her parents. She was the sole survivor. Stories about her filtered back to civilization, about a young girl, brought up by a unique sort of tribe.

"My grandfather went with a few friends and a well-equipped unit of British soldiers. She was not the only thing they were after. Tell me, did you ever read the books about a man-ape and his adventures?"

"A couple of comics, when I was a kid."

"Stories about lost cities?"

"Sure—his Africa was busting at the seams with them."

"My grandfather was looking for a city called Oparra. It is supposed to have existed since the time of Atlantis, and may even originally have been a colony, built by its refugees."

I nodded. It had a familiar ring to it.

"Oparra exists. Men have searched for it for centuries. The Bible mentions it as Ophir, where Solomon mined vast amounts of gold, more than enough for building his temple at Jerusalem. Ophir, or Opar, or Oparra."

"King Solomon's Mines," I said. "Another novel. In my world."

He smiled like I'd probed a live nerve and I found myself warming to him, the downright mischief in those eyes. "Quite," he said. "And it wasn't just gold buried under the twin mountains. There were diamonds, too. Countless heaps of them! An unimaginable fortune. My grandfather was after them." He stood up abruptly and walked over to a huge writing desk, unlocking one of its beautifully lacquered drawers, slid it open and pulled out a white cloth. He handed it over.

I unrolled it carefully and gasped. I'd revealed a clutch of diamonds, each of them bigger than any rock I'd ever seen. These were for real, and as for value, the sky was the limit. I handed them back like they'd scorched my hand. He re-wrapped them and put them on a small table.

"Morton Riderman and his companions didn't find Lavender Claywood. But they found Oparra, the gold, walls of it, and a hill of diamonds. Truly limitless wealth. Now—can you imagine how dangerous it would be for any one man, or group, to have access to such wealth, in world terms? Frightening thought, isn't it? When my grandfather discovered Oparra, World War One was some years away, but Germany was a rising power, also searching for the lost city and its resources. My grandfather brought back a fortune, but the secret of the city's location was kept shut away from the rest of the world. It was forgotten about, slipping into the mists of legend."

He refilled our brandy glasses and sat, though I could see his tale had made him edgy. He drew long on his pipe and exhaled a cloud that would have fumigated a cathedral.

"In 1968," he went on eventually, "I went looking for the city. And found it. In the renamed Democratic Republic of the Congo, buried away in the mountainous jungles of its Katanga province. Given the bloody history of the region, it was one hell of a place to get into, but we did it, and secretly, too. I had the original map and a key to get in.

"The city in our world and time is in ruins. Lavender Claywood wasn't there, but there was a statue of her, as the adopted queen of the city—from thousands of years in its past! Somehow she'd gone back—or more likely, been abducted."

I kept a straight face, sipping my brandy.

"My grandfather's expedition was thwarted by the priests of Oparra, the beast men who rule. They're huge, gorilla-like, and immensely powerful. When I visited the city, I was almost killed by them. About fifty of them must move through the various ages of the city, as guardians."

Time hopping? That's what he was talking about. Nuts. I tried not to look incredulous.

"My grandfather and his companions escaped the city with an absolute fortune in gold and diamonds. Suffice it to say, after a pretty violent battle, my own expedition withdrew, also with a substantial prize in diamonds, re-sealed the city, and came home. I visited there again in 1985, and my intention was to leave Oparra shut away in time indefinitely.

"However—recent events have stirred up every hornet's nest imaginable. There is only one genuine map of Oparra and several forgeries, all inaccurate, being part of the subterfuge, the means by which people like me keep Oparra's real location secret. And there's only one key to the city. After my 1985 expedition, I set part of my operation up here, in New York, the perfect place to secrete the map and key. My home in England would have been an obvious target for thieves. I created a dummy vault there and let it be known discreetly that the secrets of Oparra were locked within."

"Someone got wise," I said for him.

"More than that. They broke into my vault here and took the map and the key. It's only a matter of time before they attempt to visit Oparra and pillage it. I want to prevent that, and the inevitable bloodbath that would erupt, by stealing the map and key back."

"So the thieves are still in New York?"

"I gather one of them is dead." His eyes fixed on me, and again I felt that sense of mischief. Could I trust him? He picked up the cloth with the diamonds in it and handed it over.

"Take another look. If need be, have them examined. They're genuine. That's a lot of money, Mr Stone. They're yours. In exchange for what you took from Little Jimmy Ratter." I had figured this was coming.

"You want the map for these? Sounds like a deal." Like I said, I was not much more than a kid, and a tad green.

"Almost. I want the map. And I want your help. I want the key back and I need you working on that for me. In exchange, keep the diamonds. If you help me get the key, there will be a lot more."

If he really was on the level, this was going to be the biggest pay-off imaginable. Those diamonds would buy a small country.

"There is one other twist," he said. "Rather a painful one."

"There always is."

"The New York the enemy has entered is not the one in your world. It's in the Pulpworld. I'm afraid you may not know it as well as you know your home."

I looked down at my empty brandy glass. My distorted features looked back at me, as blurred and indistinct as my future. I could be filthy rich. Yeah, and probably very dead with it, I thought. Hell, I was young, fit and healthy, keen to get on, arrogant, and the brandy had washed away most of my common sense.

We shook hands and I'd taken my first steps in.

* * * *

Sir Henry provided me with a bunch of information, both about the Pulpworld, and everything he knew about the thieves. I had a limited amount of time to study it—he said it would disintegrate in a day or two. It did.

Meanwhile I had the diamonds checked out by a reliable source—even in those days I had some good connections. And those rocks were for real. I was indeed filthy rich. I also had Sir Henry checked out and what I learned about him said he was a bone fide good guy. You have to take a chance or two in life, and my guess was, I could afford to take a chance on him. I gave him the map and he was happy, up to a point.

He fixed for me to visit a friend of his, Guy Abbot, an archivist, who worked in an athenaeum.

I was wandering down a street full of abandoned houses and derelict parking lots, en route to the appointed place, when I felt the air change, as though a sudden bank of cold fog was rolling over me. It was a bizarre, brown pall, like something you'd expect in a Jack the Ripper movie, and I knew something was right off-key. I looked back the way I'd come and saw the fog closing in like a fist. There were shapes inside it, unfurling like thick ropes, writhing along the road towards me. I was thinking about tongues, claws, delightful stuff like that.

Something wanted me for lunch. I took out my twin Berettas and fired off a few rounds. It was like tossing peanuts at a landslide. Smaller shapes were emerging, the size of horses, but much wider, and greener. Some kind of nasty mutations, their own long tendrils whipping forward, cracking the air. I knew if they touched me, I was done for.

I ducked and ran. I could see the athenaeum up ahead with another bank of muck sliding forward beyond it, complete with its unsavoury denizens that would have given Mr Hyde a fit of shudders. I made it to the gate and turned in before I could be dragged back. A door opened and a lone figure peered out at the rapidly darkening day. Seeing me, the man waved me to him and we just about got inside before the fog bank slapped up against the outside like a big wave.

"Glad to meet you, Mr Stone," said my rescuer. "I'm Guy Abbot. Sorry it's such a mucky night."

He babbled on enthusiastically as though the horrors outside had been no more than a passing thought and led me somewhere deep in the heart of the crumbling old building. It must have been on someone's demolition list. The whole place was stuffed with books: some of them looked like they'd been here since men first started writing. Guy was the original bookworm. He had a deep, rich voice that boomed unexpectedly out of his thin frame. He wasn't an inch over five feet, and in his scruffy jacket looked like he came from another age. I shook hands, trying not to wince and he regarded me from eyes that sparkled with a kind of mischievous intelligence.

"I gather you're working for Sir Henry."

"Sure. I need a few leads."

He led me up a metal spiral staircase and the climb went on so long I got dizzy, plus I guessed we must have gone up into the spire of a church, it was so high. But the old building was one of those geometrical mysteries from its period, because when my host unlocked the tiny door at the top, we entered a cavernous room. The floor was so far down it was lost in shadows. I'd never seen so many books in one place. Walls of them that went up and down for ever.

"This is a very private collection. Nothing, but nothing, compares with this. Not even the Miskatonic, much to their exasperation." I could see he was loving it.

We crossed a gantry. I'm not a great man for heights, and felt my bowels clenching as we teetered along the shifting steel floor. More books loomed over us. Finally we came to an open reading area.

"I need to explain about some rather unpleasant things, I'm afraid."

"Like the things I just saw outside this building?"

"Oh, much worse."

My education began right there. I was about to have my eyes, ears and mind, truly opened. Guy spoke of a whole lot more than the Walrus ever got to tell the Carpenter, and he backed it up by fetching some of the most unbelievable books and opening up their secrets.

"Impossible to say when it all started," said Guy. "Long before Man climbed out of the seas. It's been speculated in fact and fiction for centuries that forces have come to our world from outside. Forces that have, at various times, controlled Man, or had that control wrested from them. It's a ceaseless struggle. Human life is a microcosm of what goes on across the vast tracts of space and time."

"God and the Devil," I said.

"That's just one interpretation of many. Light and Darkness is another, and probably simpler." He pointed to the huge grimoire he'd set down. "This is one of the oldest books we have. It talks about Lemuria, Mu, Thuran, Valusia and Atlantis, although not necessarily using those names. It also mentions some of the fabulous heroes of those ancient epochs, who first fought the darker powers."

I'd read a few pulps and comic books. Guy was talking about these characters like they'd been real. At that time, as a young, naïve rookie private eye, I didn't know any better. So I eyed him sceptically.

"Most myths are based on facts," he said, patiently. "Take, for example, Elak, a fabled king of Atlantis. This volume chronicles his struggles against the darker forces, which were emerging in his time, and which were the roots of what has followed down the centuries. There are the first references here to the lost city of Oparra, its beast men priests—who were originally from Atlantis.

"In Elak's time, dark forces attempted to sink the known world and create their own kingdom, perverting the course of evolution and driving Man back into either the slime, or slavery. Elak defeated them, but they rose again. As you know, Atlantis and much of its world did succumb to immolation, though more naturally, but Man was not subdued. The dark forces ebbed and flowed, always in opposition.

"Oparra endured many changes over time. It was at its peak 5,000 years ago, ruled by a white queen, who was known as Lalanda."

"Yeah, Sir Henry put me wise to her. Lavender Claywood, from 1910.

She went back in time."

"Oparra is the centre of fabulous powers, a cosmic wheel of time and space. It's all in the book." He tapped the wide pages and I could see the script beneath his fingers, dancing with its own kind of magic. "Over the centuries, the city has decayed, its priests becoming more and more debased, yet still serving its goddess. It has become a vault, an impregnable fortress for many secrets. These—and I'm not referring to the vast amount of gold and the heaps of diamonds—are not to be shared by any but the most devout opponents of the dark forces."

He closed the book and pulled another from the several he had originally taken from the mountainous racks.

"This is a summary of a codex, which we do have in its original manuscript form. The codex lists the details of what can be found in what is probably the most terrifying book in existence, the Malleus Tenebrarum, a work which describes all the artefacts of power, created long, long ago in what were certainly pre-human times. The book also describes how they may be used. We don't have the book—only one copy exists and it is guarded very carefully. The powers of darkness never cease their efforts to purloin it. If they did so, it would cause catastrophe on a cosmic scale.

"This codex is protected by ancient spells. If our enemies as much as looked at it, it would disintegrate. Among the artefacts listed are certain keys. For example, keys to the Pulpworld. These are given to only the most trusted of its protectors.

"As you know, there is a map to Oparra, which I understand you were able to retrieve for Sir Henry, and a key to the city, a key which will open the path back in time to all aspects of it. Our enemies now possess that key—it will give them resources beyond imagining. Enough to fund their numerous plots and subversion of authority, as well as developing whatever they need to wrest complete control. They will open doors to other worlds, other gods, and raise up whole armies—the opportunities, gorged on such wealth, would be limitless."

I shook my head. "So how come you want me—I'm a single maggot in an apple the size of a planet—to get these things back? Sounds to me like you need an army."

Guy smiled. "Don't underestimate the power of the individual, Mr Stone. Your analogy, while unfortunate in some ways, is very apt. But who would find a maggot in an apple that big? It would be a singularly elusive maggot, would it not?"

His words didn't console me. Who likes a maggot? Fishermen, maybe, and we all know what they do with them.

* * * *

I visited Guy several times and on the last of those visits, he tipped me off about a possible lead. He took me to one of the countless spiral staircases in the upper athenaeum that wriggled upwards like the tunnels of oversize worms to the roof. He opened a trapdoor, and I saw a circle of pure darkness beyond, starless and forbidding.

"Pulpworld awaits you," said Guy, grinning at me in spite of my evident unease.

Suddenly a face was peering at us both from the opening. It was pinched and narrow, and anyone calling the guy who owned it a weasel would have been right on the money. The eyes were very piercing, glittering somehow, and the hands that gripped the rim of the opening were gnarled, the fingernails sharply pointed. Amazingly the creature was even smaller than the archivist.

"Need to move," it hissed through teeth like needles.

Guy told me, "You'll be in Rafe's safe hands. He's a Roof Runner."

"The best," piped up the diminutive figure above. "We going, or what?"

I climbed out on to the roof and my new companion closed the trapdoor, leaving us in a half-glimpsed landscape of rooftops, garrets, skylights, turrets, and every kind of high level bit of architecture you could name, like this was the lost property office for all of them. Light seeped upwards from indistinct sources, combining to give a lurid glow to everything, a kind of greenish, swamp-like miasma. And that roofscape—man, that was the last word in bizarre.

For a start, I wasn't just looking at the roof of the athenaeum, although that was a complex geometrical nightmare all on its own, but countless other roofs that linked in, stretching as far away as the eye could see, and curiously, that was a long way. These roofs dipped and swayed, some horribly steep, others flat, some curving, still more stepped, all interlaced with cupolas, small turrets, endless chimney stacks, even a spire or two, although I'd never seen anything remotely approaching them for weirdness. Gothic had nothing on this realm.

"You're looking for something what was nicked."

I figured Rafe was talking about the key Sir Henry wanted. "Sure. What you got?"

"Come and see." His eyes flashed like jewels. It must have been part of the landscape and the way its mad light danced. Rafe danced, too, running over the roofscape like an oversized rodent, sniffing like one, and I ducked down and followed, almost slipping on cracked slates a dozen times or more. My introduction to the Pulpworld didn't fill me with awe and wonder. Already I wanted to go home.

We paused at a jumble of chimney stacks that leaned over like they were about to topple, their mortar worn thin, their bricks like fat red biscuits, slowly disintegrating. Clouds of grey smoke poured out of their pots, reminiscent of a Victorian London. In fact, looking around me I came to the conclusion that this couldn't be New York. Not mine, anyway.

Crouching down beside Rafe, I got my breath back.

"A few nights back," he told me, "I got a sniff of something. There's this big hotel place not far off. Owned by some toffs, right? Murky lot. Don't like anyone poking their snouts in. So we've got to be watchful, got it? There'll be ravens about. Big buggers. They go for the eyes, then when they've pecked them out, they drive you to the nearest edge and you goes over. It's a long way down and no one bounces."

I slipped out one of my Berettas. "Would this help?"

He beamed. "Yeah. That'll do nicely." He studied the shadowed terrain and moved us on like a couple of raiding commandos. After another tortuous scuttle across the roofs, we reached one huge area, a series of dips and rises, another Victorian edifice, squeezed in between a high rise block and a broken-down church. The city planners in this district must have been sniffing something potent when they put this collection together.

Rafe pointed to several curving, dome-like windows, a number of which glowed. They reminded me of very large mushrooms, the poisonous type. "Down there," said the Roof Runner. "That's where they meet. They worship gods you never heard the like of. Nasty. I've heard them chanting and seen a few things. Ugly stuff. Mostly I keeps away."

"They got what I'm looking for?"

He nodded. "Not here. They make plans to use it. I heard them. Said they'd be talking about it tonight. They'll be there now. Want to see?"

I looked across at the curved glass. I can't say I had a mind to venture out across it. If it shattered under my weight, I'd be delivered into the laps of the creeps in the chamber below. Not my idea of a fun night out.

Rafe was pointing at a wide chimney, ivy growing in profusion up one side; it had already dragged a couple of the bigger pots off the top and swallowed them. Not the most heart-warming image. No smoke emerged from the chimney and my guess was it was long since disused. Before Rafe could say anything, several dark shapes flapped close overhead: the ravens had arrived.

When Rafe had described them as big buggers, he hadn't been kidding. These were the size of eagles, and their claws looked even bigger. Rafe pulled something out of a pocket and held it up, a thin rod. It glowed with scarlet light. I had both guns out, but Rafe shook his head. "If they attacks," he said, "let them have it. Otherwise this will keep them off us. Those down below would hear the guns."

I kept an eye on the huge birds—now a flock—as we started the climb up the old chimney. It was easy enough, especially with the ivy offering numerous hand-holds. Once we were on top, the ravens got even more agitated, but they didn't like Rafe's scarlet light, as though it radiated something radioactive. One of the birds did make a try for the little guy, but when it got close, the red light pulsed and the bird crash-dived in flames and rolled down a sloping roof to its gutter. The other birds took a dim view of it and held back, but by now they were kicking up a ruckus fit to wake the entire city.

I knew what Rafe had in mind. He wanted us to slip down inside the chimney. Okay, he'd used it before, so I went with it, although the tight fit didn't fill me with confidence. If I'd had a problem with claustrophobia I'd have passed out, but I let Rafe lead me deeper down that black funnel. It stank of old soot and I'd need some fresh clothes once we got out of here. But we emerged in a dark room, dusty and almost empty, clambering out of its huge fireplace. I was trying not to cough my lungs up.

"Must keep quiet," said Rafe, unsympathetically. "The lot below us may have heard the ravens. May know something's up."

At the door Rafe peered out. There were lights far down below, but up here the place remained in shadow. Which suited me just fine.

"Thought so," he whispered. "Another banquet. Heard them mention the key the other night. Now they want the map."

He stooped low and slipped out onto a mezzanine. I followed. The floor was unstable, its timbers bending, eaten by woodworm, but it held. Rafe took us to a spot high above the gathering. I had to peer through the gaps in the floor to see anything. My view was not the best. I could make out about two dozen figures, all dressed in their board of director's finest, seated along both sides of a long dining table, the remains of a sumptuous meal spread over it. As the men sipped their tall glasses of wine, it looked like a multinational, about to decide on its next takeover. I didn't recognise anyone, but there were men from all over—Africans, Orientals, Hispanics, white Caucasians and others. An international selection, and my guess was, there was a whole heap of money behind this.

They wanted more—the Oparran payoff.

One of them was standing, talking. "Our best efforts to find out what went wrong with the securing of the map have led us to a blank wall," he said in a smooth American accent. "I told you last time what happened at that cheap burger joint. Investigations have not led us to the truth—who killed our collectors, and who took the map."

There was a general murmur of unrest. Rafe had been right, these guys were not amused. One of them stood up, but I could only see the back of his head and broad shoulders. He was tall and muscular, his hair dark, slicked back. When he spoke, his voice was cultured and very English. "I am convinced the map is now in the hands of Sir Henry Riderman. Who else would know about it?"

Again there were murmurs, this time of assent.

"I propose we act on that basis. Would the company allow me to put my strategy into play? I'm convinced it's the only way to prize the map from our enemy's hands."

The man opposite smiled thinly. I thought of reptiles and other cold things. "I'd support that. Subtlety does have its rewards. However, if we fail again, we'll have to visit Sir Henry Riderman with an altogether much more violent resolution to this problem."

This met with applause. Obviously these creeps would enjoy the kind of nightmare visitation being suggested. I felt like I was peering down into a big tank of barracuda.

"Need anything else?" said Rafe.

"You know where the key is?"

"Oh, they've got it. Dunno where. It'll be heavily guarded. I've put the word out among the Roof Runners. One of the clan will get a fix on it. You'll be the first to know."

* * * *

"It's something of an impasse," said Sir Henry. He'd assembled a group of his companions, a bunch of guys not unlike him, a doctor of philosophy, a military man, some others who had accompanied him on his travels—all of them I imagined useful when the chips were down. There were two women in the group, young and very attractive, but they weren't there for show. They had teeth, and like their companions, wouldn't stand for any shenanigans. And he'd secreted me in an alcove, curtained off from view, where I could see and hear what went on.

"I reckon the direct approach would be a bad idea," said Daniel Carter, a man who'd spent a lot of his time in Africa. "Too risky."

Sir Henry looked at his watch, a mite irritably. "Where is Claywood, for heaven's sake? That man would lose his confounded head if it wasn't screwed on."

As if on cue the door to the large drawing room opened and a butler entered, politely bowing. "Apologies, Sir Henry, but you did ask me to let you know when Eustace Claywood arrived. He's outside, sir."

"Thank you, Petherton. Send him in."

The young man who entered the room was stoop-shouldered, nervy as a cat on a hot tin roof, and had more than a hint of a stammer when he stated his apologies.

"Don't worry, old chap," said Sir Henry, masking his irritability. "You know everyone."

Claywood looked nervous: of all that party, this guy stood out like a cherry tree in a pumpkin patch. My guess was, he was one of the Clay-woods descended from the girl lost back in 1888.

Drinks were served, and everyone sat, the air around them taut as a bowstring.

"What d' you make of it all?" Carter said to Claywood, who jolted back in his chair like he'd been slapped.

"I disagree with your inactivity," he said, struggling to get the words out.

One of the women, Agatha Berridale, laughed, though not unkindly. "Good lord, Eustace, we're not used to hearing fighting talk from you." Obviously she relished the thought, her eyes gleaming. I had her down for a tough cookie.

"Well, I'm sorry, Sir Henry, but I have to say, my family has had a raw deal over the years. When your grandfather first went to Oparra, he was looking for Lavender, it's true. But he was more concerned about the diamonds and the gold! Poor Lavender wasn't found and no attempt was made to keep searching. Then you went there yourself, and again, no real effort was made to find a way to Lavender—"

"Goodness me, Eustace," said Sir Henry, and I could see he was un-happy about the accusations. "That's not true, you know. On both my vis-its, they were tricky situations. We were lucky to get out with our skins intact."

"Yes, but you made sure you brought a pile of diamonds with you! Well, I think we should go back and really make an effort to find Laven-der! If that key can open the past and we can go back, then we can find her. My family has grieved over her loss for over a century! Knowing that somehow, she's still alive, among those, those—savages!" It was quite a mouthful and Claywood was sweating, mopping his brow and face with a big silk handkerchief.

Carter scowled. "You want us to launch an expedition to Oparra? You forget—there's a snag."

Claywood shook his head, looking even more nervous. "No. You're wrong. You think Vanderborg and his Satanists have the key. You think they stole it, and the map. You got the map back, I know that. But what if someone else stole the key?"

Now I was getting very interested in this. Claywood's performance had been an eye-opener, that was for sure. I watched him very closely. What was I missing?

"Vanderborg," he went on, "is bluffing you. He doesn't have the key. I do."

Every eye in the place was on him. Everyone thought he was talking through the back of his neck.

"I may be an easy touch, but I'm not short of resources. The Clay-woods benefitted from the raids on Oparra, too. I bought help. I bought the thief, I over-bid you! And I've got the key to Oparra."

"For God's sake!" gasped Sir Henry. "Where is it? Is it safe?"

"It's at my estate. It would need an army to wrest it from me. Vanderborg can do his worst, although he doesn't know I have it. We can arrange an expedition to Oparra before he realizes."

Sir Henry sat back and the others regarded Claywood with a new respect. This had taken balls they didn't know he had.

"Eustace, our prime aim is to prevent Vanderborg and his cronies from getting at the Oparran treasure, knowing what that would mean. We'd be resourcing the agents of Hell itself! We must prevent that!"

Claywood looked petulant. "Well, you won't get the key from me if you don't help me rescue Lavender. After that, it's yours." He folded his arms and sat hunched in his chair like a sulking schoolkid. "You have two days! Come to my estate then, and we'll plan. Bring the map."

* * * *

"What the deuce do you make of all that?" a slightly bewildered Sir Henry said to me once everyone had gone.

"Claywood is one smart guy. I've seen him before. I didn't get it at first, but I saw him that night I visited the Pulpworld. Vanderborg's banquet. Claywood was there. Not so hunched up and nervous. He did a good job squeezing those shoulders together, and making with the stammer. He must have worked on that for years."

"He's always been the runt of the Claywood litter."

I shook my head. "Neat trick." I explained what Rafe and I had heard in more detail. "So he does have the key. And he wants us to take the map to him and plan a trip to Oparra. Vanderborg and his chums will be waiting for us!"

"You're right, of course. There's no limit to the black powers they'll unleash."

"Can anyone sneak in and check the place over?" Who was I kidding? I meant me. Rush of blood. "Could Rafe slip me down a chimney?"

"Damn risky business, but it would be worth a try. If we knew where the key was, we could take a strong company to Claywood's and make a play for it.—at least we'd have the advantage of surprise." He was bristling with enthusiasm. Me, I just wondered if I'd talked myself into an early grave.

* * * *

Two nights later, we put the plan into action. I had my twin Berettas, and some anti-Satanic stuff—charms, necklaces, a thin rod carved like it was from a Druid's temple. I also had, unknown to my new colleagues, a few items of my own. Over the last few years, setting myself up in the city, I'd got to know several weird characters, and I am talking weird with a capital W. I'd helped them through some tough times, and they'd paid me in kind. Powerful juju, they said. Time to put it to the test.

I hooked up with Rafe the Roof Runner on the balcony of a huge, silent spread adjacent to Claywood's estate, which wasn't far removed from Sir Henry's and was no less extravagant, even for that salubrious neck of the New York woods. There was something mighty strange about the atmosphere. Since that trip of mine into the Pulpworld, I'd become more sensitive to such things, and I wondered if I'd slipped across to it again.

"Interesting pile," said Rafe as we made like monkeys and crossed several interwoven branches, over a tall wall and eventually up on to the roof of Claywood's. We disturbed a few indefinable black-winged birds, but Rafe made certain crow-like sounds that scared the hell out of them. I was glad of his company.

"I've been inside the place," he said. "Reeks of money and evil power. It's got a basement, way down. Big, like a crypt. They're guarding something. You sure you want to poke your nose in? Nastiest hell-hole I've seen."

"I just want to take a peek."

He obviously thought I was a prime contender for the funny farm. "This chimney here'll get you to ground level. A mite tight, but I've enlarged it in places." He gave me some idea of the lay-out below and how to find Dracula's crypt. "You want me to wait?"

"Sure. I might need some help when I come back out."

"If any of them guardian things follow you, I won't be hanging around."

I didn't wait for him to elaborate, and climbed down into the sooty mouth of the chimney flue, a pencil flashlight gripped in my teeth. In those days I was a lot slimmer, so I was able to wriggle and squirm downwards, through a thousand spider webs, until I saw a vague light below me. There were enough brick ledges to support me and I dangled sideways to peer into what was a lavish room, thankfully unoccupied. I dropped into the huge fireplace and immediately felt the embrace of the building, like I'd slipped under the surface of a warm pool. Money shouted at me from every direction, the walls hung with a spectacular array of huge paintings, big game trophies, and shields representing the sporting triumphs of the Claywood family over the years. The pretend Eustace would have been a real oddity in his family if he'd really been a sap. The broad-shouldered man I'd seen with Vanderborg's pals was obviously at home in this place.

I sneaked out into a wide hall. I found an over-sized bathroom you could have thrown a party in and checked out another door. It led to a narrower corridor and stairs going down. No signs of guards, so I investigated. The place would have rivalled any palace, with more rooms than the Ritz-Carlton. I kept on going, checking out room after room, until, at the end of another long corridor, I saw a door that had "strictly no entry" carved all over it. Okay, those weren't the words per se, but the elaborate hieroglyphs and archaic diagrams said it all. Something in the air near the door made my flesh creep. That may be the place where the key was stored, but I decided the direct approach was a no go. If I was going into an ante-room of Hell, I'd sooner sneak in the side door.

Further along the corridor was another door. I tried it. Bingo. I eased it open and found myself in a bedroom, or should I say, boudoir? Its lights were on, soft and exotic, velvet drapes everywhere and a huge bed that looked like it could have housed a whole team of houris. Eustace Claywood may have had a harem somewhere, but thankfully none of its members were present. I shuffled through the elaborate items of furniture and tried to ignore the pungent, perfumed atmosphere. I saw movement overhead and ducked, but the entire ceiling was a mirror.

I found what I wanted beside the biggest wardrobe this side of the Winter Palace—a curtained alcove that hid a door. This one was locked, so I took out my special key, the one that would open anything short of Ali Baba's cave. No one had followed me, so I got the door open. A blast of chilling air hit me and my senses were screaming at me to withdraw. I went in.

More stairs—stone steps, this time, leading down into that cold well. My tiny flashlight couldn't penetrate more than a few feet either way, but my instincts told me I was in a huge chamber, and I do mean huge. Like I'd wandered into St Paul's Cathedral in London. I was on tiptoe, guessing the slightest sound would be magnified a hundredfold. The stairs curled around and around, until light from below threw the place into full relief. No relief for me, though. I was like an ant inside a zeppelin.

The stone walls curved upwards and opposite my precarious steps a huge statue, apparently hewn from the bedrock, glared at me from baleful eyes, its naked form, obese and grotesque, dominating the vast space. One arm held aloft some kind of tray, on which coals blazed away, while down below, between the jutting knees of the squatting monstrosity, an area opened out into a rough arena. The floor was tiled, blood-red, a wide circle enclosing several others, with numerous symbols, figures and some kind of mathematical formulae dotted around the inside. Not something I wanted to set foot on.

There were several braziers around this circle, and by their hot glow I saw what was at the heart of the circles. A narrow stand, chest high with a flat top. Thereupon sat a glowing object, and I didn't need Einstein to tell me it was the Oparran key. All I had to do was amble over and lift it. That simple.

I wasn't that much of a mug. Something protected it, and it wasn't long before I found out what. The air inside the circle twisted and pulsed, darkening until it sculpted a shape. It was almost human. Naked, gleaming, it looked like a man-high mound of potter's clay that someone had punched and moulded, with a vague idea of what they wanted the finished product to look like. It had male genitalia, so distorted they made my eyes water, as well as female breasts, bizarrely mismatched. The head, an oversized blob, had a mouth as wide as a tunnel, a totally dark orifice, and two eyes that I refused to look at. I knew it would have meant instant damnation.

At the foot of the stairs I remained in shadow. I pulled out both guns, although I was thinking they'd be a fat lot of good against this horror. It was trying to finish shaping itself, and when it spoke, its voice was a woman's, a hideous attempt at being seductive. Its eyes, brilliant as diamonds, stripped the darkness from me.

"No need for violence," it said. "Why don't you come here and relax?"

I moved very slowly around the edge of the wide circle. Relax? I'd have found that easier in a pool full of starving piranhas. I kept one eye on the demon, which was now getting the hang of transforming, becoming far more feminine and, as it thought, seductive. Too late for that. My other eye was fixed on the Oparran key. Okay, I'd found it, and could simply report back, but if I could steal it, I could prevent a pitched battle—how the blazes could I do it, though?

Blazes, yes. That might work. I knew there was no way I dared step into the circle. Mercifully, as the demon followed me, slinking around the inner perimeter, it couldn't step outside, bound by whoever had summoned it. The key wasn't going anywhere. So Claywood would have thought.

I took careful aim with both Berettas. My guess was, the key would be tough enough to resist a shot or two—almost certainly cut from Oparran diamond. Worth the risk. I fired: the combined blast shook the chamber. The demon-thing leaned back momentarily, laughing, or at least, I took the strangled sounds it was making for some kind of mocking delight. My ears rang, but my eyes widened as the shadows retreated.

I'd hit the key. It went spinning off its stand and flew across the far side of the circle. Now it was a few inches from its edge, though still inside it. The demon and I saw it simultaneously. I made a loping run around the perimeter, while the demon hopped like a giant flea across it. It was going to get to the key before me. If it did, I'd lose it.

I loosed off several shots, but it was like shooting at fresh air. So I took aim and went for the jewel. I hit it just as the demon bent down to retrieve it. Its slender fingers were about to close on it, when it skittered out of the circle and hit the wall. The demon screamed and ran smack up against whatever invisible barrier was restraining it. It turned to me, its tongue unrolling like a huge chameleon's, but the disgusting fleshy rope also smacked up against the invisible barrier. Sizzling spittle ran down it, seemingly in mid-air.

Cautiously I made my way round to the key. The demon followed me on all fours, no more than a couple of feet away, shrieking hideously, rocking the entire chamber so I thought maybe the walls would collapse. Writhing shapes had emerged from holes in the base of the chamber walls, serpent-like and deep green, cruel fangs gleaming, eager to sink into my flesh. I was surrounded and they were closing in.

I fired at the nearest of them and they spat back at me angrily. Gobbets of venom splashed the stone wall near me and I made a dash for the great feet of the idol, the only place I could avoid the slithering horrors. I leapt up, almost slipping. It would have been curtains if I had. The things had gathered in force and a blizzard of sizzling venom had me ducking the bolts of fire. The air enclosing the circle crackled, like mist being instantly dissipated in hot sunlight.

That was more bad news—the demon was free. And there was only one thing on its mind. Me. It hopped upwards, and my guess is, would have landed on me and pulped me into a fleshy, steaming mess if I hadn't scuttled up to the next level of the statue like a rat up a drainpipe. I didn't wait to hear the hissing and spitting below me, not to mention the vile curses and descriptions of what the thing said it would do once it got its poisonous claws into my wretched hide. I just climbed.

I reached the statue's lap, another elongated tray, on which two small braziers burned hotly. I kicked them over the lip and heard a shriek as coals tumbled out into the face of the demon. Chunks of flesh were torn from it, tumbling below in a torrent of steaming grue. But it kept on coming. I climbed up a fat forearm, my body level with the glaring face of the statue, which I swear had turned to look at me with the anticipation of a gourmand about to gorge itself.

So where the heck was I headed? There was no holding the demon. I looked directly above me. In the curved ceiling, a few feet above the bald dome of the statue's head, there was a grille—it was through this the smoke from the braziers rose. A flue! Hot damn, it must lead up to the roof. Maybe I could get into it and back to where Rafe would be waiting. I clambered unsteadily on to the statue's head, still expecting the thing to open its ugly mug and snap me up.

The demon was still below me, though slowed by the hot shower of coals I'd given it. Parts of its torso were burning, enough to slow it down. I looked around me. On either side of the statue's head there were two hanging steel baskets, each filled with more blazing coals. I stretched out and unhooked one. The chain was damned hot to the touch, but the hell with that. I swung it like a hammer thrower busting a gut at an Olympic final and crashed the basket and coals into the grille overhead. It disintegrated in an explosion of red hot coals. Something pawed at my feet, but I leapt upwards, my hands grasping the edge of the smashed grille opening. I swung to and fro for a few terrifying moments, then I was up.

It was a long climb up the flue, enveloped in darkness, and I knew the demon was still pursuing me, though maybe not as fast as it would have liked. Finally I was out into the cool night air. Thankfully Rafe was waiting, his face a mask of amazement. He helped drag me out.

"Better move quick," he said, "this old chimney stack is about to—"

Collapse. He was right. The bricks heaved and imploded. I'd done enough monkeying about inside to dislodge too much of the old mortar. Rafe and I watched as the entire stack folded in on itself. I allowed myself the luxury of thinking the landslide of bricks down the flue would have carried the demon with it, back into the chamber far below.

"Mission accomplished?" said Rafe.

"We need to be a long way from this place, as soon as possible," I told him. "The guardians are not amused."

* * * *

Sir Henry listened as I recounted my escapades, sitting back with a long drawn out breath as I finished. "You were lucky to get out alive," he said. "Dammit man, you shouldn't have risked your neck. All we needed was to know where the key was."

"That reminds me," I said, reaching into my pocket. "I almost forgot." I handed him a folded handkerchief. "In all that mayhem with the serpent-things, I did manage to snatch that up."

He unfolded the handkerchief and gazed in wonder at the key. "My God! You brought it out!"

I grinned—very smugly, I admit. "Yessir. It was touch and go. Let's say I did it for the diamonds."

DREADFUL APPETITE
by Franklyn Searight

For countless years I believed myself to be unequaled in the techniques of thaumaturgy. But I was wrong. There was another wizard, one with powers at his command much greater than my own. This I learned from my friend and ward, the youthful Kuthar, who has grown up almost before my very eyes to be the strong and self-reliant man he now is. It was he who revealed to me this other sorcerer, one quite competent to challenge my claim of supremacy in the craft in which I felt myself unequaled. It came about one day...

—Culled from the Runes of Tromcor

*

Rondo, an unusually strong and healthy child, braver and more inquisitive than most, strayed further out onto the meadow than usual, running and romping, and rolling in the thick greenery of the grasslands near his village home. It caused no concern for his parents, Kuthar and Lanoma. They sat at the edge of the forest, watching him as affectionate parents will, certain the lad, at the slightest hint of danger, would be on his way toward them as rapidly as his little legs would carry him.

Life was good, especially for a boy of five years old. Minutes earlier he had been selecting and picking the prettiest of flowers blooming in abundance, for his mother, and chasing the brightest colored butterflies, reaching and leaping to grab them in their flight.

Kuthar's eyes were continuously scrutinizing the lowlands and the wood side, ever on the alert for signs of predatory animals. A long toothed tiger, perhaps, or a hulking grizzly, might make an appearance, seeking midday sustenance to energize their bulky bodies. This was a constant vigil he maintained, except within the sanctuary of his home—it was only there he could relax and suspend his guard—for he lived at a time and in an area where only the strongest and the most vigilant survived. As the leader of his clan, he was well aware most animals subliminally make unobtrusive noises indicating their presence, no matter how silent they believed themselves to be. During his young life he had encountered attacks from the most fearsome creatures of the wild, and battled them with scant weaponry to defend himself. Avoiding contact with them was always his hope, but he also knew he would not flinch in the protection of his wife and son.

Lanoma shifted her position and eased her back to the ground, contented, unafraid, and fully aware the man next to her was the greatest protection she could ever hope to have. Her eyes drifted about the blueness above, and a gathering of fleecy clouds moving slowly across the scope of her vision, going no place in particular. It's a heavenly scene of placid serenity, she thought. Life was good. Kuthar and Rondo were good. Nothing could mar the perfect happiness she felt.

But destiny does not always create the most reliable of conditions. A dark speck was in the sky, low over the horizon, drawing closer and larger as she studied it.

"What is it, Kuthar?" she asked, feeling no alarm, only inquisitiveness, pointing at the object in the sky rapidly increasing in size. She sat up straight.

Kuthar had been watching a section of the forest nearby, and elevated his head to see where she was pointing. He, however, did begin to feel the prickling sensation of alarm, although he believed the sight was nothing special for them to fear.

"I don't know," he said, gripping the spear by his side and standing up, shaking off the grass shredded on his loincloth. In the following second, a flying creature zoomed out of the sky, its pointed head swinging from side to side, its gigantic wings no longer flapping up and down, but held straight out in a glide, its gigantic talons unfolded and ready to pounce upon its prey.

"Rondo!" Kuthar shouted, still failing to understand what his eyes were witnessing. "Come to me, boy!"

Its head down, the colossus spied the youngster and, as it descended, Kuthar raced toward his son, his spear clutched in one hand. He had never seen such a creature before, but he had heard of them in stories told by elders of his community around the flaring, moonlit fires—undying tales told of these magical apparitions. He knew not what they were called, only of their ability of flight which simply should not be possible because of their uncanny bulk.

His son, unaware of the creature's flight and the danger he was in, responded quickly, nevertheless, just as he had been repeatedly taught. Realizing the danger at last, resounding in the shrill tones of his father, he scampered to safety as best he could.

Rondo heard the flap of giant wings, but did not see the silent claws at the tips of long and knobby legs, thick as the stump of a felled tree, reaching forth to seize him!

Kuthar's speed to grab his son increased by the moment, and it felt as though he were skimming above the turf, just as the creature flew above the ground, its pointed beak open to screech a triumphant cry of seizure. The chieftain, fearful his weapon might harm the child, paused for a moment, but he knew he must certainly intervene. He propelled his spear anyway in hopes it would bring the determined flyer to earth ere it could snatch his child. But at the very moment of release, he stumbled, one leg entangled in a clump of heavy grass. He fell headfirst to the ground, his lance going awry.

Immediately, he was on his feet again, in time to see the bird renew its flight, his little boy, Rondo, in the grasp of its fearsome talons.

A split second remained for him to make his decision. The spear was on the ground, too far away to reach. Weaponless as he was, the hideously cawing bird but a few feet away, rising upward, he launched himself forward, both hands reaching for a tip of the wing, He could hear the flying feet of Lanoma nearing him but knew, even if she were to reach them, she would be of little aid. Grasping the three-tined tail, he was able to pull himself upward, throwing the enormous avian off balance as it struggled to rise. However, the awfulness was not to be denied its prey. It rose steadily, unhampered by the prize held tightly in its grasp. With a violent swish of its tail, Kuthar, unable to retain his grasp, was thrown to the earth. He landed in a clump, narrowly missing Lanoma who had reached him.

For a moment, they hoped the abhorrence would drop the boy close enough to the ground for his father to catch him. But it did not happen. Kuthar was forced to stand there, helplessly, fingering a long, black feather yanked from the obscenity's plumage, and watch the attacker effortlessly ascend into the sky, still clutching Rondo. They could hear the boy's cries of desperation, and were certain the blasphemy had no intention of dropping the prize it sought. The bird continued its flight in the same direction from which it had come, becoming smaller and smaller as the moments passed. Lanoma, sobbing hysterically, had fallen into Kuthar's arms, and the two of them together followed the departure of the abductor as it ascended higher and higher into the sky, farther and farther away, until it disappeared from view.

Kuthar was fully aware, as he resolved to seek and return with Rondo, the days of his incredible adventures had not ended—this was but the beginning of the next.

"Go home," he said to his frenzied wife. "Find Skaf; he's probably returned from his fishing jaunt by now, and is taking a morning snooze. Tell him of our plight. Show him the direction I go, and ask him to join me, if he will, and lend his aid as he has done so often in the past."

Lanoma nodded, wiped her eyes, and fled to their nearby village where their awesome friend would no doubt be found. Kuthar turned and began the strangest odyssey he was ever to encounter, seeking his son who had been snatched from his very grasp.

His resolve was immediate and clear: He would return with Rondo, or forfeit his own life in the attempt. The rippling muscles of his sun-bronzed body flexed with resolve as he set off in the direction taken by the awe-inspiring flying thing.

* * * *

"Yes," nodded Tromcor, while preparing his midday meal when Kuthar stopped by the wizard's cavern on his quest. "I've seen the bird you speak of—infrequently, but from time to time. It wasn't until its flight carried it close to me one day I saw the extend of its mighty girth and the magnificence of its huge wingspan, flapping rapidly to keep the brute airborne, and saw the mighty thews of its legs and body girth. I believed then, as I do now, it is a bird of magical properties. It's inconceivable the good Spirit could have conceived such a monster."

"What else do you know of it?" asked Kuthar.

"There's little more. It stays in our area not long, and returns in the same direction on an airborne pathway to the northern hills. It's there, I believe, it has its aerie, and more than likely where it has taken Rondo."

"Why? Why would it snatch him up?"

"To dine upon him, of course. Or feed him to its young, if it has a brood."

Tromcor slowly turned the spit into the flame, carefully roasting the small hare which had wandering too close to his entrapment. It was a little one, but the meat was sufficient to last him several days. He would have invited Kuthar to join him in his meal, but was fully aware the lad would decline.

"What chance have I, against such odds, of bringing my child safely home?"

Tromcor pondered the question, and then answered, "Consider the hairs upon your head. What is the chance of selecting a certain one? Your chance of success is perhaps a bit better. But we both know there is always hope, and with immense determination, anything can happen."

"What powder I have left to summon your presence in time of need is back at my home. There was no time to return for it."

"Have no concern, Kuthar. I have more—newly made"

He reached toward a lower ledge running along one wall of his rock-hewn cavern and plucked from it a small pouch he handed to the young tribal chief.

"Use it in case of need," he advised, "but sparingly."

Tromcor finished telling what little he knew of the enormous bird. He agreed with Kuthar a northward route was the one to follow because it was the direction in which he had seen it headed when returning to its home base in the evening. It was also the direction in which it had flown off with Rondo.

"I think its aerie is beyond the range behind me, but just how far I do not know."

"Well, it makes no difference. My travels have never taken me more than a league in that direction. It will be an exploratory journey for me."

Kuthar tucked the small sack of powder in one of the folds of his garments, retrieved his spear, said goodbye to his mentor, and set off on his quest. He had not gone far when he turned to his left, onto an even narrower, little-used trail, making his way up the sloping mound. Cresting the top, he could see in the far distance layers of cloud cover over the distant peaks which were his destination.

The day was not excessively hot, as it usually was at this time of the year, and he was able to maintain a steady pace, alternately taking long walking strides, followed by swift running ones. His progress was considerable, and the miles fell behind him one by one until he was halfway across the valley's floor. Sweat dripped from his bronzed, muscular body, although his exertions seemed to slow him not at all.

He hesitated slightly upon reaching the banks of a rapidly flowing river slicing across the grassy plane, disappearing into a forested area just around the bend. He considered for a moment the creatures of the deep which might be lurking beneath the frothing surge: possibly an enormous fish, large enough to consider him as prey, or one of those constricting snakes he detested. But not for long. He dove into the swiftly flowing current, clinging tightly to his weapon, and surfaced to begin long thrusts taking him to the further shore. He was not an accomplished swimmer, he knew, but made up for the deficiency with the precision of his powerful strokes and a fierce determination to let nothing slow him down.

Reaching the shore, refreshed and ready to continue, he heaved his glistening body out of the water and, without a backward glance, plunged onto the grasslands and continued onward toward the mountain, still in the distance but growing closer with every step. Kuthar hoped his footfalls would take him out of the meadowlands and the forest beyond while adequate daylight remained for him to reach the lower levels of the lofty cliffs. He noted the gradual passage of the sun overhead and increased his speed even more.

Half an hour later his swift strides carried him into the forest where he entered a glade, and paused to rest momentarily. It was then he heard a cawing, agonizing shriek of agony, followed by a thunderous thud.

Now what? he wondered, not knowing what either sound portended.

He rushed to the edge of the clearing and heard a thrashing sound coming from nearby. Rounding a thick tree, he came upon an elderly woman lying on the ground. She was struggling to get to her feet, one of her arms hanging limply at her side.

"Help me," she gasped, pointing off to the side with her one good arm. "Look!"

Kuthar swirled to see a gigantic bear emerging out of the woods. Its snout quivered slightly, and its powerful opened mouth revealing a fearsome cavity of terrifying teeth gleaming in the dim light slanting through the trees. The terrified elder, attired in a worn and fringed animal skin, waved her one good arm to ward off the coming attack. A gamy smell swept off the animal, and a mighty growl roared defiance as the man stepping between it and the woman.

He did not waver. The distance was about right, he judged, for his weapon to achieve optimum impact, either to kill it or, at the least, slow it down or frighten it away. He heaved his spear with an accuracy gained from recurrent practice, and watched it enter the body above the stomach area. Hopefully, it had struck a vital organ.

Kuthar had killed bears before, but never one of this extreme size or apparent power.

The bruin immediately lost its interest in the woman. With a snarl sounding so loudly it might have been heard a long distance away, it took one, two, three awkward strides towards its tormenter before falling on its snout with a resounding smack, pushing the spear further into its body, emerging out the back.

It lay there, shaking and growling, until its eyes glazed over and closed forever.

"Who…who are you?" the female cried, attempting to regain her footing again. She spoke with an extremely pleasant, melodic voice.

"I am Kuthar," he told her, "from beyond the mountain range. Are you hurt?"

"I fear my arm is broken," she disclosed, her voice taking on a trilling, musical quality as he gently helped her to her feet. "You are a good man, Kuthar, to aid an old woman in her distress. My name is Moro."

Kuthar laughed lightly, "It's not the first time I've bested a bear, and probably not the last, but this is an extremely large one."

"It is a big one, indeed," she agreed, giving a swift kick to its haunches with a viciousness surprising her champion.

"How did you harm your arm?"

"Why, I…why…I stumbled and fell and broke it when I landed on the stump of a tree back there."

"Landed?"

"Stumbled over a stump."

"You must be more careful," advised the young man, tugging on his spear until it emerged from the body of the bruin, its blade and most of the shaft coated with the creature's blood. "The forest is not a safe place for you to wander.

"I wish I could take the whole beast, or some of its meat, with me," he added, "but I travel fast and cannot afford delay." He wiped his weapon on nearby foliage, cleaning it as best he could until he could find water in which to immersed it.

"Don't worry about it," declared the woman. "The meat will not go to waste. I'll send my husband for it, and he'll bring it home. But, why are you in such haste?"

Kuthar told her of his quest and the deep concern he had for his young boy, as he gathered vines and fashioned a sling for her arm.

"Ooooh! Noooo!" she exclaimed, her jaw dropping, her good arm reaching up to cover her mouth. "A bird flew off with him?" she repeated. "How awful. It must have been an enormously large flying creature to lift a small boy from the ground. You do know, of course, you are in the valley of the wingers?"

"A winger? Is that what it's called? Whatever, it's enormous. The largest bird I've ever seen, or could even imagine seeing. I fear my Rondo is lost to me forever.

"There, it's the best I can do," he said, "but it should be snug enough to help you return to your home for proper care."

She nodded. "Thank you, again. But I must not delay you. If your son is still alive—oh, I pray he is—he likely won't be for much longer. I've seen this giant winger you speak of. Soon you will see, as you ascend the distant slope, its home—a colossal nest. It's not a difficult climb to reach it. Go, and good fortune be with you.

"I travel in this direction," she added, motioning and pointing with her good arm, "and you go that way."

Moro stepped out of the glen and disappeared into the woods, her grateful words of appreciation chirruping harmoniously in his ears, along with the sound of her retreating footsteps. He turned and sprinted along the course she had indicated. Already he had lost much precious time, and none remained in which to despair.

He was well underway when he heard the thunderous sweep of mighty wings above him beating the airways, and saw a blurred shadow sweep along the ground. He looked up to see a winger skimming awkwardly overhead, rising clumsily, and then nearing the ground again.

Kuthar did not break stride, but he was unsure of whether to follow its flight and see where it landed, or take Moro's advice and seek its nest.

The bird was not carrying Rondo, but might have left him somewhere with the intent of returning. Kuthar could not be certain if it had landed in the woods ahead of him, or had righted its flight and returned to its aerie. He decided to search for the bird's home, desperately hoping his son would be there. If he should locate it, he would probably be forced to dispatch the winger, despite its size.

A few minutes later he bolted from the forest and stood upon the rocky foothills of the craggy mountain before him. His eyes swept the sloping terrain, probing for the nest Moro had mentioned, or a cavern in which Rondo might be concealed. And then he saw it, just as the woman had described it, not difficult at all for him to locate. He wondered why the bird-thing had not built its nest up in the high precipices, away from marauders which might attack its mate and brood. Apparently, he decided, a bird of the size he was pursuing believed no intruder would dare to attack its home. It was all the better for him, as it enabled him to avoid a tough, arduous ascent.

Kuthar climbed the gently slanting slope until he reached the ledge upon which he had sighted the massive nest, and the sheer face of the cliff beyond. Twilight was still a couple of hours away, giving him adequate time to reach his destination before it arrived and blended into darkness. Such an event might force him to temporarily suspend his search.

It took him a few more minutes to reach the shelf upon which rested the enormous nest he had spied from below, pull himself onto its level surface, and look about. He could see, from this short distance away, it was even larger than what he guessed. The winger, perhaps several of them, could comfortably fit within, with enough room left over for a few people like himself. Just what was this mighty creature who lived within? Were fledglings nesting there, also? Was Rondo inside? He would have to first climb it and peer within to answer his questions.

Not far away from the nest could be seen the dark mouth of a cavern. Out of it, an old and withered man, scrawny and bewhiskered, was stepping from the shadows. He hobbled toward Kuthar, aided by a stout stick he used as a cane. In the other hand he held a rope trailing back into the cavern. The ancient stared at Kuthar for a moment, and then continued to advance toward the lip of the slope where he stood.

"What do you want?" he grated, eyeing the uninvited intruder cryptically, waving his staff about. "Who are you? Who dares to approach my home?"

"I search for my son," said Kuthar, walking closer. "Have you seen a small lad—about so big?" He used his free hand, elevated, to give an idea of the boy's size, clutching his spear in the other. "His name is Rondo"

"No, I have not," croaked the emaciated one, his crackling voice issuing tortuously. "My name is Armos. I live here alone, with my wife. Who wants to know?"

"Kuthar—from beyond the mountain, south of here. I seek also the enormous bird-thing which stole him away."

"So," he said. "You've come here for the lad, have you? Do you see a child? No. There's no gargantuan bird-thing around here, either. I promise you—only myself and my wife."

Kuthar looked at the nest off to the right of the man and did not believe him.

"Then you won't mind if I look inside the dwelling of straw and sticks behind you. I've never seen one of such size. I want to assure myself my son is not there."

"Ho! Ho! My word is not good enough for you?"

"No offense, Armos, but I will see for myself."

"Don't trouble yourself," said Armos, pulling on the rope he held. Kuthar was stunned to see Rondo emerge from the cavern, struggling at the end of the line, but otherwise unharmed. When he spotted his father, he began to run forward.

"Rondo!" Kuthar cried at the sight. "Come to me, boy!"

"He cannot," squawked the scraggly man, relentlessly pulling the rope taut until Rondo was near his side. "He's mine. He's secured to the rope, and I hold it."

"Rondo, come to me!" demanded his father again.

"The boy is mine," claimed Armos, chortling.

"He had better be alright, or you are dead, whoever you are."

The chieftain noted the tie binding the youngster appeared to be frayed. Evidentially, his son had managed to nearly sever it and free one arm. Possibly, if given enough time, he might have been able to save his own life.

"I can't, Daddy. The rope is holding me—tightly."

The tribal leader was amazed at his son's self control. Other lads would be in awful anguish, a rain of tears cascading down their gentle faces, perhaps, but Rondo stood there courageously, his head held high, visage defiant, unafraid and in control of any qualms.

Casually, Kuthar elevated his spear until it was pointed at his host.

"Release the lad. Now!"

"Oooh. You're so insistent, aren't you? You mean to harm me, if I defend my home and my catch?"

"No, I mean you harm if you injure my child. Let him go."

"I will not. Be gone. Do you not know with whom you speak? I am the mightiest of sorcerers. The tiny stick you want to hurl at me, puny man, will not harm me.'"

"I know about wizards, Armos, and you can be killed. My mentor is

Tromcor, from beyond the mountain range, and he's told me so."

"Tromcor, is it? A middling necromancer, he is, with limited skills. He can't do the things I can do."

Kuthar was spellbound as the man dropped his cane and transformed himself into the flying horror which had stolen Rondo. He…it…folded its wings at the side of its gargantuan body.

"There, interfering man!" it screeched, one claw maintaining a grip on the rope. "Are you satisfied?"

Kuthar stood aghast, speechless, blinking his eyes in disbelief, his arms dropping to his sides. The enormous winger stood there…Armos… its yellowish eyes, nearly as large as saucers, blinking furiously, its meaty legs shifting awkwardly from one to the other.

"What strange creature are you?" Kuthar breathed slowly, now unsure if his missile could harm the birdman.

"Strange creature am I?" it cackled hoarsely. "You have seen me turn myself from a man to a bird. Can Tromcor do it?"

"I don't believe so. But I want to know: Why did you take him?"

The birdman, confident he was firmly in control, became somewhat mollified. "At first, I thought to make him my apprentice, thinking he would grow to be a magnificent wizard, such as me, and do wondrous things, perhaps one day surpassing his teacher. I would have adopted him, and raised him to become a novice in the craft—and in time take his place in the world of wizardry. I would have spared his life, a boon I soon regretted when I realized he is so obstinate he would fight me every minute of the day.

"It would not be worth the effort to train him. What was I to do? I changed my mind and decided to dine upon him. He would be my dinner. Wizards must eat, just as normal people do, and he was such a fetching lad. A fine entrée he would make, fricasseed or barbecued. But I had dined on the way home, and had little appetite at the time.

"I took him to my nest and dropped him inside. My own brood…"

"Your nest? Your brood?"

"Well, my wife's and mine, and our offspring of three handsome flyers. They would amuse themselves, playing with him before satisfying their own appetites upon his meager flesh. But your son is a brat and attacked my chicks. He punched the largest and bravest of my children in the beak and flung it out of the nest. I intervened to end his destructive, malicious actions.

"I grabbed him and set him on the ground, swinging at me. Small as he is, the boy continued to fight. And then the stubborn tot kicked me in the shin. And it still hurts! Why do you think I hobble about, needing to balance myself with this branch? I would have chewed him up myself, then and there, and cast the remains back into the nest, but not without becoming the bird-thing again, and I was weary. I was in my human guise, and it's possible he might have bested me, even then.

"So, I bound him to the rope until ready for dinner, dragged him into the cave, and tied him down to prevent his escape. But would he stay compliant? No. He immediately tried to cut the rope on sharp edges of rock, hoping to run away. I was untying him from the rock, and holding the rope, when I heard someone approaching my home—and then you appeared and confronted me with hostility.

"Tell me how you managed to live with him the few short years of his life and cope with his impertinence and disrespect?"

"You misjudge the boy, I assure you," replied Kuthar. "Never has there been such a well-mannered, happy youth, obedient, courteous, and unfailingly loyal."

"Ha! Little do you know. The lad is a quarrelsome, unreasonable bully to his elders."

"He is not. Now turn him loose before I run you through with my bear stick."

"After all I have endured from him, you expect me to let him go?"

Suddenly, an unseen voice vented angrily from within the enormity of the nest: "Who awakens me from my rest?" it trilled. "Who disturbs my hatchlings?

"Armos, is it you, screeching loudly enough to frighten the squirrels out of the trees?" the voice tweeted melodiously, but heatedly.

To Kuthar's further amazement, an enormous feathered head, followed by a viciously curved bill, peeked over the edge—another flying winger. The bird, smaller than Armos, awkwardly levered itself out of the nest and onto the ground. Something appeared to be wrong with one of its wings, and it moved with difficulty.

Spying Rondo, it chirped, "You lied to me, Armos! Now release the boy, or must I come and slap you?"

"No. This is my dinner." trilled the birdman disagreeably, his features now contorted with anger. "Go back to the nest and take care of our brood."

Moments passed before Kuthar could recover his composure, but when he did, his decision to slay the thief who had stolen his son returned. Again, he drew back his spear in preparation to launch it at the feathered dreadfulness before him.

"Wait, Kuthar," cooed the smaller avian melodically. "He's my husband."

If the chieftain had been amazed before, he was doubly stupefied as he watched the female bird transform itself into Moro, the woman he had earlier saved from a bear. He continued to stare, stunned, his eyes growing wider. Slowly, he lowered his weapon.

What weird magic is this? Kuthar wondered. His head swiveled from the woman to the birdman. This was a feat even Tromcor could not duplicate. Or was Armos playing a mental trick upon him? Magic was something he had known all his life, practiced by his ancient friend, the greatest exponent of wizardry the Early Earth had known—but even he could not transform himself into a bird.

"After leaving you in the forest, I flew here as quickly as I could with my damaged wing," Moro explained, as soon as she had fully assumed her human shape. "I was afraid I'd be too late to stop Armos from harming your boy, but he assured me it must have been another winger snatching him. My wing is broken. It will be weeks before it has healed properly."

Her neck swiveled to face the larger bird. "Tell me, husband," she peeped, "tell me you have not harmed the lad."

"Not yet, I haven't, but I will." he squealed. "I'll snack on him this night, and finish the remainder tomorrow."

"The man...the bird...is really your husband?" Kuthar asked in disbelief, looking from the birdman to the woman, his eyes focused on her broken arm upheld by the sling he had made for her.

"He is. Our being married makes for an agreeable union," said Moro. "But not when the stubborn man is like this."

"But he intends to have my boy for dinner."

"I assure you he won't," she cooed. "Armos, turn the boy loose."

"I won't." said the birdman with equal determination, and even greater authority. "I'll be hungry soon."

"Turn him loose or you'll spend the next month banished from the nest, sleeping on the cold, hard ground."

"What care I, woman?" crackled the birdman.

Kuthar brought his spear up...

"Hold, Kuthar," said the voice of the woman, as she saw him draw his weapon back. "Do not kill him. He will release the child."

"No, woman, I will not. I caught him, and he's mine.

"Isn't it marvelous?" screeched Armos. "She's a bird who is able to turn herself into a woman, and I'm a man—the greatest sorcerer of all time—who can turn himself into a bird."

"So...now Kuthar knows your great secret and ability," said Moro to her husband in disdain. "What does it accomplish? Release the boy or I'll peck your eyes out."

"I'll not let the boy go. He is my supper. My brood needs to eat, also."

Kuthar, frustrated with the arguing, spoke up. "Harm the boy, Armos, and I'll run you through like a slab of venison roasting on a spit—and, before I leave, I'll trample and rip the nest apart. Your fledglings won't live to show off their adult plumage or even enjoy their first molting."

A look of indecision appeared on Armos' feathered face, and his voice was no longer as decisive as before. "You'd not do it...would you?"

"Test me, Armos. Test me, and see what I would do."

"I've wasted enough time," decided Kuthar, and drew his arm back to deliver his projectile into the shaman, who was at first a man and now a bird.

A smirk crossed the countenance of the birdman. One of the gigantic talons pulled the boy into its mass of feathers and enfolded its wings around him, forcing Kuthar to lower his weapon again. He dare not take the chance of hitting his boy.

"Release him now, or you'll find my deer-stick embedded in your stomach. And, as you slowly die, I'll pluck your feathers out, one by one."

"Ohhh. We'll see. One snap of my beak will end your presumptuous demands."

"Stop," said the woman. "Armos, this man you threaten is a good man. He is my benefactor."

Kuthar slowly nodded.

"Let the boy go, Armos," she said with decisive insistence.

"No. The lad is mine. He's just the right size for a few bites."

"Please, Armos. Let him be. Kuthar saved my life!"

"Makes no difference to me."

"Harm the child, and I'll leave you forever."

"Then, be gone. What care I of your silly threats?"

"You don't understand, Armos. I flew into the lower branches of a tree, earlier, and fell to the ground, my wing broken. I heard him coming, and was transforming myself into a woman, when a bear came along. I was unable to defend myself or fly away with my broken appendage...and would have fallen prey to the toothy beast roaming these hills if he had not killed it. He kindly bound my arm, enabling me to come home.

"Tonight you can dine on something else. I'm sure he will gladly exchange the bear he killed for the boy. I'll show you where to find the carcass. Bring it here, and I'll prepare a fine meal for you. But the boy goes free!"

"Hmmm," returned the birdman. "The boy for the bear? It sounds like a fair swap."

"Release the boy to him now, Armos," she demanded, her voice modulating lower.

"I said it was a fair swap, dear one. I didn't say I'd let him go."

"But you said..." began Kuthar.

"Hush. The boy is mine. There's no reason why I can't have both the boy and the bear."

"Yes, there is," peeped Moro, heatedly. "I won't show you where the bruin is."

"Oh, I'll find him, all right. Remember, woman, I'm the greatest wizard who ever lived."

"Harm my son, and you'll find my spear sticking out of your fat belly," warned Rondo's father.

"Pah! I'm a wizard. Run me through, and I'll patch up the hole and be as good as new. Remember, you're here by yourself, little man."

"Oh, no he isn't," loudly bellowed a burly, commanding and inflexible voice, coming from the rim of the ledge.

Kuthar spun around, and the birdman peered in astonishment in the direction from which the contention came. They saw an enormous head, perched on a gigantic body, glaring fiercely over the edge, one causing Kuthar's lips to part and pull into a wide smile.

Skaf, with long arms like knotted hams, hoisted himself easily onto the outcropping and walked towards the combatants, hefting his spear from one hand to the other, his eyes glaring like chips of ice, ferociously and intently upon the birdman.

"Ho! Skaf!" Kuthar shouted. "How long have you been here?"

"I've been here a while, little friend, listening to the fat-bellied chickadee boast he can defeat you in battle."

Rondo peaked out from behind a covering wing. "Uncle Skaf!" he exclaimed. "Wait till you hear what happened to me!"

"Aha!" his adopted uncle cried out. "Is it Rondo covered by the moth-eaten wing? You've found him."

The colossus continued his approach to the tribal chief. "I no longer travel as rapidly as I once did, Kuthar, but I came as fast as I could."

The two clasped each other on the shoulder, the universal gesture of greeting, and Kuthar grinned broadly.

"Armos," said Skaf, addressing the birdman. "Know this. My friend and I can and will pluck from you all your feathers and scatter them into the wind. Then, we'll dine on your brood tonight, roasting and toasting them over our campfire."

Armos stared spellbound at Skaf, its beak open wide, its reddish tongue flickering outward. The winger was much larger and heftier than Skaf, but had never seen a man of such size before. He pondered the outcome of the battle ensuing should he tangle with both of them. Nearly a minute passed as it considered its options. He glanced at his wife, then back to the interlopers. Perhaps…just perhaps…it would be vulnerable to an attack by the two of them.

"Take him," Armos said, making his decision and shoving Rondo towards his father. "The brat is probably too stringy, anyway, and too tough a portion for me to consume—unfit for proper dining."

He looked at Kuthar in disgust and waved his walking stick menacingly. "Never have I seen such an independent tot, determined to defy me and have his own way in every manner.

"Take him, and leave me at peace."

Kuthar was in no mood for further argument. He untied the rope, snatched up his son, and the three went on their way. Skaf, his head turning around as they approached the ledge, watched the wizard warily, ready for a trick of some nature. Kuthar and Rondo walked by his side, with neither a backward glance, nor word of farewell to the furious winger.

* * * *

"What did you do, my boy, to upset the man so much?" Kuthar asked a few minutes later when he set him down and they started the long journey home. "Your mother and I have taught you courtesy and gentleness all your life. You're not bratty. How is it you've changed so quickly?"

"Father," said Rondo, his hands on his skinny hips, looking up into Kuthar's eyes. "The man would have consumed me. Did you see his mouth when he was a bird? It was half the size of our house! Well, anyway, it looked quite large to me. I did what I could to discourage him.

"Besides, you told me to avoid strangers."

Kuthar patted him on the head, admiring the audacity and ingenuity of the young lad, who was so much like himself. "You're right, my boy," he said.

The sun continued its descent over the western horizon as they traveled along, and shadows began to lengthen.

"So, as it turned out," Kuthar revealed to Skaf, relating the essence of their adventure, "there wasn't even a fight. I thought there would be one when Armos decided he'd keep both the bear and Rondo, but he changed his mind when you appeared. The two of us together were too much for him to overcome.

"Rondo, it seems, can be as obnoxious as you are from time to time, Skaf. I think he used you as his model to irritate the birdman."

"Good for you, Rondo," Skaf said admiringly, reaching down to rumple the boy's hair. He looked at him fondly and told Kuthar, "I've trained him well."

"Ha! You mean we've trained him well. Lanoma and I."

"Well, yes—the two of you. But you must admit his adopted uncle is useful now and then."

"I'll acknowledge it. You're an extremely helpful friend, Skaf."

* * * *

They had covered only two miles or so when twilight dimmed the landscape and darkness began to close in upon them. Traveling without a light source would be foolhardy, the two men realized, and stopped upon reaching a pleasant clearing in the forest where numerous saplings grew along its edge. Little time was necessary to bend them to the ground, cutting and trimming them where necessary, and forming a pergola bound with jungle vines to protect them during the night if it should rain. Boughs of luxuriant foliage were laid within to add to their sleeping comfort, and a small fire set ablaze to frighten away inquisitive animals. They had no furs with which to cover themselves, but felt secure and snug in their temporary habitation. Rondo promptly fell asleep.

They awoke in the morning, scattered sand over the cold embers of the fire warming them during the night, and continued their homeward trek. The miles were consumed more slowly than the day before, and the time passed in pleasant diversion. They had been walking for barely half an hour when Rondo commented: "Yesterday was a very exciting day for me. My playmates will be envious when I tell them all the escapades I had."

Kuthar was happy to hear this declaration as it meant the extreme danger the boy experienced was no longer centermost in his mind, and was fast becoming a memory no longer upsetting to him.

"I must say," Kuthar confided later to his larger companion, "in a competition of avian sorcery between the manbird and Tromcor, our mentor would be soundly defeated."

THE HANDMAID OF THE KEY

by R.C. Mulhare

The night of her twins' third birthday and after their Grandpa's evening ritual on Sentinel Hill, Lavinia took Wilbur up to her room, next door to the one she could never let him into, not on his own. She set him on the tattered red wing chair there, sitting herself on a fraying ottoman at his feet, opening one of Grandpa's big books on her lap, holding it so he could see the pages. Once she'd made sure he had washed his hands, she let him turn the pages over, looking at the text and the pictures there, naming the beings in the plates there: Hastur in his tattered yellow robes, the mask revealing his face; Nyarlathotep, the tall, dark Pharaoh with a shadow that stretched and writhed vast behind him; Nodens in his chariot that rode the waves of Chaos; Father Dagon and Mother Hydra, laying in the deep, sending forth and calling back their kindred; Shub-Niggurath, the black goat of the woods with her thousand young; Azathoth, enthroned in the center of Chaos.

Then she paused on the plate depicting—or attempting, at the least—Yog-Sothoth, the Guardian of the Gate.

"And there's y' daddy, Wilbur," she said, touching the plate reverently, stroking the image of the strange globes entangled with tentacles or twisted beams of light, as any other woman would stroke the image of her lover. "He is the Gate. He knows the Gate. He is the gu'ahdian of the Gate. One day, he will return, Willy, and take you and y' twin t' be with his kind an' bring them across t' change this ol' worl', make it more hospitable f' you an' he. No more people starin' at us. No more whisp'rin' 'bout what we do."

"Will you come with us?" Wilbur asked, looking down into her face.

She could not help giving him a lop-sided smile, but she felt a tightening in her chest and a dampness in the corners of her eyes, as she closed the book and rose to replace it on a shelf. "Maybe. If he lets me look on him again. If he comes in a form that's easy on m' mind. You an' y' twin: y' not made f' this world, an' it's not made f' you. But you two can change all that."

"How will we do that?" he asked, sliding off the chair, his hooves clicking on the worn floorboards.

She reached out to stroke his shaggy black hair. "You don't need to know that just yet: the stars ain't come right for it. But you keep up y' studies, and you'll know when y' need to." He grumbled a bit, but the way he nudged his head into her hand, seemed to indicate he was content with this reply.

Tonight, she would let Wilbur sleep in her bed, something she hadn't allowed him since he was a tiny thing, and he had not stayed that way for long. She had expected that when he and his twin were born and yet she had still marveled at how quickly they had grown. She made up the bed for the two of them, though Willy hardly slept much. It still felt right to have him nested next to her, even while he read by the light of the bedside oil lamp. Always reading, her bright-minded boy, learning what scant things mankind knew, the better to build a bridge between his father's world and the human world.

While the lad bunked down, she started to excuse herself. "Have to see about y' twin, Will. Y' want me to warm y' some milk?" she asked.

"Yes, thanks, Ma," Will replied, already rummaging about the shelves of the bedside bookcase before tugging out a volume of Frazer's The Golden Bough.

Down in the kitchen, she found some milk still fresh in the stone cooler in the pantry, pouring it into a metal pipkin and setting it on the stove. From overhead, she heard sliding sounds and thumps from the room beside hers. The other which she had borne must have heard her moving about and now made its presence known.

She heard a key grate in the lock on the side door that lead to the entryway and the door yard, and it opened, letting in a gust of chill February night air along with her father's lanky, grizzled form. "Y' not tendin' the watch fires?" he asked, glancing to the crazed-glass kitchen window and the near-distant glow of the bonfire atop Sentinel Hill.

"Not this time, it's the twins' birthday," she said.

"They ain't yours t' keep, y' know. They're just lent t' y'."

"I know that, but just f' now, let me just be with them."

He glanced at the pipkin on the cook top of the old black stove. "Warm milk? Ain't they a bit old f' that?"

"Willy wanted some: it helps him settle down."

He looked from the pipkin to her face, his shaggy brows knit slightly. "Just remember: they're His children as much as they're yours. He chose you f' a reason, Lavinia. Be sure you honor that reason." Taking a jug of moonshine from the floor under the crockery shelves, likely what he had come in for in the first place—he and the other devotees would need it, this chill Imbolc night—he went back out into the midwinter darkness.

She could not help the wince that cut through her as he had said that, though she had done her best not to show it in the shifting of her shoulders. She knew what the twins were and from where half their substance had come, but at the same time, another half of their substance had come from her, and she would care for both sides as best as she could. How could a mother not feel otherwise? She wondered if the Virgin Mary of the Christians had felt this way toward the God born man Whom she had borne and nursed and raised to manhood. She had thought as much when she carried the twins, those strange nine months. People in Dunwich had eyed her askance, more in curiosity than contempt: folk in Dunwich took it in stride that women would grow visibly great with child, not minding from whence the child came, not like those so-called fine folk up in Arkham who would talk in shocked, hushed tones of their neighbors' affairs, hiding their women's conditions when they proved fruitful. But they all knew that she had not had a man try to court her attentions. Ainsel Carter, who had once tried to charm her by slipping his arm around her waist one market day, had sneered at her in Osborn's general store: "What man would plow your field, let alone plant a seed in it?" She had darted a glare at him without turning her head but had otherwise paid him no mind.

"You're gonna get a drawn mouth from all those sour grapes," Zadok Bishop had snapped back, in what passed for defense.

Then her father had intervened, stepping between her and the hecklers. "I reckon Lavinny's man is as good a husband as any loafer on either side o' Aylesbury. One o' these days, ye'll hear a child o' hers callin' its father's name from atop o' Sentinel Hill."

Despite her father's retort, she would hardly have told the townsfolk, then or at any time, who had planted the seed in her belly: for one, it was no business of theirs, though that snoop Mamie Bishop might have made it her business, not that she had a leg to stand on, the way she was stepping out with Earl Sawyer and still stepping out with one or two others behind his back. For another, they might not believe her, had she told them; for yet another, if she had told them and they'd listened, they might think her touched.

"Touched", how fitting a way to put it. Touched by something and someone of which the dull folk of Dunwich could barely dream, and if they did, might awaken shrieking at the things their minds had envisioned, or gone fleeing for the solace of a secure ward in Arkham's Sefton Asylum.

At her father's knee she had learned of the things under the earth and the things in the depths of the seas, the things in the air, the things in the fire, and the things in the far off spaces between the stars; the reasons why forgotten races of long ago, before man walked upright on the face of the earth, had raised circles of stone atop what the colonists of yore and the settlers of Dunwich had called Sentinel Hill and which the Pocumtuck before them had called by a more fitting name now long forgotten out of fear. Their ancestor Hugh Whateley had fled Arkham on account of his knowledge of such things, in the days when the Miskatonic River valley, from Arkham to Manuxet, had rung with cries of "Witchcraft!" borne of ignorance, though some cries came not unfounded. With him and with his son and one surviving daughter Sarah, he had brought a trove of the tomes that now ranked on the shelves of the old house, the black letter books over which Lavinia had pored and which Wilbur now studied day and night, in the very house that Hugh and his family had built. As a child herself, Lavinia had learned to read the signs in the stars, the passing of the seasons and the wheeling of the cosmos. She had learned to look past the masks that the Greeks and the Celts and the people of the Nile had placed upon those which dwelt in the spaces between the spheres, who would at times cross the threshold and move among lesser minds, leaving unchanged no mind that chanced to gaze on them. To her, his only child, her father taught the signs and words and formulae that would for an instant unlock doorways between the spheres, leading onto paths through chaos. He taught her the rites to be performed at the proper points on the cycle of the year, allowing these Elders to gaze across the void and into man's world.

From her studies, she learned of Yog-Sothoth, the Guardian of the Gate and Key to that same Gate, the Gate that would allow the seeker to look past the walls of the commonplace and gaze on what lay behind. In reading of this, she sensed the inspiration to look beyond, to pass through the gate and return with the knowledge that such a journey would bring, to return changed and wiser for it, to become more than the strange, pale woman in a backwoods town that she was. She would not say, had someone thought to ask her, that she had prayed for such a transformation or to be the vessel of transformations, for her gods were not dogs to be called by name, but she had chalked out the proper formulae upon the standing stones and made the given signs, things she had read in the Al Azif and also the Book of the Ways of Rha's-awl-Aliq. She had read of the offspring whom the Old Ones had begotten on mankind, of the strangely shaped beings who moved among mankind like the giants on the earth begotten on the sons and daughters of Adam and Eve, mentioned in a fleeting passage in the Book of Genesis. Perhaps the prophet Enoch's Watcher Angels, described in the book that the Christians set aside, served as but another face of the Elder Ones. Some of the women among her father's small circle of followers—some of them true believers, others mere dabblers looking for a thrill—had hoped to bear such a child, but despite the number of times her father had succeeded in opening the door even a crack, nothing had come of it. Some took human lovers and bore them human children; she did not fault them, nor rankle at their good fortune. Time was when it would have irked her, but she knew that she had a face and form that few men would find appealing, and she had almost aged out of desiring a man of her own. Some of the townsfolk had prodded her, asking her if she was saving herself for someone; one wag had thought her an easy target for his rustic charms, on account of her plain face and withered hand, one day when she had gone to buy flour at the store. She had shrugged off the hand paddling at her shoulder, and Pa had given him a hiding that put the fear of trying that again into him. But it still made people's tongues wag, Mamie Bishop's in particular, not that she had 'saved herself', as if her predilections were coins to be banked in a mason jar. She had given herself to one of her father's followers, during the Great Rite one May Day night, but that hardly counted in the grand order of things.

What had counted, had happened upon that May Day night four years ago, when the earth shook, when Sentinel Hill had rocked beneath them, when the sky had opened, showing colors not known on this earth to the gathered devotees below.

Then she had seen Him. He had looked into her and she had looked into Him, that flock of spheres revealing themselves as a cluster of eyes as myriad as a flock of birds flying forth, interwoven with tendrils coruscating like bending rays of light in unworldly hues, bent and refracted by those eyes, their piercing gaze.

She looked into Him and He looked into her. All around her, she heard the panicked gasps and cries and exultant ululations of the other devotees, but she looked on Him as a bride on her wedding day might look on the groom whom her parents had picked for her, as a medieval lady might gaze on the king to whom her noble parents had pledged her hand. Trepidation and wonder, fear but not the terror that veered toward madness that she glimpsed in the other acolytes. She had stepped forward, gaze turned upward, like a bride approaching the altar where her groom awaited her.

He Looked Into Her.

And then she felt it. Tendrils reaching down from the heavens and one shot toward her, transfixing her, its substance sliding betwixt and between the substance of her being, the very turnings of her mind, the very fibers of her flesh. She did not struggle, no, she embraced it, drawing some small part of His substance into her mind and body. Over the hum of strange emanations that pulsed on the edge of the doorway, she heard a voice, a pulsing that took on the form of a voice, though its accidents might not seem like words to an unkeened ear.

I know the Gate. I guard the Gate. I am the Gate. Open to me and I open to you. Unlock to me and I unlock to you.

Whatever barriers of fear or ignorance she held in her mind, she broke through them. Whatever trepidation lingered, she banished it with a laugh of joy. Then she felt his searing presence enter fully, a key fitting a lock, opening the way through her. She felt him dive into her, examining every fiber, probing every corner in mind and flesh alike, till she fairly swooned from the encounter.

When she came back to herself, she lay upon the scant spring grass, her father's blanket coat swaddled about her as he knelt beside her, putting his warmth between her and the early May chill.

"Did he see you?" Pa had asked, looking into her face.

"He looked into me and I looked into him," she said, as he lifted her gently, carrying her through the swarm of their circle. Even then, she knew she had come away from the threshold with one part of her unlocked and some of His substance left behind, melded to hers, specks that in time grew and quickened and came forth as her two children waiting above for her.

She scented the creamy odor of the milk coming close to a boil. Coming back to the present, she took the pipkin off the stove and set it on the draining board to cool a bit. Couldn't have Will scald his mouth. Rummaging on the dresser, she went in search of a clean stoneware mug, then a clean tin plate on which she placed a few of the remaining molasses cookies from a crock atop the dresser, high up where Will could not yet reach it. Filling it from the pipkin, she took it with her as she went back upstairs, back to her boys.

Will had already crept beneath the covers when she entered her chamber. "You look cozy already, Will-boy," she said. "What y' readin' about?"

He looked up from the book in hand. "The Sacred Marriage," he said, glancing back to the page.

"Good to know about: that was how y' daddy gave you and y' twin t' me," she said, setting the mug on top of the bedside bookcase where Will could reach it.

"Will I ever give a child to someone?" he asked, his dark eyes questioning.

"Maybe, if you want to and she wants a child of you," she said, knowing full well that the father of her children had other designs for them. Not time for them to know, not now, not yet. Let them be children, as much as either of them could be, for now.

She reached to smooth the quilts down around Will's form, but one tendril of his stirred under the covers and slipped out from under them, reaching for the mug.

"I'll best be checkin' on y' twin," she said, rising and letting herself out of the room.

Putting a hand to the key at her belt, she approached the door to the chamber that held the other which she had borne and pressed her ear to the leaf, listening for movement. For the moment, her elder child lay quiet, sometimes a good sign, sometimes not. Taking the key from her belt, she fitted it to the hasp and opened the lock that closed it. Raising her stronger hand, she made the Voorish Sign, not that she needed it as much as the twins' grandfather or the brother to the one within: a mother's eyes have that power to see through the veils that might hang between her and her child. But the sign cleared the last of those veils.

That which she had borne lay quietly in a near corner beside the door, close to the wall which the room shared with hers. She approached, the soles of her shoes tacky on the tarry stuff that covered the floor, and knelt, putting out a hand to stroke the damp tendrils stretched out from the body. The eyes that dotted the body, already bigger than a horse's, grew brighter and more alert at her touch, the three-lobed pupils dilating.

"Mm.... Mmmaah... Moth... Mothuhr?" the voice asked.

"Shhh, it's all right, Yog...you hungry?"

"Yyy...yah... Yess..."

"Mother's here, let me give you a taste." She crept closer, kneeling among the tendrils. Several crept about her, one sought to entwine about her ankle, but she pushed it away, with a gentle but firm hand. Another wound about her arm, reaching upwards before a barbed sucker on the body of the tendril found the side of her neck, above the neckline of her stuff-gown. The barbs bit into her flesh; she felt blood flow from her, caught up by the sucker. Just a taste would she allow, then after a long moment, she slid a finger under the sucker, ignoring the barbs, as she broke the grip. The tendrils fidgeted about her, restless, seeming to show disappointment.

"Mm...muh...more??" the elder child asked.

"No, not just now, child," Lavinia said, rising and slipping free of the tendrils before rising and backing toward the door. She put a hand out against the doorpost to steady herself. "I'll have more f' you t'morrow: Y' grandpa's got some new Jersey cows from y' cousin Curtis's pa, bull calves he had no need for."

"Nn...naow?"

"Not till mornin', you've had enough," she replied, firmer this time, as she stepped out into the hallway and closed the door, putting her shoulder to it. She felt the leaf quiver as a tendril flapped against the door. Poor creature wanted more, but she had no more to give at the moment, lest she should come to harm and lest it grow too eager and grow faster than it should. The stars had yet to come right by her father's calculations and her own examinations of the night sky by way of a spyglass he had bought in an old Innsmouth junk shop, for the time when her elder child would come forth beneath the sky, before the way opened anew to close no more.

"Mama? Yew all right there?" Will's voice called, snapping her back to reality. She looked up, seeing him peer out from her chamber door, and she put a hand to her neck, covering the bleeding mark there.

She put the lock back on the hasp and fastened it. "Yes, Will, you go on back to bed. I'll be right with you."

He looked toward the closed door before looking to her face, and she could see the concern in his grave, dark eyes. How much longer would she have the both of them like this, she wondered, and how soon would they grow beyond her keeping, when she would needs release them to do as their father intended…

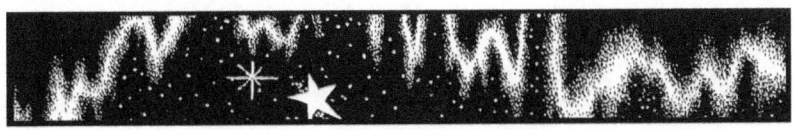

THE OLD ROCK
by Russ Parkhurst

Had seen the shore made for itself, back
When the stars were young and comets
Fell, and where one fell, those men of old,
Those ancient heroes back of all did wrought a yellow rock
Whose sides they grave with everything that was,
Magic dire and fell, technologies now lost, vimanas
Soaring through bright cobalt skies and
Flying metal cities crashed to Earth but
Over time the script had softened, ran like wax
Engulfed in flames, so much was lost that mankind
Was, it lost its name and all the knowledge graven on
That rock did weather 'way to tiny scratches, little
Bumps and sounds no man could speak.
Now it lies beside a thin and shallow creek,
A place to feast and talk and play but late
At night, when the revelers have gone their way and
Umber purples streak the midnight sky, the stars come out and
Light the scratches on the rock unto
Their old primordial meaning, the ancient sacred
Meaning carved in stone by men of old, now just
A rock men huddle to in summer's heat and
Winter's cold.

BLUE MOON
by Allen Mark Price

The hazy, murky setting sun that blazed over New England most of July was no contest for the rising Blue Moon. July was to have two full moons. The first rose on the Fourth of July and the second, which is called a Blue Moon, was expected in a few hours. Only this Blue Moon was going to turn blue like the one in 1883, the year the volcano Krakatoa exploded. Scientists liken the blast of Krakatoa to a 100-megaton nuclear bomb. Ash-clouds rose to the very top of Earth's atmosphere causing the Moon to turn blue. We were hearing this all over the radio, all over the news. I didn't know what the fuss was all about. People get all in a tizzy when there's a full moon, believing people act strange, and strange things tend to happen. Please. A bunch of nonsense if you ask me.

So I thought.

I saw her through the bow window, her silhouette pressed against the curtains. It was 7:15 p.m. Mom didn't get home most nights until after 8:30; she had taken a second job. I ambled up the dirt driveway past her clunky maroon van sitting at the base, hearing her deep-pocketed voice seep through the back screen-door as I approached. Her voice was more man than a man's, deep like Barry Whites. Don't misunderstand me, now. It wasn't deep and sultry like Barry's, it wasn't sensual either, it was ruff and raw and edgy. She was overcompensating for her lack of Y-chromosomes. She was my mother's lover.

Shaquane. That was her name. Can't you tell she's black? So I tend to stereotype like the rest of America. Sometimes stereotypes are true. Especially when it's all you've got to base something on. Doesn't mean I'm prejudice. I'm black. Man-bitch is what I called her. Trying to understand her need to be a man was like trying to comprehend why I had to go to Catechism. There was no way I'd ever believe she was a man, just like there was no way I was ever going to believe in an Almighty, merciful Father, so willing to leave his son behind and let him get strung up on a cross, like my father, leaving me, leaving me when I was barely sixteen weeks. When I asked God his reason for forcing me into a life I didn't ask for, to a mother who embarrassed me with her lifestyle, to a father who embarrassed me with his absence, He didn't answer.

Embarrassment. That's not the word I'd use to describe how I felt when my mother moved Shaquane and her daughter in with us. Try morti-fied. How was I to tell my friends when they came by to visit me? Needless to say, I never invited anyone over. This may have been the eighties, but it was not the gay eighties.

Shaquane and her daughter, Nakia, had humiliated me, the entire six years of our coexistence. I never knew what was worse: the two of them subjecting me to the bugs, to the stench of chitlins and greasy chicken, to the cigarette smoke clouding up my house, forcing me to drown my clothes in cologne to cover up the smell, or watching my dog, Sienna, drown, try-ing to catch the birds that nested in the backyard trees, raping and robbing them of their berries.

July 30, 1974. I'll remember that morning even as I lay in my coffin. It was the first month they had moved in. Shaquane was in the kitchen smoking, like always, and making coffee. She let Sienna out in the back-yard, something she was not allowed to do. She heard Sienna's crying, and didn't do a damn thing. I know this because her daughter and I woke up that morning to Sienna barking and chasing after the birds. Sienna sat on top of the cesspool lid, a bird in her mouth. The lid collapsed and she fell in— squealing, sinking, drowning in the cesspool. I stared and I stared from my bedroom windowsill down at Sienna gasping for air. I ran and I ran out the house to liberate her, to free her, but I'm still running, trying to liberate myself from the anger, from the pain. The pain. She knew not to let my dog out, only I let her out; I was the only one who'd stay in the backyard and watch. I blamed her.

I blame them all.

Sienna's body has never been recovered. Six years of draining the cesspool and nothing: no body, no bones, just chunks of her dirty white fur. That night, though I saw Sienna's face in the Blue Moon, as I lay on top the picnic table and starred up at it. Sienna's white furry face bloody, her teeth locked on Shaquane's neck as she dragged Shaquane's limp body towards me. Birds flew down and perched on the fence gazing at me. Her clock was ticking.

Shaquane and Nakia came from the Pawtucket projects and brought cockroaches that infested my home in a matter of days: little brown-legged creatures that crawled on the counters at night, in the bathtub at dawn, and on my T.V. screen while I watched, the one show I watched, The Cosby Show. It's not a pretty sight when Bill Cosby's nose looks like it has a booger in it. Killing them was pointless—the roaches not the hoodlums, although, the thought did cross my mind. I dreamed about it. You probably call it a nightmare if you kill someone in your dream. Normally I would too, but the thought of having my life back gave those deadly visions sweet satisfaction.

Hate is a strong word (so they say), but death is stronger. I wanted them out of my life, out of my house, but more importantly, out of my dreams. The more I dreamt, the more the dreams forcefully, provokingly, pushed me, uniformly to the other side. Sweet, horrifying, beautifully depicted visions, watching her slip slowly beyond the trenches of life, inside a deep, painful death only time was capable of freeing her from. Time was taking too long. There's only so long you can wait for God to come down and put his invisible hands in the situation. I figured after six years he wasn't coming.

I saw the T.V. screen's reflection through the window. She was always home, sitting in front the T.V., or in her chair at the kitchen table. No matter where she was smoke followed her. Knowing where she was came in handy. Don't worry, you'll know why soon enough. Okay, don't press me. She died fantastically. No one knows if it was accidentally.

Decide for yourself.

I felt that feeling I always felt when I saw her, twirling around inside my vessels, puncturing holes in my heart, rupturing, waking my senses. She was walking across the living room—smoke billowing through the window screen, her voice rippling the toxic air—as I entered the backyard gate. Sienna's area by the shed was as it was when she died: doghouse sitting in the dirt, water bowel off to the side, her choke chain full of dog-poo, the one difference was the birds residing in and around the doghouse. They had seized control over our backyard, over us. Tapping on my window every morning to wake me, to know the day's agenda, to wait, to watch diligently, like a predator hunting for prey. I gave them sport. They'd watched me, intimately, intently, smirking, as I'd peeked out the blinds.

I saw Nakia walking up the street. Nakia. Where do black people come up with these names? Again, don't misunderstand me. I'm not prejudice, but when you grow up in an all-white neighborhood, not knowing anyone black, even though you're black yourself, it takes some adjusting to. Nakia must have gotten out of softball practice early; she practiced every Monday and Wednesday afternoon. I heard her cleats scuffing along the cement. Nakia was a sixteen-year-old tomboy, but not gay. She had a boyfriend, as I had a girlfriend. So pretty, so well known, yet so unpopular. She hung out with the local college crowd, the college that she spent last summer taking prep courses at, which is where she met her boyfriend. She was mulatto. Her black hair slicked back, her skin smooth, her brown eyes, her long narrow nose, her high cheekbones all had people telling her she looked like Sade. She did.

I'd decided to slow my pace, and wait for Nakia. The tricks you learn to survive in a home where surviving is a way of life. Home: If you want to call it that. I no longer believed in it, believed such a thing actually existed, anywhere but in my head. Home was a place where sexual deviants ran rampant. But disassociating myself from it was impossible when mom would go to parent/teacher night with her lesbian lover. Like having the kids at school call you faggot down the hallways wasn't enough punishment.

Someone UP THERE felt I hadn't suffered enough.

I sat down, leaned up against the fence, rested my back against my bag, and heard it rumbling below me, again. I had heard it for weeks. Not earthquake tremors, this wasn't L.A. This was the bum-fucking boonies of Rhode Island. The sticks! A place no one's heard of: Foster/Gloucester, where life is mundane, and an endless stretch of woods makes life ordinary. I can't tell you how many times, during my travels, people have asked me: "Where's that?" Or "Rhode Island's near Connecticut and Mass., right? It should really be connected to one of those states." I couldn't agree more.

The rumbling grew hollowly, an echoingly pounding, pulling me in. It snapped my attention tautly, soothingly, touching the corners of my mind, digging deep underneath my clammy skin. It was hot, naturally hot; it was July. I knew where it was coming from, I knew the first time it asked for my attention: the cesspool, but none of us dared to enter the backyard. The cesspool, the yard was plastered with bird-doo and dog-poo. No, I never cleaned it up. Neither did anyone else for that matter. The only person willing to go near it was the cesspool man.

The cesspool man came every five months, but every fourth month was when it needed to be emptied; we were poor. So for thirty days, toilet flushing occurred twice in the morning and twice at night, bath washing occurred on Sunday evenings, and the cesspool lid rattled daily. The worst part was when the lid raised up and unmasked itself, unleashing its smelly dungeon. Even Sienna didn't go near it when the lid was in mode. She'd stick her nose out the cracked back screen-door, wiggle it a bit, sneeze, and back away. She was no fool.

If Hell smells that bad, I'll need air fresheners in my casket.

Funny thing was, none of the neighbors ever complained about the foul smell. Maybe it was because the cesspool opened during the day when everyone was at work, or maybe because no one in the neighborhood spoke to us. And I mean no one. Not after they moved in. I've often wondered what I had done to deserve such turmoil, such misery at such a young age.

"She's home," Nakia said, annoyed.

Nakia appreciated her mother as much as I did. Who would? Even the birds grew angry when her van pulled up in the driveway. Nakia had black-and-blue on her shoulder, another on her thigh, which were from last night's beatings. The first week of their arrival I listened to fights breakout every week and arguing occurred hourly. Nakia got all of her mother's love through beatings. Sienna's bark was Nakia's scream. Not one whimper or scream belted out of her mouth. She accepted the beatings.

"Why ya sittin' behin' da fence, Sean?"

In case you don't know, that's me, Sean. ME, with the recognizable, basic name, but I'm mulatto, too. My Dad's Caucasian, my Mom's Indian and African-American.

"Shhh," I whispered, pulling her arm, placing her hand to the ground. "Feel that?" Her brown eyes widening told me she did. Our faces locked in place, our eyes stared down the rock walkway past the picnic table in the direction of the cesspool. We slowly, timidly descended down the rock walkway. This sound was gravitationally pulling. Just three months in to the five was too early for it to be emptied, way too early.

I paused, grabbed Nakia's arm, and said, "It's different, huh?" She said nothing—her head, her eyes not moving.

"I gotta go out," Shaquane hollered, bursting through the screen door, startling us. "Behave or I swear I'll put ya both in da tub and bleed ya ta death. Got it!"

We said nothing, we did nothing, we were afraid. Okay, I lie. We flicked her off, behind her back, as she stumbled down the walkway. More like she weeble-wobbled down the walkway. She had nothing on Humpty Dumpty. To bad she would never fall and crack open like him.

She was plump. Plump? Wrong word. She was fat, and short, like five-one, a look that wouldn't even grace the pages of Lane Bryant's catalog. Her skin sagged like dead fish caught on a fisherman's net. Her hair slicked back, her oily, rubbery skin created a ragged look, due in part to her dark complexion. She was dark. Real dark. Not that dark can't or isn't attractive.

Our footfalls in line, the rumbling grew as Shaquane pulled out of the driveway. The stench built, the birds chirped and shook the branches, as we weaved in-between piles of dog-poo past the picnic table and Sienna's doghouse. I felt Nakia's heart beating in my chest; she was walking behind me, her chest flat (no boobies yet), pressed against my back. Nakia's nose pressed against my shirt, her chin rubbing my neck. The back of my neck was wet with perspiration, the bottoms of my feet dry.

I paused.

The birds all of a sudden quiet, sweetly, incredibly quiet, just watching, eyes on a sparrow, just watching. They seemed to have invited squirrels; squirrels leaping and jumping, like monkeys swinging from vines in the jungle, heartily eating the tree's berries. It was a sight, a sight out of National Geographic, one of those picture-perfect rainforests in Brazil or Africa that I'll never get to visit before we destroy them with our greed.

The lid, the cement cesspool lid shook and rose ever so slightly in the stale air. We ambled up to it, Nakia draped on me like an early morning fog, stepping on the heels of my sneakers. She was scared to take her eyes off the trees. So was I. Sweat dripped from my underarm down my sweat-induced hairy stomach into my belt-free shorts. Uncontrollably, my skin tightened, my nerves loosened, a drip of sweat fell down the center of my forehead.

My feet trembling, my toes tense, still dry inside my sneakers, I stood, we stood a foot away from the cesspool, hands over our noses. It stunk. Stunk? It reeked. A stench not persistently strong, a light wind was driving it around. But the lid had simmered down, unabashedly, visibly conscious of our presence, pushed up onto the dirt, cruddy dirt. Roaches, tons of dead roaches, encircled its edge. A patch of dirt leading into the cesspool had been dug out with scratch marks, more like claw marks along the opening.

"Are ya crazy!" Nakia asked, watching me kneel down, pulling the lid away. "Don't open it."

"There's something in there," I said, digging out underneath the lid.

"Leave it there," Nakia said curtly.

Ignoring her plea, I said, "You're just like your mother: loud. I wanna see if it's Sienna. What's the matter, Nakia? I thought you of all people could handle a little foul smell. Considering where you came from."

"Screw ya, Sean. Ya think ya somethin', don't ya? With ya white daddy and ya white friends and ya wannabe white mommy."

"This coming from the jigaboo who can't tell the difference between Ebonics and English."

We fought like that all time: her belief that because I wasn't fully black, I wanted to be white, and me fed up with her black ways. Strangely enough, all was forgiven in minutes. What else do you do when you're forced to share the same room? Nakia did drive me nuts, though: the constant bickering, the refusal to wash in my bath water, saying it would turn her white, the refusal to accept our living arrangements. After one blow out, I didn't speak to her for four months. A teenage guy and girl sharing a room: isn't that a sign of the apocalypse? Dramatic, I know, but if you saw the fights we got in, you'd think it was. I hate sharing, and as I said earlier, hate is considered a strong word.

"Ouch, damnit!" I pulled myself up, and pulled my bloody fingers out. A bone stuck out of the cruddy dirt. My flesh was cut, and covered with black crud. My fingernails were split, like a knife had sliced it open, mucus bubbled out, a fiery toxin shot in. My hand shook, my palm stiffened and swelled. The lines expanded and blood rushed to the surface turning the whites of my palm Blue.

I gripped my shaking arm. The toxin flooded my vessels, crashing against the walls, taking over, tainting my blood, my organs; my palm was beginning to peel, the swelling torturously reduce itself as fast as it produced itself. And for once, Nakia was quiet. Her mouth cracked but silent, staring with amazement, not at my hand, but at the bones, Sienna's bones rising in the sludge steadily. A warm, satiated calm angrily rushed my head, pumping my skull, forcing me to the ground.

* * * *

I woke up on the couch, awkwardly, violently, hearing the running water in the bathroom next door, the Blue Moon shining on me. It was hypnotically captivating, like when I ran downstairs, out the screen door, and saw Sienna drown, my arms in sludge trying to pull her up desperately. I hurt, ached, and God did nothing to ease the pain. Ten years, ten blissfully contented years of having a friend to talk to, to keep me company, to cry to when I wanted to die, and he sat silently in the sky. That's when I left him behind. The abysmally boring sky behaved erratically.

The Blue Moon shone down through the tree's branches, through the window screen, lighting up the couch, suffocating me. Moms image intoxicatingly visible in the Blue Moon: her reflection, as bright as the Aurora Borealis, in-between the passing clouds, smiling so gently, so motherly. Her lips disgustingly based upon Shaquane's. She was winking at me, stirring my mind, my toxic blood. I heard Shaquane, humming in the shower. Her cigarette smoke leaking out under the door, annoying me, aggravating me, she was beseeching me to do it, to let loose. And I did just that.

They found Shaquane's dead body in the tub, Nakia sitting on the toilet, vomit on the floor. Birds had ripped, torn down the window screen, stabbing, digging in her body. They were searching for something. It wasn't food. They had enough food in the trees. It wasn't about killing; she was already dead according to the autopsy report, but no know knows how she died.

We moved out in a week, a few blocks away, no one moved in. Mom disallowed me to return, not that that would have stopped me. I had no reason to return: all the birds had followed us, and all of Sienna's remains, her ashes I spread around the trees are deep in the ground now. Nakia was sent away, but I didn't know where until I had graduated from college, and married my high-school girlfriend. Mom refused to tell. She refused to tell me this morning when I stopped by. We fought in the backyard. The birds rested in the trees, standing overhead like a sexton standing at an open grave.

There was a letter from Nakia in a pile of mail on mom's coffee table. The letterhead read: Butler Hospital. That's where psychos go. Nakia wrote that the charges had been dropped against her, as they unable to prove she had anything to do with her mother's murder. Murder? The state awarded her the house, having given up trying to sell it. She wrote that she's coming back home to the house we grew up in this evening. She's excited. Not to be free, not to see me, but to finally see the Blue Moon we missed watching that night. I drove by the house earlier today: bushes bushy, paint peeling, tall yellow grass, the fence crumbling. I walked in to the backyard: trees bare, Sienna's doghouse, her water bowl hidden behind the tall grass, the cesspool rumbling, the lid rising.

I told my wife I was going hunting with the guys for the weekend. She's afraid, having woken the past two nights to horrible dreams. She's growing madder with each mention of my pleasure in hunting. She can't understand why I enjoy killing. As I lay back on the couch waiting for Nakia to arrive, I stare out the screen window. The Blue Moon's making its way across the starless sky, Sienna surrounded by an undulating light, dragging Nakia's dead corpse towards me, the birds lining up one by one in the trees, like soldiers preparing for battle, I hear my wife's words bouncing around in my head, as I think to myself: I can't understand it either.

⚡

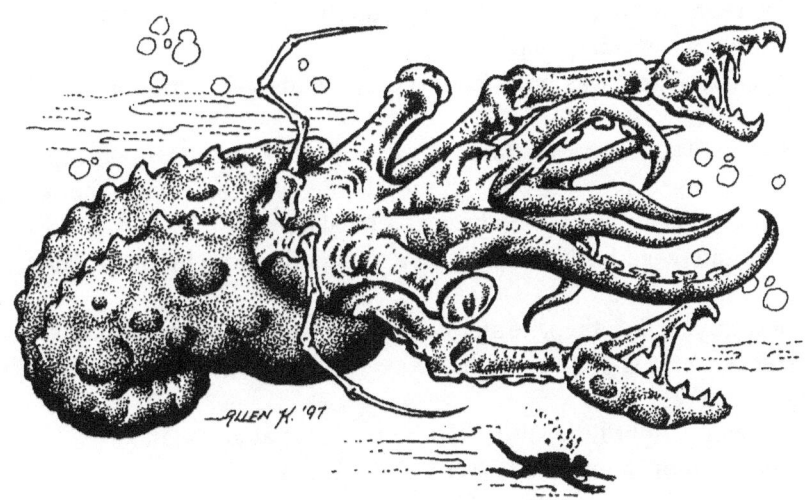

SHE WHO GIVES LIFE
by C. I. Kemp

It wasn't through a crystal ball that Sharon learned the truth about Mason. She wasn't that kind of witch.

Actually, she found out the same way most people learn such things. She saw them together, in the park — Mason lip-locked with a very bustaceous blonde. Mason didn't see her. If he had, he wouldn't have had his hands where they were.

What made it worse was that this was only days after Mason told Sharon that he wanted to spend the rest of his life with her. They'd lain in bed the rest of the night, loving, cuddling, and talking about moving in together.

You cheating bastard! I'll get you for this!

* * * *

You might think that "getting him for this" meant turning him and his new squeeze into toads or something equally loathsome, but no. Remember, Sharon wasn't that kind of witch.

What she was was an Animatrix; someone who brought non-living things to life.

Not dead bodies or anything like that. Rather, inanimate objects.

So when she saw Mason with the blonde, she knew what she was going to do. It began with a purchase at a local shop.

Then she went back to her apartment, stood before her work table, and spoke.

In response, her favorite stool walked towards her on its spindly legs.

Her book of spells soared her way with the grace of a seabird skimming the waves.

Wearing a tight little smile, she hummed an ancient air.

The phial of Manticore tears floated off its shelf.

The Megalodon cartilage, filtred and refined, launched itself into her outstretched hand.

The albino Roc pinfeather, reduced to a fine powder, moseyed out of its drawer.

They emptied themselves into a centuries-old marble mortar that had ambled on over while its partner, an equally ancient marble pestle crushed the contents into a fragrant gel.

When Sharon was satisfied with the consistency, she doused her purchase in the liquid and chanted words seldom articulated over the last thousand years. Upon completing her incantation, the purchased item sauntered out of the mortar and rested before her.

She called Mason and invited him over in her most coaxing, Marilyn Monroe-type voice. He was at her place within the hour and found her waiting in her sheerest nightie.

She told him how much she missed him, how much she wanted him, then handed him a square foil packet.

What was inside looked the same as it did before she'd animated it: a round object, roughly the size of a silver dollar, with a somewhat oily feel to it. Only now, she'd given it life.

And teeth. Very tiny, but very sharp.

Mason took it and told her "You look good enough to eat."

To which Sharon smiled and purred, "You, too."

AN IMPLEMENT OF ICE

W. H. Pugmire

I awakened in a chilly room and shuddered beneath bedclothes. At first I was uncertain concerning my whereabouts, but then I remembered the room from the few times I had visited it in childhood. My journeying to Canada was required so that I could organize my great-uncle's estate, part of which was this old café that he had transformed into living quarters. The smallish room in which I had awakened had once been the café's pool room, and my uncle had turned it into his bedchamber. Shifting in the antique mahogany bed, I became aware of the sounds and smells of cooking. I moved my legs from underneath the bedspread, stood and pulled on my trousers and socks, and then hobbled into the kitchen at the back of the establishment. Karla Ambrose smiled at me from the stove where she was creating breakfast. I watched the elderly woman for some few moments, until she signaled for me to sit at a low table.

"It feels odd being here again," I told her. "Mom always spoke so poorly about Uncle Silas, but we were always nice to him because of his rumored wealth. Then he journeyed to Burma and lived there for a year, and when he came back behaving so strangely—well, the family kept its distance. I'm glad he left you so much of his money, I think you took good care of him."

The old woman shrugged her petit shoulders. "I did what I could. He was as generous as he was difficult. No one else would have much to do with him, mostly on account of Chodon."

"That was the Tibetan dwarf he brought back with him from Burma, right? Yeah, that's when the family began to get weird about him."

"We all kept our distance. I limited my time considerably after he returned from his year away. Things had been so different before he left. We would spend many evenings together before the fire, and I would read to him. But when he came back—I don't know, he was changed in ways I can't explain. He'd become secretive, particularly about the odd books he began to study, those books in other languages. And he would dote on that disgusting runt."

"The dark dwarf, yes. Mom encountered him once, and that was the last time she visited Uncle Silas. Racial prejudice, I suppose—although her repulsion seemed excessive."

She brought me a plate of food and then went to pour a cup of coffee. Her face, when I studied it, was very serious. "Chodon was extremely ugly, but in an almost inhuman way. His face was—twisted, and it gave me the creeps to look on it. His teeth were gray and bent inward, and he had lost an eye. His ugliness seemed to have an unnatural aura about it—as if it were of an evil nature, melodramatic as that sounds. I never understood their relationship, and I stopped working for your uncle shortly after his time away. There were rumors of odd goings-on, but no one knew anything as fact. I thought perhaps Silas was tutoring the creature, for I would sometimes find them studying together and pronouncing passages from the foreign books. The freak had been seen by more than one, out there in the woods, dancing naked during snowfall and gesturing to the sky. Well, there's your breakfast." She looked about the place and scowled. "Can't say I'll miss this place. Silas was a strange one, sure enough, but he was good to me, and I'll always be grateful. But after his—change—all I could think about was how to escape his employment, much as I needed the income."

"I never took Uncle Silas for a drinking man."

"Nor was he."

"And yet he was found frozen to death in the woods, sitting against a tree in the dead of winter. He must have been on a bender and wandered out there and nodded off. My cousin had an alcoholic friend who died in similar fashion three years ago, in Montana."

"Well, Silas is gone now, rest his soul, and he's been very generous to both of us. Shall I return in the morning? We can do laundry if you like."

I nodded in the affirmative and waved at her as she exited through the back door. The kitchen area was fairly spacious, and had been the workplace when the café had been in business. Rising, I took my plate and set it in the sink next to the dish-washing machine, and then I went to look inside the larger of the two walk-ins. It had, in earlier years, been the place where café foodstuff had been kept, but there was little inside it now, and most of what remained would have to be thrown out. I exited and walked around to the smaller walk-in, but the door refused, at first, to open as I yanked on it, and I thought it might be locked. Summoning vigor, I pulled on the handle and nearly fell on my backside when the door opened at the force of my exertion. The walk-in was very narrow, not much bigger than a large closet, and its glacial air testified that it was a freezer. Stepping gingerly into the icy rectangle, I saw that there was no bulb inside the space, and the pale kitchen light did little to illuminate the icy surfaces of walls and floor and ceiling. The air seemed abnormally chilly, and I imagined that my liquid eyes were beginning to freeze. I stepped out into the kitchen but left the door open, rubbed my eyes with frigid fingers and squinted again into the dark enclosure. As I stood there, I seemed to detect a subtle yet unpleasant stench, as if something inside the walk-in had rotted. Grimacing, I searched the area just inside the doorway and found an upper switch, and when I pushed it the hum of the freezer's motor ceased. Turning on the oven, I left its door slightly ajar. The freezer would drink in the kitchen's warmth, and then I would then return to investigate it.

Walking through the main room of the building, I frowned at its dilapidated state. My great-uncle was a man of means, and yet he had chosen to dwell in this dim and dreary place. I suppose it was comfortable enough, this large room with its three sofas, antique lamps and sturdy bookcases. There were a couple of faded photos on the wall of when the place had been a café; it certainly couldn't have had room for many tables, especially since one wall had been reserved for the bar, which was probably its main attraction for the locals, who would come here to drink and trade talk after a long day of labor. Going to the front door, I stepped outside and gazed to where the road curved. It was an isolated spot, although the main section of the small town was just beyond the place where the road curved. Forested hills surrounded the area where I stood. I heard an approaching rumbling, and soon a large truck passed by.

Returning indoors, I went to make the bed, then sat on the bed and took up my great-uncle's journal. Perhaps the jottings in it would make more sense when read in the light of day, as they didn't when I glanced over them before going to sleep the previous night.

"It is true that I've become nervous—dreadfully so; indeed I suffer what I may call an ecstasy of foreboding. The damn howling haunted my dreams again. I awakened to find the Little One was playing on his pan pipe. Pah!—his smile as I approached him, the curling black lips in the jaundiced face! I tried not to look at the ugly slit that is his eyeless socket. His remaining eye, of course, captivated me again, and this time he allowed me to kiss it. An infinitesimal remnant of eye-jam clung to my lip as I backed away from him, and he was quick as he shot toward me and chewed the stuff away. His stiletto teeth sliced into my mouth, and my tongue tasted blood. I think he is especially happy because of the early snowfall. His orb—it shimmers when he's merry, like some green gem of rare beauty. But then he begins to laugh, and my eyes return to the cruel black slash that is his diabolic smile. I hate him then."

I set the journal aside and wiped my hands on the bedclothes. The room had retained its earlier chill, and I decided to return to the kitchen and its warmth. I had forgotten about the freezer, and when I again approached it its space was not so frosty. Small rivulets of water seeped from the doorway onto the floor's tile. I entered the walk-in and found it to be empty except for one curious thing that rested on a tall block of wood. Touching the object, I found it frightfully cold, and so I got a large towel from a drawer by the sink and used it to carry the object to the kitchen worktop. Never had I encountered anything so bizarre. I had, of course, seen ice sculptures in some of the fancier restaurants in which I had dined, and I supposed that the object before me could have been some such decoration. What is mostly reminded me of was a large frozen amoeba proteus composed of sparkling ice, a solid mass from which weird tentacular protuberances extended near its top. Queerest of all was the yellow face encased within the ice, a small countenance that might have belonged to a malformed child. The disturbing stench that I had detected earlier in the walk-in oozed from the object, a smell so hateful that I wrapped the object in the towel again and took it out back, where I set it and the towel on the ground. The October air was crisp, and a breeze carried the fragrant scents of autumn. I studied the wooded area that spread behind my great-uncle's abode, the woods that rose before me for some distance. A sense of intense isolation came over me, and I suffered a sudden yearning for the lights and noise of America. I would soon bring the business of my relation's estate to a close and return home.

Re-entering the large living space, that had originally been the customer dining area of the café, I considered it as a place in which a man of means had meant to spend his life; and this added to my already perplexed picture of my great-uncle, because I could not imagine anyone deliberately choosing to dwell in some dim a place, so far from real human activity. Why had my relative decided to so distance himself from the world? Was it because of something that he feared, or something he wanted to conceal about his life? I sat on one of the large soft sofas and reached for the decorative wooden box that sat on a small nearby table. Undoing the latch, I opened the box and drank in the aroma of the item that nestled within, the crudely constructed pan pipe. Taking up the instrument, I pressed its reddish wood to my nostrils and drank in the thing's ligneous fragrance. Bringing the flute's tubes to my mouth, I breathed into it and made music; and as I played my impromptu tune I was subconsciously aware of the wind outside the walls rising in force and sound, as if in accompaniment to my mindless melody. I played for a little while, but soon the music began to sound uncomfortably forlorn, and I was struck by the solitude of my surroundings, the loneliness in my life. Removing the instrument from my lips, I gazed for some moments at the moisture from my mouth that lingered on its tubes; and then I returned the implement to its box, rose to walk to the bedroom and reclined on the bed, determined to nap.

The rising gale shook the window panes, and the bedroom air was cold. I rose and put on a sweater, and then I noticed my great-uncle's odd journal and, sitting again on the bed, glanced through its leaves. As I read,

I seemed to comprehend that my relative had not been merely over-imaginative—he had been a little crazy. I knew no explanation for an entry as bizarre as this:

"His eye stays open as he slumbers—wide, wide open—but wears a glaze that shimmers like ice in firelight. The Little One likes the frozen snow that falls after he has called to the Wind-Walker with that accursed flute. He has taught me the phrase we studied from the ancient text, but I have trouble mouthing it precisely. I have seen the Old One through the blizzard, that ill-formed Behemoth of Storm, with its eyes of burning embers. Flaming eyes—and the eye of jade that glints in parchment of yellow flesh. Awakened by moan of wind, I find the horror on my chest, like something out of Fuseli—a nightmare indeed! I pushed the squat fiend from me, forcefully, and he did not rise from the floor. His pallid mask—so deadly still. How easily it is removed, with aid of smooth cool blade. And 'though the pygmy husk is buried deep within the woodland, there are reports of a Little One dancing between trees during snowfall. Well, let it frolic as it will. That butchered face can no longer mutter the words of calling to the Old One, encased as it is in dark frigidity."

Setting the journal aside, I listened to the wind; and coaxed by its song, I walked to the kitchen and out the back door, into biting storm. The snowflakes were large and lovely, and I giggled as I caught some on my protruded tongue. Pursing lips, I whistled the odd tune that I had played on the pan pipe, and I raised my hands to whiteness and did a little dance, until I slipped and fell against the sculpture that I had removed from the walk-in. The thing still stank atrociously, and it looked more weird than ever, half-melted yet still frozen, with some few of its protruding spears still intact while others had broken off due to my crashing onto it. The hideous mask was soft and easily removed from its cavity of ice. I could not ascertain the fabric from which it had been fashioned—pigskin, perhaps. One eye socket had been damaged. Getting on my knees, I pressed the mask against my face, to which it clung; and I fought the urge to gag, the smell was so revolting. I could feel the gash that was its mouth tighten against my own, it lips curling and opening as if it wished to speak. One of the tentacular spears of the ice-sculpture lay near me, and I picked it up and admired it. Some distant thing moaned above me in the storm, as if it begged summoning. My face felt as if it was shrinking beneath the fleshy mask. I listened to the thing that pulsed beyond the wind, and allowed the mask's mouth to utter phrases in a language I could not comprehend. I raised the implement of ice to the storm, and then I stabbed its sharpest point into my eye. Oh, exquisite pain. Ah, how vision blurred and turned crimson. I laughed as my scarlet liquid became icy, as the world became a kaleidoscope of blood and slime and snow.

Although my eyesight was blurred, I could just make out the thing that pranced about me, the small and faceless phantom that frolicked in the snow. Together, it and I made sigils with our fingers to the sky, and I pressed our twin lips together as we whistled a weird tune to the curtain of storm, behind which, subtly, I could almost see the monumental presence of monstrous doom that had been summoned.

NIGHT OF THE CIRCUS
by Sharon Cullars

Orwell, Nevada 1957

The rustling at the tent opening signaled that something was about to happen. The flap pulled back. In the light of the moon, a shadowy figure stood at the entrance.

The moon pitched a fluorescent glow that settled over the tent, a soft yet ominous aura that highlighted the red and white nylon structure standing in a lonely field. Outside the flap stood a growing line of patrons eager to get inside. Most of them fidgeted in the dark, their murmurs traveling the night. The silhouettes were of women, men and children, the denizens of a town that had seen better days. But those better days were long past, having seeped away with the closing of the chicken processing plant. Along with the disappearance of the jobs that had been a ballast to the families of Orwell was the death of prospects, the death of hope. Which was why they stood now before the large tent in a dark field, the time approaching midnight.

The flyers around town had said that the tent would provide an answer to their bedraggled lives and many were putting their faith that something miraculous was going to happen tonight.

"Welcome ladies and gentlemen, young misses and lads. The show will begin shortly, so please do come inside and take a seat," the shadowy man announced with a sonorous boom that quieted all the murmurs.

The line moved forward, a march of bodies pushing toward the unknown. Interspersed in the prevailing silence were titters of excitement, or the occasional whimpering of a child intimidated by the strangeness of it all.

Just past the flap, glaring lights settled on a semi circle of benches to the left, rows that tiered upward just a few feet short of the tent's roof. The bodies moved toward the wooden seats, filling the gaps in an orderly fashion, as though orchestrated by an invisible hand. Strangely, the shadowy figure was no longer at the entrance. Somehow, he had slipped away before anyone could put an eye on him, size him up.

It took nearly twenty minutes for everyone to be seated, their focus on a wide circle of light fronting the rows of benches. Whatever was to happen would probably take place in this circle of light.

As silent as the horde had been outside in the dark, the welcomed lights loosened tongues. Neighbors seated within earshot of one another greeted each other with smiles, bits of laughter, a litany of 'how's it going?', 'haven't seen you in a month of Sundays.' The smattering of exchanges meant nothing but was somehow required to keep the sense of community, the illusion of oneness. It allayed the nervousness.

Another good twenty minutes passed, during which the jovial talk began to change it's tenor into strains of impatience.

A tall, odd-looking man emerged from a backdrop of the tent that remained in shadow. His sudden appearance curbed the tongues. The wait was over.

The man stood nearly seven feet, his lithe body outfitted in green silk pants and jacket, both accented by a yellow silk vest. A green silk top hat completed the ensemble. The colors juxtaposed the deep, rich ebony of the man's skin, the black orbs of his eyes. Here stood the Master of Ceremony, the Ringmaster.

Murmurs of surprise punctuated the boom of the Ringmaster's welcome to all, the words spoken as though by rote, as though memorized from being spoken millions of times. As, indeed, they had been. Obviously, the pale, bedraggled assemblage had not expected the black man standing before them.

"What is this?" came a question from one of the top tiers of seats.

The Ringmaster smiled. "Yes, what is this, you ask. What this is, ladies and gentlemen, is your salvation."

"How is a nigger gonna save us? You ain't got no power, boy!" This interjection came from a man, now standing, overalls stained with dark spots, a dingy gray poor-boy hat atop his head, wisps of blond hair escaping the rim. A chorus of assenting voices joined the man's accusation.

The Ringmaster smiled with beautiful white straight teeth, teeth that could outmatch any that belonged to the horde before him.

"So you say I have no power, but what power do y'all have? None, from what I can see. The reason you came out of your shotgun houses this hot June night, loaded your families in your broken down cars or walked miles in your turned over shoes is because of hope, or rather the promise of it.You sit here in this place, bereft of any hope for the future. And I'm here to offer you a way out of your predicaments."

The aggravated man standing in the bleachers began pushing his way to the end of his row, stepping over those still seated, his trajectory moving downward until his foot touched the tent ground. He was dutifully followed by a silent blond woman, her face young but worn from the burdens of a hard life.

"I ain't got time for this," the angry man exclaimed as he headed for the now closed tent flap. He tried to open it, but it would not give with his effort.

Several men and women were standing now, all determined to leave. The man at the sealed exit turned to the Ringmaster.

"You better let me outta here nigger or else I'm gonna tan you blacker than you already are!"

"Y'all don't seem to understand," the Ringmaster said calmly, a cane mysteriously in his hand from nowhere. "There's no leaving until the show is over."

"What show are you talking about boy?" the young woman asked, her tone without anger, just tired, the strain of it that of someone who had been beaten by life's vagaries. There must have been a time when she sounded young and carefree. But that must have been a while ago.

"We came here tonight because we were promised that we would be given work, a new life," she continued. "That's what them flyers said."

Now several couples stood near the exit, their children in tow. Others still sat, seemingly more curious than angry. This was a spectacle they had not expected, not on this hot June night, so hot the crickets had gone silent and the edges of scraggly lawns had already turned brown. Given the drought, Mayor Youngston had ordered that the water in the town's reservoir be rationed, leaving everybody and everything lusting for water.

Despite the heat emanating from the intense lighting, the temperature inside the tent was not as fevered as the sweltering heat outside. But blood boiled in its confines as those who had ventured from their homes found themselves captives.

"If you folks would just be seated again, I will tell you all what you came to hear."

There was a sense of threat in the air. Toward the Ringmaster first of all. After all, how dare this nigger hold good white folks hostage!

But there was something else, something almost palpable, felt by the adults here this night. A sense that their well-being was somehow in this black man's hands. And that feeling was not settling well with most of the folk beneath the tent.

The angry man stopped his attempt to exit and resentfully turned to the Ringmaster.

"Tell us whatever shit you got to tell us then let us go or…"

"…or you'll tan me blacker than I already am. Yes, yes, I know. So, ladies, gentlemen, if you would take your seats, I will begin."

The group at the sealed entrance grudgingly made their way back to their seats, at least for now complacent enough to listen to the Ringmaster. Anything to get this over with. Who knew, maybe he had something worthwhile to say.

Unexpectedly, the lights dimmed leaving everyone in shadow. A child whimpered in response. This wasn't what the little ones had expected. The circus was supposed to be fun. They didn't understand their angry parents, and the strange black man.

The Ringmaster began.

"These years have been hard for a lot of you folks. A drought that seems to never end, no harvests from your farms, all the jobs gone like tumbleweeds in the wind. And I'm sure all of you have asked yourselves why. Why are these things happening to good folks like yourselves?"

In the dimmed lights, several heads nodded. The last tinges of anger quelled at the Ringmaster's sympathetic words. Yes, why were these things happening to them? They were good, hard-working folk. Why indeed had God turned His back on them?

"I can only say that fate is mercurial, if you will. Goodness is often rewarded with egregious cruelty while the most heinous acts go unpunished. But I'm here this night to let you know that not all murderous acts go unheeded by the universe. That time and circumstance have a way of providing due dispensation."

"What the hell you talkin' about?!" came a voice from the dimmed area of benches.

If the audience could have seen the Ringmaster clearly, they might have seen his smirk.

"Oh, so you ask what I am talking about. So, let me tell you. I stand here in the stead of Ruby and Frederick Gaines."

A gathering of murmurs moved through the dim tent, settled at the core where the Ringmaster stood. He listened at the excited whispers.

The audience had reason to know those names, names that would be forever etched in blood in the soil of Orwell.

A scream pierced the whispers.

"I'm on fire!" shouted a woman.

And truly, several could smell the pungent odor of sizzling flesh.

The same smell that went up that awful night.

A shadowy female figure jumped from several tiers up, fell to the ground. Then the figure disappeared. That caused a stampede as bodies rose from their seats in a panic, trying to find the exit. But as they found before, the tent would not open.

"What is this?!!!"

"Who are you?!!!"

Questions rose, as well as screeches from the women and children.

"You can call me by my true name. Justice," the Ringmaster said without elaboration or fanfare.

Another voice pierced the dim enclosure, a dimness that had darkened even more in just a matter of seconds.

"Justice! What justice are you talkin' about?!! We've done nothing!!"

"Tell that to Fred and his wife. Tell it to their orphaned children."

"I had nothing to do with that!" came a male plea.

"Ahhh, but that isn't true, now is it. For Roger Gilmore, you were there. You even kept a souvenir. The bone of a finger if I recall correctly.

"And Milton, I believe you took over the farmland you coveted, the rich soil you lusted for, envied. Isn't that why you told the Sheriff that Fred raped your seven-year-old daughter? So you could set your neighbors on poor Fred and Ruby, take what was rightfully theirs.?"

The Ringmaster's voice was an indictment, any pretense at conviviality now gone. No, this was not a true circus. There would not be fun and games, animals and tricks. Neither would there be the offered hope that had lured them all here. No jobs, no restitution for their desolate lives.

Panic were (was) in the voices of men, women and children as they tried to escape. Only the children were blameless. Well, not all of them. There were those who had stood next to their parents as Ruby's body had been set to the flames. They had smiled at the spectacle of a body becoming nothing more than cinder and molten blood.

One man moved toward the Ringmaster. The one the Ringmaster had named Milton. Not surprisingly, the very man who'd been the first to protest, the first to try to leave. Even in the near dark, the Ringmaster saw him clearly. The poor-boy was gone from atop his head.

"I'm gonna kill you nigger!" the white man spat with venom.

The Ringmaster simply blocked the oncoming fist with his larger hand. Crushed bones. Took pleasure in the scream of pain. Much like the sound that Fred had sent into that night over a year ago.

Milton collapsed to the ground.

"I didn't mean it," the injured man moaned, nursing his broken hand as he rolled back and forth like a child seeking solace. There would be none given.

"Why(,) murderers never mean what they do. Especially when it comes time to pay the price."

The screams quieted as the bodies realized there would be no escape. Mothers gathered their children close, as their menfolk hugged their respective families. Tonight there would be retribution they finally conceded.

"You're not human…" Milton moaned. "How can you do this to children?"

"Good question."

A scream pierced through the now utter darkness as a woman called out, "Where's my baby?!!"

Sure enough, her arm baby had disappeared as had several of the smaller children. More anguished cries went up.

"Please, give us back our children! They don't deserve this!"

"And that is why they have been released."

"Released? From what? What hell is this?!!" Milton asked as he sat up with measured breath, still holding his broken hand. His question was punctuated by similar questions from the darkness, from mothers wailing their loss, from fathers trying to quell their own fear.

"Strange you should ask. Hell is here, this moment, this place."

"But...but..." Milton began.

"Yes, a little confusing isn't it. No brimstones, no fiery lake..."

"But, I'm not dead. Neither is my family or all these folks here."

The Ringmaster's laughter was a sound of mirth, satisfaction...and just a barely perceptible anger.

"That's where you're wrong. Ironically, in this drought, a sudden downpour of much needed rain swept away your town. Some survived. You and your family, these folks here, did not. Unfortunately for you."

"Are...are you saying that we're dead."

"Yessum boss. You is dead, dead, dead!" Justice the Ringmaster said with glee before throwing his head back and laughing.

"Noooo!" came a chorus of voices. "It can't be true!" "Why did this happen?"

"Yes, Hell is a subjective...I don't know why I use the word when you're too stupid to understand...so let's just say that Hell is a personal experience, meted out according to the sin. Now y'all thought it was shits and giggles and just plain ole fun as you strung Fred up that old oak tree that his grandpappy had planted on their own land. As you menfolk, in front of your women and children, did dirty things to Ruby, in front of her screaming children whom you had the trace of grace to leave alive. One of you poured kerosene on her as she lay there begging, pleading. Another struck the match. And your children, those old enough to know and enjoy, laughed with glee. Some of you even brought baskets of food for the spectacle. After all, it was a family gathering. Those same children are here with you right now while the younger ones too young to know have gone on to glory."

"This night(,) you died as the rain came down. Now your women will feel the flames lick their flesh, while you men will feel the grate of rope tight around your necks, as you gasp for breath as your necks finally break..."

And then the Ringmaster was gone.

And the light shone...the light from several flames that permeated the very flesh of the women, the children...

And from the rafters of the tent, figures dangled.

* * * *

Milton, poor bedraggled Milton, who'd never had much in this world, who had looked at a nigger making a go of it with land that should have belonged to a white man, building up a fine farm, a handsome family... well, something had to be done. Especially when he'd caught his seven-year-old Lulabelle playing with one of Fred's nigger sons. That'd been the last thread in the rope they tied around Fred's neck. And Ruby...well... she'd been a fine-looking woman, so why not?

After hours had passed, Milton finally realized that Hell was eternal. The rope bit his flesh something awful. An eternity of your neck stretching, slowly breaking while smelling the searing flesh of your wife, of all the wives, while hearing their perpetual screams, screams that morphed with that of a black woman one blazing night...

Outside the tent, the flood gathered the detritus of the town, swept it away in a deluge of water. But the tent, visible only to those trapped inside, remained.

⚡

ALLEN H. '17

WOLVERS HILL
by Tim Jeffreys

"Next left," Fergus said.

Bisma glanced across at him. He held the road map only inches from his face and squinted at it. "Are you sure?"

He didn't look at her. He hadn't looked at her for the past fifty miles, and had only spoken to give directions. "One hundred per cent."

Bisma rolled her shoulders. Her back ached. "Maybe we should pull over and look at the map together. It's going to be dark soon. I'm tired. I don't want to get lost again."

He gave her a sideways glance. "Don't you trust me?"

"Of course I do, but—"

"Next left," he said, his voice blunt with irritation.

"This one?"

"Next left, didn't I say? Next left. You're gonna miss it."

"Okay, okay," Bisma said under her breath. The left turnoff was a narrow entrance between two fields. She probably wouldn't have noticed there was a turnoff had Fergus not alerted her to it. Something about it didn't feel right to her, but she took it anyway, not wanting another argument. The narrow road was overhung by trees on either side, which created a tunnel effect, and the sudden switch from sunlight to shade gave her an added sense of uncertainty but she said nothing. Deep down, she knew it was a matter of pride for Fergus. He could no longer drive but navigating gave him a feeling that he was contributing. She understood that it was difficult for him having to live with his worsening eyesight. First he'd had to sell his accountancy business, then been forced to give up his driving license, and now he had to rely on her to be the breadwinner and to drive him wherever he wanted to go. None of this was easy for a man like Fergus. She knew he felt like he was losing his manhood along with his sight, but as much as she tried to understand there were times when she struggled to control her irritation with him.

Light rain patterned the windscreen. She turned the wipers on. Shifting her gaze from the road, she noticed on the right-hand side the grave-looking entrance to an estate. A rusting iron gate hung between two stone balusters, both of which were topped with a small statue of what looked like a dragon. Beyond she glimpsed a dirt track leading into the grounds of the estate.

"That looks gloomy. I wonder who lives there."

"What's that?"

"Never mind," she said, realising he probably hadn't seen the estate entrance. He'd hadn't been able to see anything in his peripheries for years, and now also had growing blind spots in his vision. His GP said that in five years he would be completely blind. Bisma still felt bad that her first though on hearing this news was that he'd no longer be able to see her. She'd always known she was an attractive-looking woman, some people even said she was beautiful, and soon her own husband wouldn't be able to appreciate that. Though she never voiced this concern with Fergus, he must have sensed something because one day when she was brushing her hair in the mirror, getting ready for work, he'd told her how beautiful she was and how soon he'd only be able to appreciate her inner beauty. This had surprised her, as he usually didn't like to talk about his chrolodermia. It also worried her, and she hadn't been able to stop thinking about it all day. Eventually, she realised why. Though people had been telling her how pretty she was from a young age, of her inner beauty she was less confident.

The sun set somewhere behind the trees on the left, and the road they were driving grew darker still. The misty rain added to the murk. Bisma had to squint to see the unmarked road. She had an unpleasant thought which she immediately pushed away, that they had taken a wrong turn and Fergus had somehow steered them into his own darkening world.

"I don't recognise any of this," she said.

"It's been ten years since we were last here, Bis."

"Maybe we should turn back."

"I knew you didn't trust me."

"Look, don't start Fergus, okay?" She was always surprised by how sharp her voice could suddenly become. "I told you this trip was a bad idea."

"Why was it a bad idea?"

"Because…"

"Say it."

"I…"

"Because we're not the same people we were ten years ago? Is that it? Because we're not as happy as we were back then and coming back to Somerset now will only highlight that?"

She was stunned at how accurately he'd summed up the thoughts that had been turning in her mind ever since they'd left London. Had she communicated this somehow, or had he been thinking along the same lines?

"Fergus, I just don't see the point in going back to the same place, the same hotel. The last time we came here we'd only just met. We barely left the hotel room, remember? We hadn't even meant to come here, we were just driving. We were still in that honeymoon period. You never get that back, but what we have now is something more…"

She trailed off, seeing him reach forward to turn on the radio. She knew it was his way of shutting her out. He jabbed at the buttons but all he found was static.

"I'm not saying we're not happy anymore, Fergus. I'm not. I do wish you hadn't kept quiet about your condition for so long though."

"Can't find a damn thing," he muttered, keeping his gaze lowered. He continued stabbing one finger at the radio buttons. "What's wrong with this? There's no signal."

Bisma let out a long sigh. She knew it was useless trying to talk to him in his current mood. She felt weary thinking of the days ahead, holed up in some hotel having to pretend she was enjoying herself whilst all the time knowing that one careless word could uncork the resentments bubbling in their relationship. She drew in her breath and tried for a more positive tone when she said, "What's the name of this road we're on, Ferg?"

Leaving the radio to its hiss of static, Fergus sat back in his chair and picked up the map again. He held it close to his face for what seemed a long time. When she reached up and switched on the dashboard light, he tutted and threw her a dark look. "Wolvers Hill."

"Are you sure this road is going to take us up to the Mendips? Ferg?"

"Maybe you should have married a Muslim like your father wanted. He could have found you another dentist to chat about the different types of handpieces with. You could've had an arranged marriage."

"Fergus, don't…"

He leant forward to toy with the radio buttons again, but before he could touch it a sudden sound broke through the static. It sounded like a kind of snarl, followed by laughter and it gave Bisma such a start that she lost control for a second and the car swerved toward the right side of the road. There followed what sounded like a scream, broken by bursts of static, which continued until Fergus jerked forward and hit the off button.

Bisma switched her gaze to her husband. She could tell by his expression that he'd also been given a fright. "What on Earth was that?"

"I don't know. Interference."

"Interference? It sounded like…I'm turning the car around."

"What?"

"I don't like this road. It gives me the creeps."

"What're you talking about?"

"We're not getting anywhere, Fergus. I can't just keep driving forever. We're getting low on petrol. Look—the warning light's on."

"Well, I did say we should stop at the Services before we left the motorway."

"That's before I knew you'd have me driving around in circles for an hour."

"That was my fault, was it?"

"Of course it was, Fergus, you're navigating."

He fell silent, turning his head to the side, away from her. Bisma slowed the car in order to turn around, but as she did she noticed a figure walking along the right-hand side of the road ahead of them.

"There's a man," she said to Fergus, although the figure was just a dark blur against the trees and she couldn't tell if it was a man or a woman. She slowed the car. "We can ask if he knows where the hotel is. Check we're going in the right direction."

Had it been up to her, she would have simply turned the car around and gone back to the main road, but she saw an opportunity for Fergus to redeem himself. He was already winding his side window down as she brought the car up alongside the pedestrian. The man had been headed in the same direction they'd been driving, his back to them. He wore a long dark coat and his shoulder-length hair might've been grey or blond. Though it wasn't fully dark yet, Bisma decided to switch the car headlights on. They lit the face of the walking man as he turned when Fergus called out, "Excuse me."

At once, Bisma felt a lurch in her chest and she jammed her foot down on the accelerator. For a moment, she struggled to regain control of the car as it swerved to left and right in the road. She could feel her heart pounding. All she could see in her mind's eye was the man's face. Once she had control of the car again, she began to take deep breaths to steady her breathing. She was aware that Fergus stared at her.

"Bis...what the hell?"

She shot him a glance. "You didn't...?"

"I thought we were gonna ask for directions."

"Fergus, you...you didn't see?" But of course he hadn't. Most likely he couldn't see a thing in this gloom.

"What's got into you?"

"I...his face."

"What?"

"You didn't...?" But now she began to doubt what she'd seen. Perhaps she'd just imagined it. It was this road, and those weird noises on the radio. She was spooked, that's all.

She took a deep breath. "Do you want to go back?"

He turned on the dashboard light again, and his eyes examined her. She knew that he saw how white her knuckles were as she gripped the steering wheel.

"Let's just keep driving."

"How long is this bloody road? It just goes on and on."

His voice was subdued now. "There'll be a turnoff soon. You'll see. Shall I try the radio again?"

"God, no."

He reached one arm out and stoked his hand on the back of her neck. "It's all right, Bis. We're close now."

She looked at him, showing him her uncertainty.

They continued along the road. The car's headlights cut eerie funnels of light from the suddenly full dark. Bisma couldn't help but imagine forms and faces in the patches of illumination ahead of them. Seeing something on the left side of the road she eased her foot off the accelerator.

"What is it?" Fergus said when he noticed the car slowing.

"Another estate entrance." The car headlights picked out the iron gate, and the stone balusters topped with leering dragons. "It looks exactly the same as the one I saw earlier. Only before it was on the other side of the road."

"What're you saying?" Fergus said.

"Nothing. Just that it looks the same. Could we have got turned around somehow?"

"That's impossible."

"I'm going to…don't be offended, Ferg, okay. I'm going to pull over and we're both going to take a look at the map. Okay? I just want to check we're on the right road."

She glanced across at him and he shrugged. Taking this for agreement, she slowed the car and pulled up at the side of the road. Saying nothing, Fergus handed her the map. She studied the map for a long time, checking the index a number of times whilst he sat in silence.

"Ferg," she said at last. "There's no Wolvers Hill on this map."

"What? Of course there is."

"There isn't."

"I'll show you."

"Fergus, you can't see," she said. "Why don't you just admit that you can't see? We should have got SatNav or something. Now we don't know where the hell we are." When she finished talking, she found she was breathing hard, struggling to keep her anger in check. Fergus only stared at her.

"I'll show you," he said again, in a small voice, holding out his hand. She thrust the road map at him.

"It was here. Wolvers Hill. It was here."

"For God's sake, Ferg."

"I'm telling you it was here."

Something heavy bumped against the rear of the car and Bisma let out a scream.

"What…?" Fergus said, twisting in his seat, but she was already starting the car. She performed a tight U-turn in the road then accelerated back the way they had come.

"What're you doing?" Fergus said. When she didn't answer, keeping her eyes fixed on the road ahead, he fell silent. They passed the entrance to the estate again, now on their right, but Bisma kept driving. By the time she realised there was something in the road ahead of them it was too late. There was a thump against the front of the car and she saw something roll across the windscreen and she screamed again. Fergus began yelling at her to stop, but instead she was pressing down on the accelerator. She was aware of the car pulling to the left as they rounded a bend, she saw the needle on the speedometer inching past 60 but still she didn't slow down. Eventually, Fergus' yelling brought her to her senses and she eased her foot off the accelerator. She looked at him. He sat twisted at the waist, facing her. He didn't look himself. His eyes were wide and manic, his face more lined than she'd known it to be previously. She remembered how much she'd enjoyed letting him take charge when they first met, how she was attracted by his surety and his confidence which offset her concerns about him being more than a decade older. Throw a few things in a bag, he'd said that day when she'd come home from the dental hospital after finding out that she'd failed her mid-year presentation. You need to get out of London for a while. Then he had just driven with no destination in mind, and it was exciting for her. She always gave so much thought to everything she did, but just to ride in the car with him and not know where they were going was such a thrill. By sundown they were blasting through a landscape of green hills with the top down, both of them looking at each other and laughing. She could remember how her hair had fluttered around her face. She could remember how the whole sky had turned a dreamy-orange colour as the sun dipped below the horizon and she'd felt like she was a million miles from the stresses of London.

This was different. This was just a dark road with no end in sight.

"You have to go back," Fergus was saying.

"What?"

"You hit something, Bis. You need to go back and see what it was."

"Are you serious? I'm not going back there."

"You have to. What if it was a person?"

"It's not my fault. What were they doing in the middle of the bloody road?" Before he could answer, she leant forward in her seat and said, "Bloody hell. There it is again."

She hit the brake and both she and Fergus were jolted forward in their seats. Then she reversed the car a short way along the road until they were parked alongside the estate entrance. The glow of the headlights reached far enough to show her the rusty gate and the balusters topped with stone dragons. The dragons' heads were positioned in such a way that they appeared to be looking directly at the car. Directly at Bisma in fact.

"What're we doing?" Fergus said. "What is it?"

"Look."

"You know I'm nightblind."

Bisma felt a twinge of remorse. "It's that same estate entrance. The same gate. We've passed it four bloody times now."

"It can't be."

Bisma noticed that there was a dark square fixed to one of the balusters. She flipped open the glove compartment and routed inside until she found a torch. She directed the torchlight out of the window.

"What're you doing?" Fergus said.

"There's a name."

"What does it say?"

She took in deep breath and let it out slowly. "Wolvers Hill Estate."

He could have gloated. He could have said I told you so. Instead he remained silent. Eventually he said, "What do I hear?"

"Hear?"

She watched as he lowered his side window a few inches then moved one ear closer to the gap. Bisma listened intently aswell. For a short time there was only silence. Then she heard it. An odd sound. Animalistic, but human at the same time. It sounded like someone yelling in anger or perhaps despair. There were no words, just a kind of Ra! Ra! Ra! Another sound answered the first, a strange repeated call, low and guttural, and hearing that sound coming out of the dark made the hairs on Bisma's forearm bristle. She decided she'd heard enough, and reached forward to start the car. But when she turned the key in the ignition nothing happened. The fuel warning light still blinked. The gage pointed at 0.

"I don't believe it. I don't believe it. We're out of petrol."

"That can't be," Fergus said. "This car can go forty miles with the warning light on."

"It's been on since we started on this road, Ferg."

"Oh Jesus."

Hearing the dread in his voice was too much for her. "Shit!" she said, hitting the driving wheel with her palms. She began to weep, rocking back and forth in her seat. Words bubbled out of her as well as tears. "I shouldn't be the one driving, Ferg. You were always the driver. You were always in charge. It should be you sitting here, not me. You wouldn't have let this happen. I can't do it, Ferg, I can't."

"Shush," he said, reaching across and drawing her closer to him. He put both his arms around her and held her. "It's okay. We're fine, aren't we? We're doing ok. None of this is your fault."

"The thought of everything getting darker and darker for you, Ferg. I just can't take it. It breaks my heart."

"Hey," he said. He kissed her forehead. "Let me worry about that."

A bang on the roof of the car brought them to their senses and they both jerked upright in their seats.

"What was that?" Bisma said.

"Nothing. Nothing. It was a bird or…something fell from a tree, maybe."

"It didn't sound like a bird." Bisma pointed the torch light out of all the car's windows, but she saw nothing.

"I'll get out and take a look."

"Don't be an idiot," she said. "You're blind."

Catching the hurt look on his face, she felt ashamed. "I…I'm sorry. I wasn't thinking."

He settled in his seat again.

"Turn off the headlights," he said after a pause. "You'll drain the battery."

Bisma flipped the switch to turn off the headlights. Feeling that it drew attention to her, she turned her torch off also, plunging them into darkness. She strained to see in the black beyond the car window. She realised she shook, a quiver that ran the length of her body.

"I know you're still angry about the accident," Fergus said.

Bisma laughed under her breath. "Are we really going to have this conversation now?"

"Lots of drivers hit cyclists. Plenty of drivers without my condition. We have a weird blind spot to people on bikes. All of us in cars."

"A literal blind spot in your case."

"I'm just saying, it could have happened to anyone."

Bisma shook her head in the dark. "You shouldn't have been driving, Ferg. You should have told me about your chrolodermia a lot sooner."

"Would you have still married me?"

She said nothing.

"I'll understand if you wanna separate."

"What?"

"You're only thirty-five. You could meet someone else. Who wants to be stuck with an old blind man for the rest of their life?"

She was quiet a moment. Then she said, "I do love you."

"Enough?"

"I…I don't know."

"Well," he said. "It seems to me we've got two options. We can sit here and wait for daybreak, or we can walk up to that estate and see if there's anyone home."

Bisma turned her head towards where the estate entrance was, although she could no longer see it in the dark. "After what we just heard out there?"

"That was just an animal. Fox or something. You'd be surprised at the noises they make."

"I don't think it was a fox, Ferg."

"Well, I'm getting out. I'm tired of sitting down. It can't be very far to the estate house. Worth a try, I reckon. You coming?"

"You know you can't go alone."

She heard the clunk as he unfastened his seatbelt, then the sound of him springing the passenger side door open and her heart lurched suddenly. Don't go out there! she wanted to tell him. This road we're on... there's something wrong. Don't you feel that? But for some reason the words died inside her. She switched on the torch then pointed it through the windscreen, searching for him. He stood in front of the car with his arms folded, waiting. The sight of all the blackness surrounding him made her want to cry.

"You coming?" he said again.

She didn't want to go, but she didn't want to stay alone in the car either. She unfastened her seatbelt and climbed out. Pointing the torchlight toward the gate, she took his arm and led him towards the entrance. The gate hung at an angle on one hinge and was stuck half-open in the dirt. She avoided directing the light at the dragon statues, fixing it instead on the dirt track that led inside the grounds. There was a large stone in the path and she stumbled over it, letting go of Fergus' arm and dropping the torch. Luckily, it was undamaged. Grabbing it from the dirt, she pointed the light ahead. Fergus had walked on a little way without her. The darkness appeared to be swamping him from all sides, consuming him almost. She hurried to catch up.

"Fergus! Ferg!"

"I can't be that far," she heard him say. He walked too fast, leaving her behind. "Bis...where are you? I can't see you."

"I'm here. Wait. Wait."

"I can't see."

"Fergus! My darling...wait."

He was gone then, beyond the reach of her torchlight and she felt a thread of panic. She heard a weird shriek from somewhere distant, and the thought passed through her head to return to the car. She could go back to the car, lock all the doors and wait until morning. But then she thought of Fergus, that day she'd failed her presentation, saying Throw a few things in a bag. You need to get out of London for a while.

So she ran on, following Fergus into that darkness which had taken him, pointing the beam of her torch in all directions, calling his name. Then…there…there…her light found him. He had strayed off the track and crouched in an area of long grass to one side of it. She ran to him and helped him to his feet. She was alarmed to see that he was weeping.

"Fergus what…what happened?"

He wiped the tears from his face with his fingers. "I'm sorry…I got scared. There were sounds…shrieks. I felt something touch me. I'm sure I did. I couldn't see…nothing. I couldn't see, Bis."

Bisma could feel her panic threatening to unravel again. Taking a deep breath, and gripping his hand in her own, she led Fergus back to the dirt track. She moved the torch from side to side so that the light arced across the track and into the grass on either side of it. Then she began moving quickly forward, tugging Fergus by the hand.

"Where are we?" Fergus said, sounding calmer, more like himself now. "All I see is black."

"I'll guide you," she said. "Stay with me. I'm here."

⚡

RAFTS

by Lorenzo Crescentini

translation by Lisa Kramer Taruschio

That night, the blind dog spoke to the boy again in the boy's sleep.

"*Your voice,*" the dog said, with words that weren't words, "*is like a blade slicing through the dark. It makes me dream what I had started to forget.*"

The next morning, the boy asked his mother if a blind dog lived in the building.

"I don't know, why do you ask?"

He said never mind.

On his way downstairs, he looked at the doors, wondering if the animal invading his thoughts in the darkness lived behind one of them.

It spoke to him only at night, and he knew why. For the blind dog, life was darkness. During daylight the world was full of sounds, smells: people moving, homemade bread baking in the oven, children who made fun of his big, white eyes that stared and saw nothing. At night, in the silence, the darkness turned into nothing. And the dog reached a paw out into the void to confirm its own existence, to stop its own self from becoming nothing.

"*Give me lots of action; I need it so I can leave this dark plain. At least for a while.*"

For a while; the time to get through another night.

Sometimes the boy slept at friends' houses, and before he drifted off, he would think of the dog. What would he do if he looked at night and didn't find him? Would he send his prayers elsewhere? Was there anyone else in the building who could hear them? And he—why could he hear them?

He never spoke of it to anyone, because what was there to say, after all? He couldn't even admit it to himself. Still, when the dog called, he answered.

He worked hard at pulling shining images into his head, fields as green and endless as he had maybe never even seen, and he did his best to send them toward where the dog was speaking in words that were like matches about to flicker out in the dark.

In the morning he couldn't remember what was real and what was only a dream. And if it was the latter, he wondered if it made any difference.

"Laugh at me, play with me, tease me, pity me. But talk, and I will follow your voice."

* * * *

One night late, standing at the window looking out, he saw the man who lived on the second floor.

He was holding a large dog with a shiny black coat on a leash. Without thinking, the boy whistled softly. The black dog stopped immediately.

It turned and looked at him from the ground up with its big, white eyes. The dog's owner said something, but the dog ignored him and stayed still, its face turned toward the open window where the boy was standing. Then the dog's owner started walking again and the dog followed behind.

The boy lay down on the sofa and dozed off, dreaming of the sounds of steps in the stairwell. He awoke when he heard scratching at the front door. He stood and went to open it.

The dog was waiting for him, sitting in the shadows—because a blind dog does not need a light to climb up to the last floor of a building.

It was looking at him with its beautiful empty eyes, and he bent over to take the animal's face in his hands and pet him.

"Spark!" The stairwell flooded with light and approaching footsteps clicked on the marble floor.

"Spark! Ah, here you are!" The man from the second floor appeared on the landing and saw them. "I'm sorry about the time, I don't know what got into him. He's a wonderful dog, but when I opened the main door he suddenly leapt ahead and ran up the stairs. Maybe he smelled something, or whatever."

"I'm sure that's it. He's really very handsome."

"Yes. I'm going to miss the monster. The vet says he hasn't got long."

The boy nodded, but said nothing. He kept staring at the dog. It seemed as though they were exchanging looks.

"Let's go, Sparky, leave this young fellow alone. It's bedtime. Sorry again to have disturbed you. Goodnight."

* * * *

In his dream there was an open door and a luminous figure, posed in the doorway, radiating a warm light all around.

"You."

* * * *

It was the last time he heard the blind dog's voice. A week later he met the owner from the second floor who told him that, sadly, Sparky had passed away.

"He was a good dog," the owner said. "They say that when an animal knows the end is near, it behaves strangely. Maybe that's why he came to find you the other night."

The boy nodded.

That night, he thought about the dark plain. He could see it, broad and obscure, and within it the dog, floating like a raft on the sea looking for a voice to follow.

*Dedicated to the Memory of Lisa Kramer Taruschio.
A true artist at translating without whose assistance and enthusiasm this story would not have been what it is.*

CLEAN SWEEP
Edward Ahern

The catnip spray made her naked form easy to find. Her ectoplasmic hands clutched at the back of a sofa. Gaunt and wrinkly. Would be nice to extract an attractive ghost for a change.

Ralph lumbered over to her, activated the acetone spray, set the wetvac nozzle against her hands, and broke her grip on the fabric. Her drug-addled wail was faint but audible as she was sucked in. Every time, he thought, I get shaky every time.

He walked out the front door of the house and slipped between the plastic sheeting that covered it. Mrs. Calassi was standing in the driveway waiting for him, dressed like she was going to play tennis. She'd been watching his performance on a tablet. Her expression shifted between frightened and disgusted.

Ralph set down the wetvac, which shuddered, turned off the camera mounted on his hood and pulled his head gear off. "There you go, Mrs. Calassi, the ghost is gone."

"That's terrible! Her face—she could have been my mother."

Or mine. "Don't feel too bad, Mrs. Calassi. She was infesting your house. But she's drugged, trapped and gone. And with Hauntfree ongoing inspection coverage, we can suck up any recurrence."

Ralph stepped over to his van, grabbed his cell phone and sent a text. "The crew will be here shortly to pull off the sheeting and hoses and vacuum up the Catnip. "There's a balance of seven thousand for the extermination and sixty-five hundred for the two-year inspection agreement."

She stared at the quivering wetvac. "Ah, Mr. Cramden, about the inspections, the cost of your exorcism has cleaned us out. We really can't afford them."

Ralph knew what he was supposed to tell her. That houses once haunted are apparition prone, and that without the coverage they'd be charged full price for another removal. But ghosts weren't house bound, and almost never moved back into a house that'd been fumigated. And he knew from their credit check that the couple were almost completely buried in debt. And she'd been nice.

He shrugged. "Mrs. Calassi, we recommend the inspection coverage, but it's not mandatory. If you like I'll take it off the bill.

Thelma's relief was apparent. "Thank you." After Ralph revised the bill down, she touched her phone to his and Visa took over.

Once stripped out of the hazmat suit and back in the van, Ralph called his office. "Hi Sarah, one for the toilet, paid like you see on your screen. Anything else?"

"Hey, Ralph. The beta crew just wrapped a house on Longview for a late afternoon fumigation. Want some overtime?"

"You know I could use the money." For the Bitch Queen's alimony.

"Couple's name is Norten. They've paid in advance so just suck 'em up and drop 'em. Nobody'll be there, but they've given us the code for the security alarm. Are you gassy enough?"

Ralph checked his gauges. "Got plenty of acetone, but I'm low on toluene and nitrous oxide. Powdered catnip should be topped up as well."

"Swing by. You can flush your critter while you get gassed."

"Will do." As Ralph settled behind the steering wheel, he could smell the chemicals that had infiltrated his suit. He'd wondered about slipping under the tarp and getting high on happy juice and glue solvent, but he'd seen too many whacked out ghosts with frozen screams. And it was a contact high for the non-breathing ghosts, while Ralph could get his lungs eaten out.

First stop once back at the facility was to hook his wetvac up to the tank, reverse the suction, and squirt his new friend into the holding pen. Company PR said that the ghosts remained incarcerated at the facility, but Ralph suspected that a few ghosts built a tolerance for the catnip and were able to sneak off. We're just gamekeepers, ensuring that enough ghosts are loose that we always have work.

The nitrous oxide and acetone were no problem to handle, flammability aside, but toluene was different, more poisonous and volatile. The powdered catnip, soporific of choice for cats and ghosts, was merely messy. Once his van was replenished, Ralph called the office back.

"Sarah? Armed and dangerous, and on my way back out."

"Stay suited, Ralphie."

"Aw, you care."

"Don't be a dumbass."

* * * *

Under the plastic sheeting the bones of the house looked old, but the owners had gentrified it beyond architectural principles or good taste. Ralph rang the doorbell and waited, but there was no response. When he opened the door the alarm started beeping, and he quickly keyed in the code.

Step one was a walk through to establish the nozzle placements. He found some light switches and turned them on, then walked from the entry hall into a great room. And dropped his tablet with a clatter.

An old ghost with a scraggy Van Dyke beard was seated in a leather easy chair. He didn't float up. "Mr. Cramden, I've been looking forward to meeting you. Please don't try and run out, I've bolted the door. If you'll listen for just a few minutes I'll explain how you can earn a great deal of money."

Ralph pulled out his emergency aerosol of Specter Spew and pointed it at the apparition. "Easy or hard, spooky, you're the one that'll be leaving." Then he hesitated. "It's daylight still. How the hell can you appear? And how do you know my name?" He squeezed off a quick warning spray of holy water.

The ghost flinched back ten feet behind the chair. "Call me Ed Norten, good as any name. Daylight's excruciatingly painful and draining, so I have to be quick. Tell me Ralph, do you know the effects your drugs have on ghosts?"

"Sure. Our chemicals knock the ghosts unconscious, we contain and remove them. No, wait, do you mean how the ghosts feel? They're high as hell, so great."

"Your cocktail produces an ecstatic high, but it's also viciously addictive. Once the ghosts come back down they spend their spectral existence trying to repeat the narcotic effect." Ed Norten smiled, not pleasantly.

Get a grip on your dick, Ralph told himself, you're the one that's armed. "Look, whatever you are, you mess with me and the whole company moves in and treats you with special attention."

Norten waved a hand that Ralph could just see the drapes through. "Relax, Ralph, there's no point in my driving you insane. I have a proposition."

"No deals, clammy. If you're not gone by the time I start spraying I'll be taking you with me."

"That's almost what I want you to do. Hear me out. Want a drink? I can load up a brandy snifter for you."

"Drop really dead, you mind fart."

"Ah Ralph, always listen to a proposal before reverting to unthinking. The Nortens are expecting a cleansing, and you'll give it to them. I'll be gone beforehand."

"So why are we still talking?"

"Because two extra ghosts will be here for you to drug."

"I don't understand."

The ghost sighed. "So dense. You're going to become my dealer. You'll tip me off about the next drug spraying and I'll insert an extra ghost or two so they can get high."

"Why would I do that?"

"Money of course. With your free hand, reach over to the bookcase and take the money from the middle shelf."

"Ralph reached over, picked up the wad, and one-hand riffled through it. Mostly twenties with a few hundreds, maybe two grand.

The ghost nodded. "Future payments would be the same. All you have to do is tip me off as to time and location. I'll take care of the rest. You just do your job."

"I'll get fired. No way!"

Norten's expression flicked and Ralph had a peek at something rotted. "How have you survived this long, Ralph? As we've been talking I've keyed into you. You could move to Ecuador and not lose me. If you continue to refuse I'll make your life the kind of hell the living pay you to get rid of."

Ralph felt sweat on his neck and forehead. "Why would you want to make addicts of your own kind?"

"They're already addicts, Ralph, I'm just helping them along."

Ralph put the Specter Spew back in its holster. "But you don't need money, what's in it for you?"

The ghost glided over in front of Ralph. Ralph smelled dry corruption. "You wouldn't understand the words, Ralph, but here's the sensations." It touched a finger the color of milkweed sap to Ralph's forehead. His senses caught fire, tinted vision of shifting, moving beings, smells of earth and rot, touch that reached inside another, couplings with complete penetration of each other's bodies. "My God, you can do with the women?"

"And much more. When you encounter ghosts they are as most of them died, old and ugly. But they live night after night in the times and forms they prefer, nubile and intelligent, acutely aware. Your drugs give them an ecstatic overload that they desperately want to get back to."

The white finger moved away and Ralph nodded. "I understand I guess, but you don't need money. What's in it for you?"

Norten's expression was more leer than smile. "Our currency is emotional. Ectoplasmic sex, revenge for slights, power over another ghost. What I exact from them is none of your business, but it's exquisitely pleasant and manipulative. I have two manipulees waiting. Shall we proceed?"

The ghost's senses had clouded Ralph's thoughts, and he shook his head hard to clear it. All that money meant a new car, hell, a whole new life style. "How do you get the money?"

"Ghosts drift in and out of secret compartments and hidey holes all the time. If you'd rather I could arrange payment in jewelry or gold coins."

Ralph realized that his arms and legs were trembling "I'll take that drink."

"Of course."

"So," Ralph continued as he sipped, "you're telling me that ghosts don't stay confined in our holding tanks?"

"Most do, but not all. You keep them tranqued on catnip, but some develop a tolerance, slip out of the tank and come looking for me so they can get high again. Who am I to deny them?"

"Why would your customers use Hauntfree rather than Ghost Be Gone or any other service?"

"Some business you'd continue to get from your company's routine sales efforts. Ghosts who've approached me would use their powers of suggestion to steer the homeowners to you."

"Oh. How long would I have to do it?"

"How long do you want to be rich?"

Ralph hesitated, but there didn't seem to be any downside. The addicted ghosts had no incentive to rat him out.

"Okay, I agree to tip you off to my cleansing schedule, and let you bring in your Jonesing ghosts."

"That'll do nicely. Finish your brandy and let's get to work."

* * * *

Ralph didn't even have to make phone calls to Ed. Once he was given his schedule he visualized Norten's appearance and the ghost picture would nod once it learned the destination. The money would appear on the kitchen counter of Ralph's apartment immediately after he'd sucked up the druggies. Management was happy that Ralph had gotten more efficient in extracting specters and gave him a decent raise. The new Escalade treated Ralph well, and he found attractive company he could rent. Life was good.

Almost good. Ralph began to recognize repeat business. Distended limbs; blotchy, haggard expressions; suppurating pale wounds, incoherent. Increasingly, eternally maimed by each iteration. He sensed that he was condemning these spirits to an ever-worsening hell.

Late one Thursday evening, Ralph rolled in from a gentlemen's club to find his hidden money stash piled on the kitchen table. A voice rumbled from behind him. "About time you showed up, fatso. We know what you're doing with that swish spook. You want to keep this money you're gonna be working with us."

Ralph had almost muddied himself. With no aerosol handy he was at the mercy of whatever psychological torture the spindly ghost wanted to inflict. He visualized Norten, but saw that Norten was being held by two large spirits. He was on his own.

"Ah," Ralph said. It was a start. "Ah, who are you?"

"Call me Preston. And I already shit canned your spray bombs, so don't bother looking. Here's the deal. Norten already admitted after a little prodding that he pays you three grand a visit."

Good for you, Norten.

"You don't do nothing with Norten anymore. We're going to addict him and let him help pay his way. You work for us, same money."

"Why would I do that?"

"Because, you shit-brained air breather, we're going to addict your buddy and turn him into a paying customer. You want the money, you work for us."

Ralph's used-to-be-Catholic conscience had given him the glimmer of an idea. "Well, you already got Norten, so I guess I have to cooperate. But if I understand this stuff, Norten's got to take his focus off of me so you can put it on, right?"

"Yeah."

"I've got calls scheduled tomorrow, but the day after I can get to the Norten's house and we can make the swap."

"Cancel 'em."

"You don't want me to do that, it puts my job at more risk."

Preston screeched like rusty subway wheels. "All right, the day after afternoon at Norten's house. Keep the money, carrion eater." Preston's ectoplasm flaked and dissolved.

Ralph was too scared to sleep, so he put the night to use, getting more efficient as he sobered up. Then he called in sick and kept working on what he needed.

* * * *

Preston, his two after death goons and Norten were all waiting for Ralph in the great room of the Norten house. "In here, bowel boy," Preston ordered. Ralph walked in carrying a paint gun.

One of the goons giggled. "You gonna shoot at us with that?"

"Yeah," Ralph replied, shouldered the gun and fired three quick shots into Preston and his friends. Their screams were the scrapings of steel nails on glass, almost piercing Ralph's ear drums. He pumped several more pellets into the writhing ectoplasms, stopping only when their shapes deflated into saggy bags decorated with spots of seeping yellow-green paste.

Norten, no longer being held, drifted over. "What just happened?"

"Last rites."

"Huh?"

"A mixture of catnip to slow their reflexes and holy water as bon voyage. As the pellet passes into the ghost the holy water vaporizes. Bitch to get it into those pellets. " Ralph swung the pellet gun toward Norten. "We're renegotiating the contract."

"Ralph, thank you so much for getting rid of those hoodlums, but we already have a deal."

"I'm changing it. From now on, when you get repeat business, they're going to exit without recycling. You can promise them one last rapture before they move on. They're desperate for the fix, they'll take it. I gas them just like usual, then use Bertha here to dispatch them. Lets me feel better about myself."

"But Ralph, your business will suffer."

"Not much. People keep dying, ghosts keep showing up. We drug them up the first time, if they come back we dispatch them the next. Tidy."

Ralph smiled. "Oh, and I want that three grand a house you told Preston I was getting."

⚡

SLEEPING WITH MAD SHADOWS
("Under A Sadness Moon")

Frederick J. Mayer

"Descend the way that leads to hell infernal
Plunge in a deep gulf where crimes' inevitable
Flagellated by a wind driven from skies eternal
Where all your torments, and for all the ages
Mad Shadows never at the end of your desires
Shall never satisfy your furious rages,
And your chastisement be born of loveless fires."
—Charles Baudelaire

Darkest wet blue blood flowing
softness sky
Broken mirror stars flamming
up on high
Bless the soul sad of diamond
candle light
I like moth to star striving
fiery flight
Cacophony of silence
chrysalis
Mournful fluid arising
carol bliss
Atrical song and sun burst
finger tips
Insinuate their way to
touch my lips
Flowing crimson hair strands viens
blood pulsates
Brain transcends body and stays
peace creates
Infinite fingers coiling
caressing
All about my being soul
and bringing
Me down to desert night sea...
Strangelss colors made of tears
Jackalope
Insane says it's dark down here
with some hope
Yellow and red lizard sings
soft The End
Guns fire smoke roadrunner near
once again
Gets no crimson meat thristy
flows evening
Mysteries of the dark sun
eyes pressing
Dark sun glasses death head stares
deathfulness
Transformation dark paradise
godfulness
Arizona Middle East
Dominion
Tears of Eros glass diamonds
communion
Sympathy symphony from

Faith's gold horn
Saving, apocalyptic
music born
Cyclopaedia voices...
Holy Fool body and soul
upon hill
listening Glow of dark stars
outland will
desert garden of delights
subtle sphere
Christian Isis unveiling
ears to hear
tongue her flower entices
horn of spheres
Red mist rises to greet warm
evening here
Angel or fragrant demon
I don't care
future in hole of dying
old whore fair
red tide twilight eucharist
blood hues night
of Dissolution creature
heads praise flight
ears to hear all subtle sounds
swirl up mound
One of fool sees through her breasts
soft full round
through her tender exposed ribs
raw fleshless
passes sand rocks turning forth
embellish
cavern of the heart diamond
sympathy
my chrysalis ending no
grounding me
I am Dark Butterfly.

LEAVING MALAGA
by Cynthia Ward

Set in the "Rite of Passage" universe created by Milton Davis and Balogun Ojetade. Used by permission.

Casco Bay, Summer 1876

The stars came out as Eliza and Frenchy wrapped live lobsters in wet seaweed and steamed them on the little fire they'd built.

"There's no place on earth better than Malaga Island," Eliza told Frenchy. "I never want to leave."

Frenchy raised his eyebrows. "We left Malaga this mornin to gather lobsters." He grinned. "And who says we'll ever get off this speck a granite in the middle a Casco Bay?"

There was no place closer when their dory sprung a leak and started taking on water too fast to row anywheres else before it sank. They'd drug the dory up on the rocks and hoped some ship or boat would pass in hailing distance before night. As the sun got low, they built the fire and waited for someone to notice flames on the uninhabited islet and come to investigate.

The firelight showed Eliza's smile. "You know what I mean, Frenchy." Her face grew sober. "I keep havin this dream I'm leavin Malaga for good."

"'Leavin Malaga for good'?" Frenchy said. "You mean, cause of somebody kidnappin you? I know a Negro girl's disappeared from the maroon village on Huss Island, and some white folks be missin from other islands, but that don't mean they was kidnapped. You know what it's like when you live on the ocean, Eliza. Them folks prob'ly just drownded and nobody's found the bodies."

Frenchy's words failed to lighten Eliza's expression. His stomach tightened. He'd knowed Eliza since they was born on the same day, seventeen years ago. She wasn't prone to worrying—or worrisome dreams, neither.

The youth jumped abruptly to his feet, brandishing his work-knife with a flourish and a smile.

Eliza looked at him in surprise.

"I know what happened to them missin people," Frenchy announced. "They was kidnapped by pirates."

She burst into laughter. The Maine coast hadn't seen a pirate in decades.

"Don't worry, Eliza," Frenchy continued, his smile widening. "I won't let anybody kidnap you."

"I know." Eliza's smile faded. "I don't dream about gettin kidnapped," she said. "I just dream I'm leavin Maine."

Frenchy couldn't help staring. "You leave willingly?"

"Not cause I want to," she said. "I'm leavin cause I'm needed somewheres else."

"What?" Frenchy said. Her words made him shiver, though the night was calm and warm. "Where? Why?" He realized he was still standing and made himself sit down. "What's goin on in your dream?"

"Dreams," Eliza said. "Sometimes I'm walkin. Sometimes I'm on a huss, or in a steam locomotive, or airship, or paddle-wheel steamer. But it don't matter if I'm walkin or ridin. In every dream, I'm travelin to Nicodemus, Kansas."

"Why'd you dream that?" Frenchy was so startled by the outlandishness of Eliza's statement, he almost dropped his work-knife, which he'd been using to prize open a segment of his lobster. "I never heerd of no Nicodemus, in Kansas or anywheres else."

Eliza laid down her own work-knife and raised her hand to the pendant on a leather thong round her neck. The pendant was a small wooden disk, painted the color of open ocean and carved with symbols. Frenchy saw a little cross formed of tiny stars on the left side of the disk, and a little crescent moon on the right. Between the images was the stylized outline of a fish.

"I never heerd of Nicodemus," Eliza murmured, "'til Grammy Darling give me her necklace."

"I seen you was wearin her necklace, last few days." Frenchy said. "But your grandmother ain't from Kansas. She's from Malaga, same as everyone on the island 'cept my grandma."

Frenchy's father's family was free people of color since before the War of the Rebellion, but his mother's mother was a Frenchwoman from Phippsburg on the mainland, who'd married into the Johnson family. That was why people called her grandson Frenchy instead of by his name, George Benjamin Griffin.

Life was hard on Malaga Island, and worse for fatherless families. Eliza and Frenchy were little when their fathers was killed, serving in the 54th Massachusetts Colored Regiment, and two years ago the consumption got Eliza's stepfather. Their kinswomen took in laundry from Phippsburg, 'cept for Eliza's grandmother, who was the island's herbwoman; and Eliza's stepbrother worked on a steam-powered lobster smack out of Phippsburg and sent money home. Eliza and Frenchy used her stepfather's old dory to collect lobsters off the shores of unsettled isles in Casco Bay and sell them to the canneries springing up on the mainland.

No matter how hard life got, Frenchy loved Malaga Island. He couldn't imagine leaving. Eliza must hate them dreams.

He swallowed his last bite of lobster. "So," he said, "why'd your grandma give you her necklace, anyways?"

Eliza's expression turned wary. "Harriet Tubman tole her to."

"What!" Frenchy stared at Eliza. "Moses never been in Maine that I heerd of. Even if she was, she never set foot on Malaga Island."

"She appeared in Grammy Darling's dream," Eliza said quietly. "Tole Grammy, 'Time to give Eliza your necklace. She's got work to do.' Grammy thought—hoped—the dream didn't mean nawthin. But Moses come into Grammy's dreams three nights runnin, and repeated what she said. So Grammy knew it wasn't no ordinary dream, and give me her necklace."

Frenchy felt the hairs stir on the back of his neck. Eliza's herbwoman grandmother sometimes knew things others didn't. But he made himself shrug.

"So your grandma dremt about you havin a task to do some day." He spoke like the thought of Eliza leaving didn't turn his stomach to a lump of ice. "What's that got to do with you goin away to someplace nobody ever heerd of?"

"Every night since Grammy give me her necklace—seven nights now—I been havin that dream of travelin." Eliza looked down, touching the pendant again. "And I hear a voice in my dreams, and it's sayin, 'You're needed soon in Nicodemus,' and I know Nicodemus is in Kansas, and the voice is Moses's."

Frenchy shivered as he understood Eliza wasn't having a dream.

She was having a vision.

As he stared, he realized she'd gotten thinner.

Collecting lobsters off the shores of islands wasn't nearly as hard as hauling traps, like Eliza's stepbrother did, but it still worked up an appetite. By rights, Eliza should of polished off her lobster supper as quick as Frenchy. She hadn't taken a bite since she mentioned her dreams. Now that he thought about it, she hadn't finished her midday meal all week.

He whispered, "I'm sorry, Eliza."

She raised her head and give him a puzzled look. "You got no reason to 'pologize, Frenchy. It's just the way it is, that I got to go to Nicodemus."

She smiled.

She wasn't in her dress, with her hair done up in a neat bun. She was dressed for work in her stepbrother's loose-fitting hand-me-downs and floppy-brimmed old hat. But Frenchy understood—startling as the sun breaking through a midnight blizzard—that Eliza Araminta Perry was the prettiest girl he'd ever seen. Why hadn't he noticed before?

And now she was supposed to go away?

Leaving wasn't the same as dying. But Frenchy felt the same way he did when Eliza's grandma told him her herb-lore couldn't save his brother's life.

Abruptly, Eliza got an expression on her face like she felt even sicker than Frenchy did. She looked scared, too. Mostly, though, she looked determined.

"I got to tell you a secret about my family," she said fiercely. "But you can't tell nobody what our secret is, Frenchy. Nobody!"

"A'coss I won't, Eliza," Frenchy declared. "I won't tell a soul. I swear it on a stack of Bibles and Jesus send me straight to Hell if I break my word."

Eliza got a look almost like pain on her face. She drew a deep breath. "It's about me and Mumma and Grammy Darling."

Frenchy's brows drew together. What could three good Christian women get up to that would qualify as a bad old secret? Nawthin, he was sure.

"What's the secret?" he said.

Eliza drew another breath, her gaze searching his face.

Finally, she said, "We ain't Christians."

"Wh—what? A'coss you're Christians. What else is there to be, 'cept Jews?" Frenchy said. "Do you mean you're Catholics, like my grandma was, afore she married my grandpa and converted?"

"Not Catholics. Not Jews." Eliza was shaking her head and looking more nervous than Frenchy had ever seen her. "This—" she indicated the carving on her pendant "—is the symbol of the goddess Yemonja, ruler of the heavenly waters, and—"

"Goddess?" Frenchy said. "What do you mean, goddess? I don't understand—"

"Mumma and Grammy Darling and me," Eliza whispered, "we practice the religion of our Yoruba ancestors from old Africa."

Frenchy stared, trying to make sense of her words.

When he did, his heart set to racing like he was being chased by a catamount.

"You're heathens?" Frenchy shouted the words, leaning away from Eliza. "You cain't be heathens. You're good people!"

"I don't care if you nigras is heathens or Ingersollists or devil worshippers," said a new voice. "I just want you to put your knives on the ground. Then the both a ya better put your hands in the air and keep 'em there."

Frenchy and Eliza jerked and looked around.

In the light of fire and moon, a scruffy stranger stood between two of the six white pines that ringed the islet. The stranger was a white man, tall and bony and stubble-faced, and paler than anybody Frenchy'd ever seen. The stranger wore the clothes you'd see on a mainland farmer, but he didn't look like a farmer, with that ancient blue Union kepi on his tangled locks and that Springfield rifled musket with attached bayonet. He had the rifle pointed at Frenchy's head.

Frenchy immediately looked for an escape route for Eliza and himself, and discovered there was a second stranger on the islet. He was a white man, too, but except for showing the same extreme pallor, he didn't look like the first. Short and stocky, he wore a city man's bowler cap with a fisherman's oilskins. His chubby face was clean-shaven, but straight red hair stuck out from under his bowler like pieces of straw. A length of rope wound several times around one shoulder. His Spencer repeating rifle was aimed at Eliza's heart.

Frenchy saw how they'd got to the islet without him and Eliza noticing. There was a little boat tied to a root sticking out over the water, and the pair of oars in the boat had wet cloth wrapped around the blades. The cloth would of muffled the sounds of the oars entering and leaving the water.

The first stranger—the one with the rifled Springfield—addressed Frenchy. "Put the goddam knife down, boy, or I'll shoot you dead."

"You'd be wise to take his advice, me lad," said the red-haired man with the Spencer. Unlike his taller companion, he had an accent and an amiable tone. "My friend's not famed for his patience. As you be worth something to our sires only when alive, I'd prefer he not be spilling your blood on the sod."

Frenchy's eyes narrowed, and he spoke hotly. "Slavery's been outlawed for years!"

"Sure, and it's illegal in your fine country," the red-haired man said agreeably. "But the Old Ones have their own law—"

"Irish, you talk too much," said the tall man.

"'Old Ones'?" Frenchy said. He'd never heerd the term before. "What—"

"Grammy Darling tole me about the Old Ones," Eliza whispered. "Unnatural creatures—kill humans by drinkin them dry—"

"Now don't be unjust, lassie, " said the red-haired man. "It's not only Old Ones who are vampires."

He and the tall man grinned, revealing long canines.

"Vampires!" Frenchy sprang to his feet, pointing his work-knife at the tall man aiming the Springfield at Eliza. "You touch her and I'll—"

"Enough!" The tall man sprang forwards, far quicker than he looked, and jerked his rifle down.

Pain turned the night as white as the heart of the sun.

* * * *

Pain returned first to Frenchy: a strong throb at the curve of his brow. Then it was smells—the resin of pine and the complex blend of shore odors that land-lubbers misnamed "salt." Then he heard waves surging against rocks. The noise worsened the throbbing.

Why did his head hurt? Why was he lying on the ground? Where was he?

Cautiously, Frenchy opened his eyes.

He was sprawled face-down on a mat of fallen pine needles. He felt bruises where his arms and legs and chest had struck the granite beneath thin places in the mat. He couldn't see the ground beneath him, but a sharpish point sticking through the needles pressed into his cheekbone, just below his left eye. The pressure was sharp, now he'd noticed it. Lucky he didn't land on the stone point with his eye.

Holding motionless, he shifted his eyes to look to one side. He saw the fire-lit trunks of pine trees and the starry sky behind them. He couldn't see the waves, but they sounded awful loud for a calm summer's night.

Frenchy remembered he was on an island too tiny to have squatters, or even a name. It was nawthin but a junk of granite that stuck above the water, hardly big enough for him and Eliza to beach their leaky dory and find enough dry wood to cook a pair of lobsters.

At the thought of Eliza, memory flowed over Frenchy like a storm tide. It washed everything back to him 'cept the knowledge of how he'd wound up face-down, his head beating like a blacksmith's hammer and his workknife gone from his hand.

Frenchy slid his gaze in the other direction. He found the tall vampire looming over him, with the Springfield upraised. The vampire held his rifle at an angle, butt pointed at Frenchy's head. In the flickering light, the vampire watched Frenchy carefully, like he was waiting for movement. Frenchy couldn't recall the blow, and he didn't see any blood on the rifle stock, but he understood now why his head was pounding.

How long had he been senseless? Where was his knife? Where was the Irish vampire? Had the Irishman already carried Eliza away?

The last question was like a jolt of lightning. Frenchy almost couldn't keep still. Sweat rose on his brow.

It occurred to him that not even a vampire would wait for minutes on end with his rifle in the air. He'd want to tie up his captive before the captive woke, not after. That meant Frenchy couldn't of been unconscious more than a few seconds.

Frenchy shifted his gaze and found Eliza. She hadn't moved since he'd been knocked down, 'cept to close her hand on her grandma's pendant. Her lips was moving slightly. He suppressed a shiver at the thought of Eliza praying to heathen gods.

Frenchy was relieved she wasn't trying to get away. The Irish vampire stood next to her. He had her work-knife stuck in his belt, and had his Spencer rifle pointed at her heart.

The unseen waves seemed to be growing louder.

Frenchy wanted to charge the vampires. But even if they was human, he wouldn't reach his feet before the tall one dealt his skull another blow. Before the Irishman shot Eliza through the heart.

Frenchy drew a breath and raised his head.

"Take me and let her go," he said hoarsely to the vampires. "She won't tell nobody about you, I swear to God—"

"I tole you to shut up, boy," rasped the tall vampire. "You need another blow to that thick skull a yours?"

"Let me handle this." The Irish vampire beamed down at Frenchy. "Do be heeding my friend's orders, laddie," he said jovially. "He's a hard one, he is." He returned his attention to his companion. "The sea's getting loud—"

"You Irish worry too much," the tall vampire snapped. "It's a calm night. Get the nigras tied up."

The waves crashed noisily on the granite shore as the Irish vampire smiled down on Eliza. He smiled in a way Frenchy had only seen once before. It was the time he went all the way to Portland with his uncle and saw a fancy-dressed white man buying a huss. The fancy-dressed man smiled at the huss the same way.

The Irish vampire spoke pleasantly. "Get yourself flat on the sod, me bonnie lass, and stretch your arms at your sides."

Frenchy was surprised he could understand the Irish vampire's words. The waves had gotten as loud as the breakers of a winter storm. The air was still, though, and the sky was just as clear as it had been when Frenchy and Eliza were dragging their leaky boat out of the water.

Eliza stopped praying and let go of her grandmother's pendant. Moving slowly under the unwinking gaze of the Irishman's rifle, she stretched herself on the ground. She lay with her face to the stars and her arms against her sides.

The Irish vampire glanced at his comrade. "I must confess," he said. "I thought you'd taken leave of your senses when you told the Old Ones there were squatters all over Casco Bay that nobody would miss. But we found chickens ripe for the plucking, we did. Ripe for the plucking, I says—and convinced the foxes do be all extinct! I take my hat off to you, sir—or I shall, once we have these maroons stowed on our smack and bound for the Portland docks."

A smack? Frenchy thought. The vampires is lobster-fishermen? Then he thought, a'coss they ain't.

The vampires was using a smack cause, on the wide waters of Casco Bay, another lobsterman's boat wouldn't stand out, even at night. Too, a smack was big enough to let a pair of careful vampires move a few captives under everyone's nose. It wouldn't look out of place on the busy Portland waterfront, neither.

Frenchy's heart pounded as loudly as the unseen waves.

The tall vampire looked at the Irish one. The latter didn't appear quite so jovial now. He was looking past the pines again.

The tall vampire said, "Stop starin out to sea, and get the nigras tied u—"

The leather-tough sole of Frenchy's foot slammed into the the tall vampire's calf.

He shouted wrathfully as he toppled, the Springfield rifle flying from his hands.

Ignoring the spike of pain in his head, Frenchy lunged for the flash of firelight on fallen steel.

The Irish vampire turned away from the water, exclaiming, "What the devil!"

Frenchy didn't know if it would do any good against an inhuman creature, but he raised his knife and coiled to spring at the Irish vampire.

Noticing Frenchy, the Irish vampire raised his Spencer rifle—

Eliza's trim foot struck his calf.

As he fought for balance, a shadow swelled behind him and Eliza and the pines, blotting out stars.

The moon disappeared.

Then the wave crashed down.

* * * *

When Frenchy regained consciousness, he ached all over. The wave had struck with almost enough force to pound him flat as a flounder. He'd thought he would drownd.

The pine needles around him was soaked. The sun was just rising above the eastern horizon. So why was he dry, like someone who'd been lying in the sun for hours?

And where was Eliza?

He raised his head and found her kneeling by his side. Her hat was still on her head and her pendant was still at her throat. She was as impossibly dry as he was.

"You're all right, Frenchy," she whispered, placing his knife-hilt in his open palm. "And neither a them vampires is gonna be doing anything again."

Frenchy wasn't spleeny, but it took some effort to restrain a groan as he stood up.

"Where's the vampires?" He looked around. "I see their boat, caught on a rock, but I don't see—ah."

Both vampires lay, soaking wet, on the fallen pine needles. They no longer held their rifles. They no longer moved.

They was barely visible.

Frenchy was a Nazarene, not a Catholic, but he crossed himself like his French grandmother used to do.

He couldn't see much of either vampire. He knew they was dead—or dead again—but not cause they wasn't moving. Their bodies was covered with a living carpet of lobsters, and lobsters eat flesh.

Gingerly, Frenchy felt his brow where the tall vampire's rifle stock had struck.

"My head ain't hurtin any more," he murmured. "Ain't got a dent or bump, neither. Not even a scratch."

He looked at Eliza.

"Me and you got hit by a wave," he murmured, "but we're dry as the sun. Ocean's cold as snowmelt, but neither of us is shiverin. The wave wasn't enough to drownd us, but the vampires is both finished. My head got hit by a rifle, but it's all better. What—how—"

"Salt and movin water are powerful purifiers," Eliza said softly.

"But—the wave. I don't understand. There wasn't a cloud in the sky. What happened?"

"With Yemonja's blessin and talisman—" Eliza raised her hand to her grandmother's pendant "—some women of my family been able to summon the ocean's waters for generations. Now my grandmother's passed this gift of the goddess on to me."

Frenchy felt like a ghost just run its ice-cold fingertip down his spine. "'Gift of the goddess'?"

"I summoned the wave." Eliza looked at the bay, which lay nearly as calm as a lake. "Thanks be to Yemonja for answerin my call." She turned to Frenchy with a grim expression. "Them vampires won't be troublin anyone any more."

"But trouble ain't done, if Moses is summonin you to Kansas," Frenchy whispered. "You ain't got to go there alone, though. You all right with a Christian goin with you?"

Eliza smiled.

Frenchy returned her smile, though he knew she wouldn't of been summoned halfway acrosst the country just to fight a couple of vampires.

Something far worse waited for them in Nicodemus.

CATTLE CALL
by Gregg Chamberlain

"Well, let's get back to the monster hunt, shall we?"

In a small corner office room at Burnaby's Bridge Studios, a man with a pair of Lennon glasses perched on his nose shuffled the few pages of a sheaf of paper in his hands, tapped them on the table once before laying them down. Getting nods from his two companions on either side, he spoke into a desk intercom: "Next!"

The door on the other side of the room from the trio opened. A young man entered. He was reed-thin and a bit gawky as he walked across the room up to the table and took the lone seat on his side of it. He was dressed in jogging pants and a discount-store golf shirt. He also wore glasses, which emphasized the broad dome of his forehead courtesy of a receding hairline. He leaned a bit forward, hands clasped between his knees.

The man behind the table bent his head a bit to check the display viewscreen of a mini-digital camera mounted in front of him near the far edge of the table. The screen showed a wide-angle view of the young man seated in the chair. "Interview number 33," he intoned loud enough for the camera pickup mic to catch, "for Hellbeast 4: When Hell's Angels Ride. Interviewers Doug Scotia, Lesley Lavington, and Tash Elias." Looking to either side, he saw that both women were also checking the display screens on their cameras set at opposing angles to his own. He picked up the top sheet of paper, squinted. "Ah, Darren Milligan, right? Well, then, Darren…"

"Doran."

The man looked over the rim of his glasses. "Pardon?"

The young man's feet shuffled a bit on the carpet. With an apologetic smile, he said, "It's Doran. Doran Mulligan."

"Uh huh, okaaaaaaay," replied Scotia. He glanced over at his companions. Lavington, the red-haired woman on his left, shrugged and smiled. Elias, a coffee-and-cream-complexioned black woman, gave a rueful shake of her head, gesturing "go on" with one hand.

Scotia flicked a finger across one eyebrow. "Alright then, Doran, according to your file, you've done stand-in work for Monster Madness and for Hellbeast 2. You also had a walk-on speaking role in Creature Commandoes?"

Doran smiled wide with a vigorous nod. "Yeah, that was real cool, I got a good scene with Erik Shear just before my character died."

"Well, that sounds great, Doran," replied Scotia, leaning forward, arms resting on the table. "Okay then, show us what you've got."

Doran Mulligan stood up quickly, knocking his chair back. Too late, he turned to try and catch it before it toppled over. Smiling sheepishly, he righted the chair before starting to take off his shirt. He draped the shirt over the back of the chair, then slipped off his shoes and tucked them underneath.

For several minutes he stood there behind the chair, clad only in his jogging pants. Tash Elias began drumming her fingers on the table top. Lesley Lavington lifted one milk-white wrist to glance at an antique gold watch. Doug Scotia stared through his glasses at Doran, now fidgeting beside the chair.

Suddenly Doran's head snapped up, mouth stretched impossibly wide open. Throat muscles quivered as pained grunts emerged from his yawning mouth. His body shuddered, arms flung backwards, shaking. A series of small twitches ran all over his body, fast changing to spasms. He half-bent into a crouch as hair began to sprout all over. The grunting changed to a whining growl almost unheard below the sound of bone cracking and scraping, as his nose and jaw lengthened into a furry muzzle.

After ten minutes, a werewolf stood erect, gasping and panting, tongue lolling, threads of drool dripping onto the carpet. There was a noticeable bald patch in the downy fuzz between Doran's upright pointed ears.

Scotia sat back in his chair with a loud sigh. He glanced at his companions. Elias' fingers still drummed on the table as her bored gaze regarded the ceiling. Lavington smiled and shrugged again. Scotia nodded and re-shuffled the sheaf of papers in front of him before looking back at Doran.

"Thank you, Mr. Milligan," he said. "If you'd mind…" He gestured at the chair with Doran's shirt draped over the back.

Doran picked up his shirt. "Um, it takes me a bit more time to change back," the werewolf rasped, lips wrinkling in an apologetic lupine smile.

"I see," replied Scotia. "Well, that's alright. We'll get in touch with you when we've made our decision."

Tugging the shirt back on with some difficulty over his now-furry form, Doran backed away then turned and shuffled stiffly across the room. The three behind the table waited a few moments after he exited and the door closed behind him.

"Well?" asked Scotia, polishing his glasses.

"He tried," offered Lavington. "Post-production editing would help."

"'Tried' is the word," scoffed Elias, shaking her head. "Transformation still took too long, and with less-than-impressive results. If he was in Creature Commandoes, then he must have worn a helmet all through the movie.

That bald patch was almost blinding. Lot of fake fur needed to cover that up. That or some careful and constant ceegee work."

Scotia nodded. He tapped a finger on the sheaf of papers in front of him. "So, then, that's a no. Shall we do one more interview then break for lunch?"

The other two nodded. "Make it a long lunch hour," suggested Elias, not bothering to stifle a yawn. "These cattle-call auditions really wear me out."

"Could be worse," said Lavington, still smiling.

"Indeed," agreed Scotia. "We could be next door with Steve and the others, doing call-back interviews for Ultimate Zombie Apocalypse 3."

⚡

THE LIQUID PROFESSOR
by Jeff Barnes

His concession to the
conventional is that he opens
his office door when he
could more easily ooze
under it.

As he flows to his
classes, students—mindful of
wet feet—scatter to either
side of the corridor, allowing
him a wide passage down
the middle.

Occasionally someone will, in
cold weather, open a window,
that the chill air might solidify
him, but always the sun returns
him to his fluid state.

And when he evaporates, the
division chairman places
a bucket outside and waits
for him to return with the next rain.

⚡

ABOMINATION IS HER NAME

by J.N. Cameron

Saturday at 7:30 a.m.

I sit in the back yard under the awning. My coffee is in one hand, and a Marlboro silver is in the other. The coffee is cold, and a gnat floats in it. A suicide.

A cool drizzle has been falling since "the ex" dropped June off several hours ago. My June-bug is now asleep on the soft leather of the living room couch. The prattle of the Cartoon Network comes through the screen door. My bleary eyes are kept open by the nicotine and caffeine as I enjoy the autumnal moment and the most unusual storm I have ever witnessed.

A fierce yet silent lightening has been dancing in the hidden spaces above a black overcast. It has been building up, and it burst just seconds ago. It still flashes, and blue electric veins through a monstrous nebula of darkness. It is the mother of all storm clouds.

The intermittent explosions from the formation cause wet leaves to sparkle like jewels in the fence corners of their neglect. Among them are oak, ranging from crimson ruby to fiery orange spessartite, as well as the brilliant yellow-citrine of hickory. There is something alien about the colors; they are almost too vivid. The fescue has not been mowed in weeks, yet it glistens a crisp, neon green. I start to wonder if I am experiencing low-level visuals from sleep deprivation.

I have been up every night for the past month until after 2 a.m. engrossed in bouts of online poker. The resulting workweek in the cubicles is a living hell. Last week, I lost $375.00 and was late to work twice. Having June over every other Saturday through Tuesday helps. She forces me into bed at 10 p.m. and reads aloud until I drift away.

The sky continues to darken, and the silent lightening again intensifies with bursts that ricochet and spread through the heavens. I have never seen anything like it. When the ember burn of my cigarette dies, I consider going inside for more coffee. I should also wake June-bug. She will want to see this.

As I stand, an incredible thunderclap shakes the earth. The swing set rattles. The aftershock of the blast suspends in eerie silence before car alarms burst forth in a shrill din. Dogs howl.

"Daddy!" June-bug cries out. She runs to the screen door. Her adorable brunette curls are in disarray. "What happened? Was that an earthquake?"

"No, it was thunder. You should stay inside, bebé."

The storm is unnerving, but I cannot turn away as a bizarre scene unfolds. From under the lightening-marbled leviathan, a lower level of charcoal cumulus spills out and rolls across the sky. It is as rapid as the darting, spastic movements of time lapse. Something about that unnatural motion is unsettling. Fear takes over on a deep, instinctual level.

In a few seconds, the miasma has covered the sky. All hint of morning light is gone. It is as dark as midnight.

"Come inside, daddy!"

"Get away from the door! Go back to the couch!"

June starts screaming and joins the cacophony of the car alarms. She points to the sky. I follow her finger.

I drop the coffee mug.

My heart feels like it seizes up in my chest. My mind tries to grasp what my vision feeds it. I force myself to inhale and exhale.

Crimson spheres materialize and shine through the lower clouds. There are hundreds of them. They appear to be automobile-sized, red arachnid eyes. They hover as a much larger arachnid eye, a half-mile in diameter, takes form in their midst. The colossal orb is pulsating and grooved with darker rivets of intense red ochre. Its gaze radiates a bloody hue and an unmistakably insectoid and diabolical intelligence. It is a mothership peering down through the sheen in vile hatred.

The smaller eyes begin to circle the large one like satellites.

June's screaming is reduced to harsh intakes of breath. I cannot turn to go inside. My feet are as heavy as cinder blocks. The eye with its myriad of spawn drifts lower and lower and grows larger. It stops above the valley—over the housing editions from north of the highway to the rise of the Birch Hills.

Behind the giant orb, I perceive the silhouette of a gargantuan bloated body. Glistening silk hawsers the width of tree trunks unfurl from its underbelly. They stream to the earth by the dozens. Like rappelling ropes, the strands drop onto the houses and yards around us. One drops in my neighbor's backyard.

And down the lines, the creatures descend.

Against a red pall, I see bodies the size of cows. Eight long legs sprout from each body. I find my resolve, and my own legs finally obey. I run through the back door and scream out for June. I find her on the couch, holding herself in a shivering ball.

"Bebé, don't go to the window!" I yell. I am running to the hall closet when the lights cut out. I feel along the wall until I find the door. I pull the clothes out and grab the smooth walnut stock and take the box of shells from the top shelf. My eyes have adjusted enough that I can run back to June. She shakes in terror. I grab her shoulder and tell her to snap out of it. She looks up.

"Daddy? What is that?" she points at the window. Thick, white coils of a viscid substance spray down from somewhere above and splatter the outside of the glass. A "thud" shakes the roof; chalk from the ceiling dusts our heads.

"Daddy…something is on the house!"

* * * *

We are in the garage. We crouch behind stacks of boxes in the corner. I hold my June-bug in my arms. I have wrapped a blanket around her. The laces are untied on her favorite candy-red tennis shoes, so I tie them into double knots.

There is no reception on my phone, and the electricity is out. The only light is from the ruby glow through the dirty garage door windows. The world outside seems on fire. June whimpers, but I hold her tight and kiss the top of her head.

"Shhhh, bebé. It's important that we stay quiet," I whisper. The thudding on our roof has stopped. I listen for movement from outside, but the car alarms are too loud. I think I hear yells and screams. Staying put seems the safest option for now.

It has been a long time since I comforted her like this. She has grown up fast, especially after the divorce. Holding her brings back memories of when she was born. When she was swaddled in her hospital blanket, my first thought about her was, my little June-bug.

My phone battery dies, so I am not sure how much time passes. It feels like hours. Eventually, the car alarms stop.

Now someone is at the side garage door. I can hear a hand testing the locked doorknob.

I push June down in the corner behind me. I stand to see above the boxes and raise my shotgun.

The door slams inward, kicked by someone wearing cowboy boots.

"Roberto? June?"

It is Phil Lee.

* * * *

Hours later.

None of us speak in the shadows of the Lee's basement. Disarrayed, dirty, and dazed, we huddle back-to-back. June-bug and I watch the barred door at the top of the stairs. I have my shotgun and two shells left. I dropped the box outside in the madness. Phil Lee faces the window to the south of the house. He has a 9mm handgun. Mitch and Linda watch the north window. Linda has a Taser. Her tortoise Vera Wang glasses are twisted on her face and the right lens is shattered. Mitch is freezing in nothing but shower flip-flops and white, piss-stained boxers. He grips a metallic-blue baseball bat with both hands.

Both small windows have thick rose curtains pulled shut. A vague shadow theater reveals the outside horror. The cries of our neighbors have stopped, but we hear the prodding and searching. Earlier, Phil opened the curtains a crack when we heard Chuck Johnson run shrieking from his front door. One of the demons pounced on Chuck from a tree. Phil quickly closed the view before we saw what happened. But we heard it. The sounds of slaughter.

Phil Lee is the reason any of us are alive. After finding us cowering in our backyards or garages, he led us to his basement. Here, we seem forgotten by the invaders.

Any reason we have for what is happening is conjecture. Linda swears she saw the monsters attach people to the silk strands to be sent back up into the sky. Phil saw one of the creatures rip his wife apart. He shot at it five times. All five bullets sparked off the cupreous hide of the giant form. The gunshots still seemed to frighten the abomination, and it jumped away with the pieces of Mrs. Lee. Phil told us the beast had no head and no eyes or a mouth. It only had a body and the stilted spider legs.

We have not spoken in what seems hours. Phil is no survivalist, but at least he stored bottled water down here. We pass it around in silence. Junebug has fallen asleep, her head against me. Finally, Phil whispers.

"I don't hear them anymore."

"They could be waiting for us to go outside," Linda warns. Phil thinks about it a half-minute before replying. He scratches at his red-grey beard.

"Why would they need to ambush us? I watched them rip off the Garcia's roofing and pull the entire family out of the attic. Mitch saw one of the creatures overturn the Wright's car. It tore the wheels off and pried the undercarriage open like a tin can."

"Where would we go?" Mitch chimes in. "The creatures landed everywhere! How will we make it to the highway?" He looks at me. They all look at me. "Roberto, what do you say?"

I calm my mind and grasp for logic. I try to consider all the possibilities.

"We are the mice, and they are the cats," I reply, and no one disagrees. June sits up and rubs her eyes. "We need to do what mice do to survive and take advantage of our smaller size. We will stick to the crevices and tunnels underneath the cat and other predators. How long has it been since the rain stopped?"

"It ended over two hours ago," Phil answers.

"Then we should go out back and jump the fence. There is a storm drain in the creek. We could crawl through, but it would be too small for one of them."

"Where does it lead?" Linda asks.

I don't answer because I see the smoke waft up from the corners of the basement door. A seaweed-green slime is eating through the wood and metal from the top down. I point it out to the others, and I push June behind me. Phil and I stand at the bottom of the stairs with our guns pointed up. We watch as the door dissolves away.

The only light we have is the one attached to Phil's 9mm. The yellow beam shakes as if he has tremors. The sturdy oak and crossbars melt like ice-cream, but no puddle remains. The doorframe glistens in a fetid substance. In the darkness beyond the aperture, we hear something move.

A bristled arachnid leg as thick as an elephant's trunk probes through the opening. It feels the concrete wall and the wooden stairs. Another joins it, searching in the darkness. Phil's light dances over the legs, and my chest aches again. I fight back bile in my throat and keep the shotgun up and pointed at the doorframe. I try to scream at June to move to the back corner, but my mouth will not make the sounds. I can hear Mitch whimpering.

"No, dear God! No, dear God!" Linda starts a soft chant.

All eight of the giant legs reach inside of the doorframe and then splay open like fingers, pulling the tumid body through. The copper-colored skin is thin enough to see pulsing black veins underneath. The beast squeezes inside. The legs stretch out again and find footing. It turns around 180 degrees and blocks the entire doorframe.

A pale woman's face blinks at us through the milky eyes of death. It is Wilma Lee, Phil's wife. Her blond hair is tangled and crusted with blood. Her decapitated head has been attached by the neck onto a stump-like appendage on the monster's body. I hear a hideous moaning. It is Phil.

Wilma Lee's mouth opens, and she speaks. It is her voice, but it is not her voice. It is her voice as if it were a reed instrument blown by a malignant wind from hell.

"The Great Mother needs servants. Come out of your hiding place. Let me teach you her secret name!"

A gunshot rings through the basement. Phil crumples to the floor. His 9mm falls from his mouth. The arachnid makes a sudden move forward, and I aim the shotgun at Wilma Lee's head and pull the trigger.

Her face is smeared away in a crimson splattering. The creature falls down the basement steps into the corner, writhing as if wounded. I step back to avoid its swinging legs.

I turn to grab June, but she is not there. The north window is open. I look out and see her dashing through the yard with Linda.

"Come on! Let's get out of here while it's down!" Mitch is screaming at me. He has picked up Phil's 9mm. "Hurry! Linda and June will meet us at the storm drain!"

We run up the stairs and through the doorframe. Mitch moves with the gun pointing ahead. I hold my shotgun ready. We run through Phil's house to the back door. The yard is dark. Nothing moves.

"Turn the flashlight off," I tell Mitch. He fumbles with the gun for a few seconds before the light clicks off. "The creek is ten yards behind the back fence. Make a run for the corner, there's a gate. Head south when you reach the creek. The storm drain is close by. You can't miss it. Are you sure Linda knows where it is?"

"She said she did. Are you coming with me?"

"Our odds are better if we split up. I'm going to jump the side fence and cut over to the creek from that backyard. Ready?"

"I'm ready."

"Let's go!"

Mitch dashes out the door, straight across the backyard. I follow him a few yards and then take a hard right towards the side fence.

I glance over my shoulder, and I see a shadow on the roof lumber onto multiple legs. I ignore it and keep running. Mitch has almost made it to the back gate. The shadow jumps, and the ground shakes when it lands on Mitch. The 9mm barks out twice. Mitch screams. I jump over the fence and roll in the wet grass. I leap into a crouched run and stick to the overhang of the azaleas. Through the foliage, I see the alien legs prodding Mitch's limp body. I keep running. I run through the gate and continue through the high grass to the creek.

At the creek, a candy-red shoe is alone on the muddy bank. June must have left it as a sign for me. I pick it up. I step into the cold stream and head south. The water is a few inches deep at most and does not slow me down.

When I look back over the neighborhood, I almost stop to stare. It takes every bit of will left to press on. The great, pulsating eye still hovers above the valley. The miniature orbs still circle it. Below is a nightmare seen through a gory, apocalyptic tincture. Body parts are strewn through-out the streets. Cars and houses have been torn asunder like paper, and the spider-horrors still stalk in the shadows. The one that jumped on Mitch has returned to the rooftop.

Ahead of me, the four-foot tall and three-foot wide archway of the drainage system opens from a concrete tunnel into the creek. Above it is a slope and a copse thick with brier and cane.

"Daddy!" June calls out from the brush. I can see her face and I run faster.

"Climb down and meet me at the opening!" I yell back.

I reach the drainage opening, but she has not climbed down. Linda is nowhere to be seen. June's curls are as wild as ever as she smiles down through the cover of the umbrage.

"Daddy, don't go in there. Come up to me."

Her eyes give it away.

Her eyes are locked in a straight stare that is void of life. Empty. Then I see the swollen body behind her head and the long, spindly limbs intertwined with the branches. I see her bloody neck and the appendage sticking into it. I know what must be done.

I run underneath her and raise the shotgun.

"Bebé!" I call out. Her face turns down towards me. I pull the trigger.

I jump into the tunnel as the body of the arachnid crashes to the ground behind me. I hear its legs reach inside and thrash against the walls in consternation. It is too large to squeeze inside.

I splash into the darkness of the drainage system, almost on my hands and knees. I am numb. I look ahead. I move forward. I pass branching tunnels, but I keep a straight course. Hours pass and I emerge, exhausted and crawling through an opening on the western side of the Birch Hills. There are no monsters here.

I climb a gentle slope overspread with blue grama until I can see beyond the local horizon. The arachnids are shooting back up their silk strands at fantastic speeds. The hawsers break away behind them into floating particles of ash. The queen eye absorbs her troops. Finally, she ascends into the heavens like a sanguine moon that glares down in judgment.

I sit on the grass and watch for a long time. I watch until that eye shrinks away into a marble sized orb. Soon she is a distant, insignificant twinkle amongst all the other distant, insignificant twinkles. I watch the sky until sunlight creeps over the defiled land and bleaches the landscape into lighter hues.

Only then, do I start to think of my June-bug. I begin to weep.

I weep and do not stop.

⚡

KACHINA

by Kenneth Bykerk

A Tale of the Bajazid

He lurched forward as if his foot failed to find a step, a rifle cracking beneath him. It was not his foot though that failed to find purchase but that of his horse and it was not a rifle which sounded but the snapping of a thick bone. A rabbit hole in the tall grass had sent him flying forward over his horse's head as it shrieked in agony. He had time in the air to be thankful he had been riding free of stirrups before he crashed to earth. He felt pain shoot up his leg and he felt the hatchet on his belt thrust under his ribs as he rolled. When he stopped, his face was an inch away from a jagged stone the size of his head.

His blood was up. He scrambled, pain bursting through his leg as he lunged for his horse. With a grunt, he fell back to ground and began crawling as fast as he could. He needed his rifle and that was on his horse. Thankfully, she was lying to her left; he tied to her right. The pained beast turned her head to him and screamed. Her agony was evident. He couldn't see her leg but he feared the worst.

"Sorry Lara, I'm so very sorry."

As he crawled, he pulled the hatchet from his belt. He had a brace of converted Springfield '17s but figured he might need one of those for himself. If his pursuers caught him, his death would not be kind. When he reached Lara, she implored him with screams and eyes mad with pain. In reply, he raised up and brought the poll of the hatchet down hard right between her eyes. She jerked, screamed and struggled with a new fear maddening her gaze. He dropped the hatchet again, then again. He felt bone crunch and Lara's struggles waned though she yet lived. Reversing the hatchet, he pulled himself closer and brought it blade down once, twice, thrice on her neck before she succumbed and ceased her struggles. Ginny, the mule tethered in train, snorted her disapproval as the smell of blood filled the air.

Only then did he look up. He was in a mountain meadow, one under other circumstances he might have appreciated the beauty of. Now he was preparing to fight for his life. He had raced into the meadow from the south and west in a blind gambit to reach safety or advantage. Now he was undone, caught lame and without means of escape. He knew they were coming. He had been surprised to see them. It was by luck that he caught sight of them, enough of an advantage to mount up and ride. He had been about a mile downstream filling his canteens in the creek. A glimpse of the desert below heralded this caution. Summer was approaching and even now the heat of this place was monstrous. When he saw them, their intent was obvious. He had betrayed them in a manner deserving their wrath. It was only luck that aided his escape. An arrow still stuck from one of the wrapped bundles atop Ginny.

The pursuit had brought them to this place. When he broke through the meadow, he had made his way fast to the cottonwood-lined creek. The fording was unimpeded, his attention focused behind him. How had they managed to not only find him but keep up with him on foot? It had been six days and countless miles since he'd stolen their gods, their katsinas, and they hadn't even been in the village when he'd ran. On the other side of the creek, he pushed his horse as hard as he could. The ground had leveled out for a good distance, distance he hoped to use. The rabbit-hole had been an unexpected twist of fate.

As he pulled the long rifle free from its bindings, he saw shadows moving beneath the cottonwoods and through the tall grass. He always kept the rifle loaded. Each time he'd shot, each rabbit he'd taken for dinner, he'd reload it. This was a long-standing habit, one which had saved his life more than once. He'd felt himself safe for three days. As soon as he began the descent from the rim, he'd figured himself free and clear. Off then to the south where he would circle back to civilization, or at least that which the southern states had. With what he had atop Ginny, he knew his fortune was assured. There were institutions back east and even over-seas willing to pay handsomely for rarities of aboriginal craft. What he had was just that, something unseen before by white men. He just had to stay alive this day.

It was Makya he saw first, breaking from the cover of the trees with Sikyatavo close behind. Neither seemed winded from their run. Instead, they both wore predatory smiles as they broke into a sprint. Horatio Parsons, a man who dreamt of a return to civilization, cursed vapidly upon discovering his fall had dislodged the percussion cap. Out of precaution, he had left a half dozen in his vest pocket should he need them quickly. As he scrambled to lay hold a cap he heard shouting. It was Hototo. He was yelling not at him but Makya and Sikyatavo. There was distress in his tone. Parsons secured a cap over the nipple where once he would have poured powder in a pan. Pulling back the hammer, he swung the rifle over the corpse of his horse and took aim. Death was coming, hatchet in hand.

Instead he saw Sikyatavo and Makya standing halfway to him, facing and arguing with Hototo. Three others, all faces he knew from his stay in their village, stood back with Hototo, expressions unreadable. There was an argument going on which he couldn't follow. His time with them had been instructive and he was quick with languages, but this was of a tongue he had never encountered and of which he had still only a rudimentary understanding of. The argument was shouted and flew by at a pace far beyond his comprehension. Only a few words could he pick out, words with meanings such as "evil" and "forbidden" and "blood". Hototo kept pointing behind him, back to the creek. His voice grew in urgency and the three with him began adding their voices. Makya appeared uncertain and was backing up slowly, cautiously. Sikyatavo remained adamant, pointing and gesticulating angrily in Parsons' direction. Parsons returned the sentiment with an aim on Sikyatavo's naked torso.

Hototo's argument held greater weight. Makya's defection and the urging of the others convinced Sikyatavo and he abandoned his advance with a glare back at Parsons. Parsons didn't know any curses in Hopi, at least nothing he could shout with conviction so he relied on one he'd picked up from the Sioux on his way out west. Either Sikyatavo had an unusual understanding for foul language well beyond his local vocabulary or the tone of the sentiment was evident enough. In a flash, Sikyatavo spun and loosed from his short bow an arrow straight toward Parsons. The arrow buried itself deep into Lara's body just inches from Parsons' face, close enough to make an unflappable man flinch ever so slightly.

He spat a choice curse as his shot went high. It had the effect of making the Hopi duck, all but Sikyatavo. He raised his hatchet and began to run again at Parsons. Parson's powder-horn had fallen free of the saddle and was lying a few feet away. His shot was in his saddlebag, the side crushed beneath Lara's flank. As with caps, he had taken to keeping a couple balls as well handy. This wouldn't help. Sikyatavo would be on him before he could secure his horn. As he fumbled for one of his pistols, Sikyatavo was again delayed in his advance. Hototo was insistent in his demands. Frustrated, Sikyatavo turned and walked back to his tribesmen, his back brazenly exposed in open defiance.

This was the chance he needed. Parsons set both his pistols, capped and cocked, on Lara's neck and scooted over to where he could reach his powder-horn. New pain awakened in his left leg and he feared for himself that it might be broken. If it was, Sikyatavo might just end up doing for him as he did to Lara. He wasn't going to go down without a fight though, and with that thought, began the ritual he knew so well. From a position propped against a dead horse, the procedure was not so smoothly performed. All the while he was reloading, he was watching over his shoulder what his former hosts were doing.

At his distance, Parsons could not make out words. The gesticulations though told all he needed to know. Something about this creek marked a line Hototo felt shouldn't be crossed regardless the nature of the crimes they were avenging. Sikyatavo apparently felt otherwise, pointing contemptuously at Parsons throughout his deliverance. Then there appeared to be a consensus of sorts reached. At Sikyatavo's command, all the braves but Hototo brought up their bows with arrows in hand. Parsons saw what was coming and fumbled desperately for a cap.

Here it came, death delivered in naked brutality. Sikyatavo, bow in hand, began running; not a jog, but a full sprint. The four archers behind kept their bows at ready and Hototo stood in imploring prayer. Parsons had the cap in his hand and placed it over the nipple, his hands steady and unfailing. He raised the rifle over the corpse of the horse and brought it to bear. As he did, three arrows fell and buried themselves into Lara's chest and neck while a fourth tugged at his right leg. He flinched, but he knew their plan. Where he was, they could fire arrows all day and cause him great distress should they choose. Sikyatavo didn't have the patience for that and was using the archers as cover. Well, fuck that, Parsons muttered as he raised the hammer to full cock and steadied his aim on Sikyatavo's chest. Sikyatavo, seeing this, let loose one arrow at a dead run, a shot meant to distract. Parsons squeezed the trigger as the arrow, truer than hoped, slammed into the horse just beneath Parsons' hand.

White smoke roiled forth from the long rifle and Sikyatavo was down, rolling through the grass. Parsons was at first unsure what he hit as Sikyatavo half appeared to stumble as he loosed and, having recovered from his roll, stood disoriented with that bow broken in his hand. The Kentucky long rifle was an extremely accurate weapon in the hands of one trained and practiced in its use. The ball his used was small and the speed great. It does not wander lost if the target intended is no longer there. It continues until spent or a new target intercepts its course. Back beneath the cottonwoods, as the four archers were preparing another sally, Hototo staggered back, a scarlet flower blooming in the center of his dun tunic.

All present knew then where that shot had landed. Hototo staggered, the .40 caliber ball having crushed through his sternum, and fell straight back into the stream. The four archers stayed their bows, disbelief on their faces. Sikyatavo watched Hototo fall and turned to Parsons. Knowing the rifle took time to reload, more time than it would take for a fleet-footed rabbit to cross that distance and not even the quickest of rabbits could match a Hopi runner burning yellow with courage and the willingness to die with honor, Sikyatavo pulled his hatchet from his belt and charged. His scream was one of rage and unarticulated challenge. There was no meaning greater but it encouraged support as the four archers drew back to give cover.

They were shaken, the archers. Their arrows flew uncertain and each landed safe enough distance to not warrant concern. Parsons hadn't given them thought in flight either. His attention was wholly on Sikyatavo. Never had he seen a man run so fast. He dropped the rifle from his hands and picked up the first Springfield. The explosion was enormous and the cloud filled the air between. Through the smoke, Parsons could see Sikyatavo still. If he had hit, Sikyatavo would not be standing. With a curse hurled into the war-cry assailing him, he snatched up the second pistol and fired hastily as Sikyatavo sprang forward in a great leap, hatchet swinging.

The Springfield model of 1817 fired a .69 caliber ball, a comparatively slow-moving hunk of lead. Parsons, impressed with the ease of use which the percussion system had lent his long rifle, had the frizzens and pans removed and modified his brace of Springfields with percussion technology. It had served him well over the years, particularly in rain and wind. Now it granted him speed and confidence, for a shot fired from flint and pan would have failed. It was a shot of desperation, un-aimed but for haste in the direction of the threat. It sufficed, and better than intended. The huge ball bore through the diving Sikyatavo's palate and back through his mouth to the base of the skull, blasting the atlas vertebrae completely and tugging the body back with enough force to halt the forward momentum of the dive.

When the cloud of red-stained smoke cleared, there were no live Hopi in sight. Sikyatavo lay dead, his body up against Lara's belly and his head, what was left, hanging on by torn strips of flesh. Over by the creek, Parsons could see Hototo's corpse lying half in the water. Of Makya and the others, he saw nothing. They had disappeared as if they were never there, leaving their dead before the bodies even had the chance to cool. Parsons wasn't a trusting man though. Out of fear that they would return, he hurriedly began reloading his firearms. He was still exposed and any archer worth his salt could make his life hell.

After the last ball had been driven home and the last cap applied, Parsons still hadn't heard a sound from the direction his pursuers had last been seen. All around he listened, his ears regaining their clarity after the explosions of the guns. Nothing other than a babbling brook and birds singing in the trees and Ginny munching grass and farting. Outside of this, not a sound was heard beyond his own making yet he could hardly allow himself to believe the assault was concluded. His heart was still pumping, still racing from the excitement just past that his senses were attuned to all things about. Still, not a sound unnatural to a pleasant spring morning disturbed the air nor any awkward movements of fowl or fauna from the forest gave indication that anything was not as it should be. He sat for some minutes there beside the bodies of Lara and Sikyatavo listening to the tale the forest told.

As he listened, he ran an inventory of his injuries. The tug he had felt on his right leg had been but an arrow pinioning his pants to the ground. That was an easy remedy. It was his left leg that worried him. He probed and prodded, stretched and flexed and determined at last his leg remained whole, unbroken. He had sprained it and bruised it and it was going to hurt, but he had to move, had to travel on and sprained, he just might be able to. Ginny was quite laden as it was but he'd pack what he could from Lara's load onto her. Then he'd continue up in the direction opposite the Hopi's last flight, head north-east and deeper into the mountains in hopes of finding a place to rest.

Warily assuming the Hopi gone, he set to work. He cleared what he could from Lara's corpse, the saddlebags taking the longest to secure. Then he began working on the horse itself. To Ginny's displeasure, Parsons began carving great slabs of flesh from Lara's flank and laying them atop the mountain already piled on the poor mule. Parsons wasn't sure when he'd get a chance at meat other than rabbit and squirrel or even a chance to hunt if his leg acted up on him during his planned convalescence. From Sikyatavo there was nothing he wished to take other than the turquoise necklace and the hatchet which was meant for his own skull. After a moment's thought, Parsons used that hatchet and scraped off what scalp he could from the ruined head.

His rifle in one hand and the other holding firmly to Ginny's neck, he set off, angling his path east up the meadow along the tree-line to the north. He moved at a slow limp, always cautious, always wary and listening close for any sounds. Each pinecone which fell or nut dropped by a dissatisfied squirrel sent his gaze searching. This caution kept him as he continued up the valley and beyond the meadow, forced by roughening terrain further and further from the stream. Soon though his guard began to slip as did the barrier that kept his thoughts from streaming forth aloud in a garbled mumble.

As he limped along, his mind began to wander, focusing at last upon his apparent fortune and misfortune. Unfortunately, he had had to put down Lara. He felt bad about that, not out of any deep love for the animal or of the breed in general, but because now he was left afoot and one of those was lame. He needed a place to hole up for a couple of days, not just to rest but to inventory his load. He could not continue as such. He had too much for one old mule to handle on her own and he was going to have to get rid of some things. The katsinas, those he was keeping no matter what. That was his fortune and his fortune did him no good except back east.

He had in his possession something he was sure no white man had ever seen before. Of all the tribes he had encountered in his exile west, he'd never met any like the Hopi in temperament or tradition. In temperament, they were hospitable to a fault and the least war-like people he had met in his travels. In tradition, they differed for they were a sedentary people, established generations in a singular place. Most of the tribes he had known were at least semi-nomadic in nature. The Hopi, their buildings and their villages were meant to last unmoved, grounded to the earth and to their beliefs for time eternal.

Of those beliefs, Parsons had only the vaguest understanding. He was not a philosopher or a natural scientist or any form of scholar and held no true interest in the study of other peoples. He was educated and rather well at that having attended, uncompleted, courses at a small, exclusive university downriver from his family's land. His father had high aspirations for him. This education had been wasted though as he had no interest at all in the teachings of musty tomes or the droning of disciplinarians. Exposure did have its effects and though he was loathe to credit that drudgery, he understood the value of those artifacts which his hosts so venerated. He knew there were those who would treasure such aboriginal curiosities and he knew that there were institutions which would pay well for their acquisition. His alma mater was one such institution but unfortunately, not even were he to gift the packages he'd stolen would his return be welcomed with anything less than a noose.

His journey west had been an escape, not one taken for adventure, exploration or profit. At first, his existence had been unsteady and uncertain. The whole of New England was forbidden to him and his infamy as he fled south to Pennsylvania followed on his heels. He lived close to his spine then, scraping for bits until a new reason to flee would bother him. Always with hot rumors at his back, he continued further and further from the reaches of those who suspected him of heinous things until he was swallowed up by the forests and mountains. He traded furs on the edges of civilization, traveling always ahead of echoes of old complaints and fresh ones vehemently espoused. In 1829, eight years after he shamed his father and first fled exaggerated accusations, Parsons paid in pelts to convert his Springfields; a fortuitous decision. The next year was the last any white man saw of him. He had stolen a half-gross of caps and an equal number of balls and with other supplies he'd come to rely on, disappeared into the uncharted west with three packed mules in train and a corpse locked in a storeroom. Now, after nine long years in the wilderness, Parsons felt he had a means to return a new man, unknown, recreated and free of those lies which had driven him to such distant extremes.

Presently the terrain grew tired of rolling ravines and broadened out into a valley choked with juniper, oak and pine. For this he was thankful as his leg had been threatening. Fear of an attack urged him ever onward despite being reduced to surrendering his rifle to Ginny's pack and taking up a stick for balance and strength in its stead. At the bottom of the shallow valley he paused to rest his leg and drink from the stream that flowed. In a pack that was thankfully easy to reach, Parsons pulled out some strips of aspen bark. Shoving most into his trouser pockets, he began chewing on one of the strips. Fear of ambush remained and so he pressed on, his leg protesting each step.

He remained in awe of the Hopi and mulled upon their discovery of him after so many miles and so many days. Previous pursuits had all terminated within a day or two, even those by the native tribes among whom his presence had become vehemently rejected. The longest he knew of a search following him close was his final flight from civilization, and that was three days. That these Hopi were able to not only track him but also match his speed on foot left on him a stark impression. Being that he knew these men had begun their chase with a distinct disadvantage of being a day yet out of their own village when he fled sent a shudder down his spine. Their endurance was extraordinary, men born and bred to run. They had displayed their pride often during his months with them. They prided themselves on this ability where the men of other tribes boasted skills as warriors. Where he had only been politely impressed before, now he feared with great respect their endurance.

He followed the stream until it began to narrow, rising steadily on his left until that wall became an impassable barrier taller than the pines at its base. The day was getting long, shadows stretching in the afternoon sun when the stream finally closed to him. The terminus was a small glade which formed on his right beside five descending pools, none greater in diameter than a man is tall and formed of great rocks which flowed from the earth. Huge boulders of granite lay tumbled at the head of the pools, the stream trickling through in short falls. There was no further advance possible. A man alone and unencumbered could navigate that perilous pass but lame and with a laden mule, that way was blocked to him. Across that small sward of lush grass to his right, a ridge rose by shallow degrees. He glanced up to the heights of the precipice on his left and his decision was made. If his pursuers wanted, they could trap him here or if they chose, climb above and torment him through simply dropping stones. Without pause but to survey his path, he headed across the glade and off up the ridge to the south.

For an hour he made slow progress, limping painfully along a game trail that followed the deepening ravine he had entered. Presently he was forced to seek a higher trail as boulders and the rotting remains of fallen trees had begun to gather in the channel. He was exhausted, slipping often on the ages undisturbed carpet of pine needles. Ultimately the floor of the ravine rose to meet him and the passable path narrowed. The game trail rose impossibly high, too much for a man in desperate need for rest and an over-laden mule. The ravine had ended at a jumble of large boulders and a steep incline beyond. His leg was hurting and the relief he got from chewing the bark weighed on his most ready canteen. He could go no further. At least here he had the cover of rocks at his back.

He looped Ginny's guide to a clump of manzanita and left her to munch on the grass growing beneath the largest stone, a giant tooth jutting from the mountain. The ground was uneven beneath that monolith. It sloped at an uncomfortable angle, one which he could endure if needed. Caution demanded he seek the best defensive position possible and curiosity, driven to some degree by a desire for comfort, led him to investigate the narrow way the great stone left between it and the steeply sloping bank of earth it overshadowed. The passage was broad enough to walk with ease, wide enough even for Ginny. It extended back roughly three yards before wrapping around the stone. When he pulled himself around that corner, he smiled. He could defend himself here.

He was looking in at a small alcove in the rocks. It was not large enough by any means to be called a canyon, but it certainly was an enclosed box. The earthen wall had turned, halfway around the bend, into a solid rock sheet rising no less than forty feet before sloping steeply away. None, not even the surest of foot, would find safe purchase up there. The space within the recess was only large enough to allow a beast like Ginny room to turn. It was a small stable of stone with a lush carpet of green grass. A thin, spindly oak grew beside a pool of water no larger than half a yard across fed by a thin trickle from the rocks above. On the back wall, about eight feet above the ground was a ledge and what looked like a small cave. Running the length of the ledge but for a means of entry was an ancient wall such as those he'd seen the summer prior when his travels had taken him to cliff dwellings long abandoned. There was even a ladder cut into the contours of the stone.

Gingerly he raised himself high enough on those steps to see over the edge. His expectations were exceeded. The incidental light from the late afternoon sun lent just enough to see clearly into the cave. It was no more than six feet at the widest and four deep where a curtain of rock almost concealed a crevice reaching deeper. As with the rest of the recess, the ledge showed no sign of recent use from man or beast of any type.

He brought Ginny down the passage and tied her tight to the spindly little oak. Before the light failed him, he hauled the entirety of Ginny's burden piece by piece to the walled ledge. In the last light offered, he foraged for wood amongst the fallen, rotten logs that had rolled down to the gutter that began the ravine below. Leaving a modest pile of wood crowded beside Ginny, he climbed aloft. He hadn't left himself much room up on that ledge. That didn't matter. He couldn't leave Ginny weighted so. He needed her services. As far as he knew, she was the only mule within a thousand miles and there was no way he could carry his treasure without her.

As he'd suspected, there was more to this cave than met the eye. The faintest flow of cool air blew steady from beyond that curtain and through that crevice. With a torch from Ginny's load before him to light the way, Parsons scooted through the crack. The passage was short, opening almost immediately to a larger chamber, one which left Parsons standing awestruck for the first time in his life. It was a low, elongated natural chamber which diminished before the light of his torch. The furthest recesses disappeared in the darkness leaving only indistinct clutter visible on the floor furthest. In the center of the room was a ring of rocks long unused, the dust of forgotten fires in their center. This was all the room contained but for two things more. A body, centuries frozen in death, lay mummified and withered on the floor of the cave. This he noticed in the briefest glance for it was beyond the ring of stones and beyond that sere host Horatio Parsons' gaze was fixed. There, reflecting the glow of his torch, was a thing of gold.

He knew it at once to be a katsina but that was just a passing thought, an unconscious recognition of form from association. He did not care what it was, what it was shaped to represent. His eyes saw nothing other than the gold blazing beautiful like an angel in his torchlight. Oh, his fortune! He cried out in joy as he scrambled fully into the cave and limped over to the object of his desire. It was beautiful to behold. It stood nearly two feet tall and was created from multiple sheets of hammered gold, each one perforated with small holes interlaced with other sheets and folded in upon one another, sculpting the figure. That alone, the gold, was the fortune Parsons saw. Some philosopher back east might care for the aboriginal arts or the chance to guess at something they knew nothing about, but he didn't care for such things. He had stumbled upon an old grave or temple or what, he couldn't care. All that mattered to him was the gold; a ticket to return to the world wealthy beyond suspicion. Here alone was more gold than any one man could carry. He chuckled, realizing his misfortune. Oh, he'd find a way, he mumbled, even if he had to take the damn thing apart, there would be a way.

Parsons had lived on the edge of and then completely divorced from civilization as he had known it for almost all his adult life. Practicality was something which had become an innate trait, one which had saved him more than once. He knew he was going to be sore the next morning, maybe even invalid so he set about preparing his new home while he still could. It was exhaustive but he worked with stoic precision, his mind otherwise waxing fancy and taking stock of his new position. With wealth such as he now possessed, he could buy himself a Barony and be invited to great balls with the Senators and the Lords. Or perhaps a plantation where he could do whatever he wanted with his property and oh, he would have property and he would do what he wanted to do with it. Those peculiarities of his nature which had driven him further and further into the outlands and wildernesses would be visited upon his own private property and therefor nobody's business other than his. Yes, these were rich thoughts for a rich man; daydreams of decadence and deprivation visited from his own hand unto others. These were cruel thoughts indeed.

His bedding he laid towards the entrance along with the other bags and burdens Ginny had borne. One such bag would be dearly parted with; the remaining lead balls from his last day amongst the civilized. Then he had three mules and a horse. Now he had but one mule and Ginny was no longer the feisty young thing she was when he stole her. He wondered often how many warrants in how many places there were for him still existing and under how many names. He was Horatio Parsons born and baptized but in his flight west, before he disappeared completely, he had adopted more and more names as each replaced soon bore fresh infamy. Starting over, he could be whomever he wanted and he was enjoying the thoughts of being Southern gentry. His yellowed, rotting teeth grinned savagely under his great bush of a beard at thoughts of young belles lined before his door, their fathers trying to marry them to his wealth.

He reset the stones to suit his needs and hauled the wood up from where he had left it at Ginny's side. Very soon his torch became redundant other than for exploration. That was short lived. There was a deeper chamber somewhere beyond the back wall for he could feel a steady, gentle draft but it was beyond fissures too small to access. What else he saw at the back of the cave convinced him he needn't concern himself with that portion. The ground at the rear of the room was covered, in places piled, with bones both animal and human. Of those human, they comprised an equal portion of those present and in that flickering light, Parsons was able to see the tell-tale cuts which marked the work of a crude butcher. No less than two dozen grey and dusty skulls poked through the detritus to reveal their caps or grins to the light. The back of the cave could keep its own; he had no use for it.

At last, he looked down at the old corpse. It had lain there this whole time, a thing on the ground frozen in the death that took it ages ago. It was left in a posture crawling, sprawled with its arms reaching out and fingers splayed. The expression it wore, beneath skin stretched back to the skull, was one of madness. He told himself that any skull so dried would look thus but still, it was an unsightly thing. If he was going to be stuck in this cave for his convalescence, he might as well get the trash out of direct view. He grabbed one ankle of the thing and was surprised at how light it was. Still, with his leg stiffening, he set the torch down and used both hands to raise it up. The corpse was so dry, so stiff, that there was no movement at all in its joints. It was more like dragging a dry branch than a body. The hands, clawed talons, drew furrows in the dirt as he pulled it to the heap at the back of the cave and promptly forgot about it. He was getting hungry and his leg needed attention. The aspen bark provided only so much relief.

He put a steak from Lara's flank on a wire frame he'd carried across the continent, a simple grill but one of his most prized possessions. The horsemeat filled the enclosed chamber with the mouth-watering aroma of cooking flesh as he dragged the four bundles over to the golden katsina one at a time. There he unwrapped them and placed them flanking his golden treasure, two on a side. Oh, they were all prizes. Those four he stole were yet of great value though their importance had diminished greatly in his eyes. They were but trinkets, curios in the court of that golden thing, but he had gone through a lot to get them and that mattered of its own. Even if he had to strip the gold from its form to carry it home, the four katsinas he had stolen would make that journey as well.

There was a prize just in the telling of the tale. If he made it back east, there would be fame enough in his adventure that he would never dine a pauper. Without any to call him out, he was free to create the tale he wanted to tell. For starters, he outran a whole war-party, not a half-dozen of the most peaceful people he had ever met. And he took them, the katsinas, in a brazen theft from the heart of their city, not sneaking out at night after all the men had left the village. Yes, the story needed to be larger. It needed to be as big as it could with half a dozen dead by his rifle alone. And not just six days but a dozen as he fled and fought his way to freedom. If only he had gone back and taken Hototo's scalp to display alongside Sikyatavo's. Two scalps would improve the telling. He determined he'd keep his eye out for any opportunity to acquire another on the way back east.

The katsinas, they were unique. They were strange and they were beautiful and oh, how those professors he had known would philosophize and theorize were they to see them. They each stood about two and a half feet tall and were carved from the soft roots of cottonwood trees. Parsons had seen several, maybe as many as a hundred katsinas in the small Hopi village which took him in for the winter. These four were not unique in aspect or display, just in quality. Where most had ranged from primitive carvings to impressive, even stunning work, these four were truly unique in their craftsmanship. Of the aspects of their divinity he knew next to nothing and he was distinctly aware of that now. His heist had not been planned long in advance.

He paused for a moment to admire this bounty. The four katsinas carved from cottonwood roots he had traveled so far with were truly beautiful things. They were works of art and craftsmanship which he was sure would buy him a modicum of fame if not a small fortune even if their feathers were ruffled in transit due to bindings. They had value and they were surprisingly light which was good for the gold was not and he had a long journey ahead of him. He figured it would be long enough to spin some good yarns about what really happened and come up with some mighty stretchers to tell about the katsinas. Lead those high and mighty professors down a primrose path of fantasy and let them philosophize to their hearts content and their wallets contents.

He flipped Lara's flank to char the other side and went outside to check on Ginny. She was content. The grass beneath her was lush from the spring and the water was cold. Parsons expected her to be his first line of defense. If she was assaulted where she was, she would bray and could only kick back in defense. Being the only way to reach her was from the rear, she was safer than anywhere else he could think of. As an added precaution, he piled small cairns of pebbles every few inches apart across the top of the ladder and along the parapet. It was a faint hope but pebbles rolling in the dark had saved him before. If Makya and the others were still hunting him, it might be enough.

His thoughts were on the Hopi, his stomach and his leg when he crawled back in the chamber. The smoke from the burning meat had clouded the room, filling it faster than it could blow out on that gentle draft. He took the steak and placed it on a battered tin plate. With the fat and blood off the fire, the specter of smoke began to wane. With thoughts not of heat but creating a good bed of coals for a slower cooking of the remaining steaks, he placed several larger logs in the pit. The fire took to the dry wood immediately, the flames rising higher and brighter, flashing quicker and more violently off the surface of that beaten gold thing. Through shafts of flickering light and reflections just as sharp from the face of that katsina, he did not see that which he had no interest in seeing, no thought that it should not be there. Preoccupied as he was, he paid no attention to old bones and didn't notice the absence of those he had himself placed.

Horatio Parsons was a man who grumbled under his breath. Since he was a man alone in the world, the only he had seen in years who even understood his native tongue, he spoke freely and near constantly when alone. When he was fleeing the perceptions of hysterical people, he could be deathly silent. When he felt himself comfortable, it was a constant dialogue. The whole of his thoughts, his planning, his desires and the lusts that hid under them, they were all delivered forth in a low, muttering ramble. This was not the only idiosyncrasy of his character which would prevent any true return to what he thought of as civilization. Over the years of solitude, he had developed many habits that run contrary to most societal norms. This was not even the most outlandish or offensive of his peculiarities. It was however the one that undid him.

The fire sent coruscating waves of light through the smoke-filled chamber and reflections from the golden katsina pierced the haze in hypnotic patterns. The pain in his leg was adamant, throbbing to heartbeat rhythms. A ravenous hunger had taken hold, the toll of a day unfed in flight. His rambling had increased in volume and tempo to match the patterns of light and the drumming of his heart, a beat he felt pulsing through his leg. Picking up the steak-laden tin, he turned to the treasures he had acquired. There they were, lined in an arc with the golden one glowing in the center.

That katsina, that singular figure looked startlingly different in this light. Here he could imagine all the little holes in the outer sheets as eyes winking in the light reflected off inner panels. In this glow, it looked joyful, excited, expectant. Then, as the firelight flickered off the golden form, those thousand winking eyes caught a singular glow and turned all to him. They did not flash. They did not wink even as flames played over its surface. The color, the inner light in these manifold eyes, burned a brighter and then deeper red before descending into infinite colors beyond comprehension. He stood staring, transfixed, mesmerized and mumbling disbelief into his beard.

It was when his steak slipped from his plate and flopped into the dirt at his feet the spell broke. He shook his head. He had been staring at that katsina and lost himself. Grunting, he bent down and picked the steak up. He brushed it off, shaking his head at his foolishness. What was he thinking? That was a statue and it didn't even have any real form. It was like someone drank some cactus juice and started hammering out his nightmares. Yes, nightmares. In this light, it looked more and more sinister in shape and form. It had no coherence of shape though it was clearly meant to represent a god of hideous design. But who would create such? What madness inspired this and what craft, what art infused it for no mere doll, no mere thing could stare so malevolently. Neither could the withered man standing in the shadows to the rear of the cave yet hate was writ on its face as well.

As soon as the thought went through his mind, his focus came clear for this was beyond the realm of illusion. It couldn't be, but it was. The mummified body, that long dead Indian that he had dragged to the back of the cave, stood staring with empty eyes directly at him from beyond the arresting gaze of the katsina. Then the thing moved and Parsons heard for the first time what he should have heard before…the creaking of the dry, leathery skin as it protested the movements of the bones beneath. It was a low creak as the grinning thing raised its arm to Parsons as if in accusation. Then it sprang and the flesh binding those dead bones screamed in protest.

The corpse, that dead thing that couldn't be, lurched forward and Parsons dropped his plate to the ground. His Springfields! Where were they? He turned and dove for his bags and the brace atop. His game leg failed him and he collapsed to the ground, his agony filling the chamber. The thing was upon him. It attacked without mercy, without strategy. It slashed wildly, shredding Parson's shoulders and back as he tried to protect his face. It clambered atop him and grabbed him tight. Then it began tearing again, tearing, biting and the cruel use of petrified claws stabbed like daggers into his flesh. He struggled and fought back. He tried to tear it off but its grip was iron bound. He rolled on the floor hoping to crush it with his weight for it had none of its own. Though the body was dry and sere, though it was light to touch, the bones within were powered by more than mere muscle. The undead thing grasped him and tore at him and opened the flesh of his body, raking and severing his own muscle to the bone.

It was an accident that set him free. He had rolled to the edge of the firepit in his final struggles. He was torn and bleeding and those fingers, those bony daggers, had shredded more than his mere flesh. They had gouged out his vital means and he knew it. Still, the desperate struggle until they can struggle no more and during this fight, Parsons found himself up against the barrier stones of the pit. Desperate, he pushed himself up and rolled himself into the fire as the thing on his back chewed through the muscles of his neck.

The mummified body, though preternaturally empowered, was yet just a mummified body. It burst to flame in the instant and the bones lost their bond. With a shriek, Parsons flailed and threw himself out of the circle of stones. Hysterical beyond pain and rational fear, he crawled to the nearest wall. The entrance was to his left and the katsina to his right. Before him, the old ash pit burned with relish as it ate the corpse that had lain beside it for ages untold.

His vest had protected his back from the flames though his hair had singed and blisters on his arms and hands were forming already. He was bleeding from multiple lacerations. The thing that mauled him had not been merely scratching but tearing deep into muscle and the vital regions beneath. He feared the taloned claws of that thing, that impossible thing, had torn him to the true. He could feel pain deep within him where one should never feel such. He tried to scoot himself higher against the wall but his body didn't respond beyond the impotent, flailing kick of his uninjured leg. He needed bandages but he hadn't the strength to rise, to even crawl to his packs. Seeing the blood pooling out and around him, he feared no amount of bandages would suffice.

He lay with his back to the wall bleeding his life out. There was no staunching the flow. He was dying and he knew it. He was dying and he was afraid. What had happened was inexplicable. What happened defied even what his diseased mind could interpret much less conceive. He stared at the firepit and the skull charring black therein. That could not be. That thing, that ancient, dead Indian…

A flicker of light drew his drowsing eyes. The flames still rose from the pit and the bones that fed it. Those flames flickered and cast their light upon that katsina sitting dominant amongst the others. From there the flicker came and it was there Parsons' gaze fell. That katsina, that golden treasure, stood center to the others, each now decrepit in appearance beside it. That katsina, that golden god, glowed like an evil dream. It pulsed, throbbing to match the waning beat of his heart. And with each of those beats, those thousand eyes carved within the thin sheets of gold winked and flashed and told secrets the dying man did not want to know.

He knew now why Hototo had wished to turn back, why his courage withered when he recognized this place. This was damnation. This was a unique and singular hell. As he lay there beneath the cruel gaze of his host, that golden horror, he knew the truth of this place. He knew the secret name of the demon whose likeness shifted before him in radiant display. He knew it to be forbidden. He knew it to be beyond his tongue, but he whispered it still. And as the indecipherable name fell from his lips, his corruption compelled it show no mercy in the consumption of his soul.

Out beyond the entrance to that cave, in that little recess below, Ginny farted and tested lightly her lead. Satisfied, she resumed munching the grass beneath her, in no hurry to resume her burdens.

⚡

FLAT IS FLAT AND THAT IS THAT
by David J. Gibbs

"How long will all of this take?"

"I have no idea. Look, kid, just relax. It won't be much longer. It'll be over soon," the older man said, huddling next to the loose bale of hay, trying to stay warm as the rail car clicked on through the night.

"How do you know?"

"I just do," the old man said, tugging his hat down over his eyes.

Tyler wasn't sure what to make of Billings. He was a little rough around the edges and pretty crotchety, but his new found traveling partner had been right about everything else so far, so he figured he'd stay put. Besides, he had nothing to lose. There were no other prospects. This was it, his last chance.

Flipping up the collar of his wool jacket, Tyler thrust his hands beneath his armpits for extra warmth. It didn't help much. He looked down at his feet, noticing the dirty sections of tape holding the sole of his shoe on. Tyler sighed.

"You should find some hay to cover yourself with. It'll help you keep warm." Billings didn't bother looking at him, only the top of his knit cap visible.

The other men were walking around the rail car, some stamping their feet, while others blew into their hands. They all had the haggard, road weary look of too many miles in their eyes. Tyler shivered, watching the plumes of their breath being yanked away by the icy fingers of wind.

Times were bad, and from what the papers said, it was going to be getting a lot worse before getting better. It was bad all over. That's why they were all on the train. They were all hoping that it would be better a town or two away. Each one of them was looking for a chance to turn things around. He'd never even considered hopping a train before. The mere fact that he was here was a testament to how bad things were.

"Old-timer?"

The old man didn't move and didn't look at him.

"Hey, old man."

Still nothing.

"Billings?"

"That's a little better."

"Sorry. Look, how many times have you done this?"

"Don't know, son. It doesn't really matter now does it? We'll find something at one of the stops. I've done it before and made it back and I'm doing it again. Flat is flat and that is that."

He gave up and sat down, pulling together some of the loose hay like Billings suggested. As much as the old man irritated him, he had given him the tip about the train and the possibility of work. He'd also shared the scrap of bread he pilfered from the bakery. He supposed he owed him some gratitude.

Leaning against the remains of the hay bale, he pulled his collar around him tightly and nestled down as best he could. The bucking car and the sounds of the track slipping beneath made him think it would be impossible to fall asleep.

He was wrong.

* * * *

At first, Tyler thought someone was attacking him, the rough hands grabbing handfuls of his jacket, pulling him to his feet. Slapping the hands away, he heard shouts and commotion while still trying to wake up. He quickly realized that everyone was jumping out of the car.

"What's going on?" he asked, bewildered. His legs were cramped and his mind wasn't working yet.

"We gotta get off now kid. They're rousting us. Gotta go!"

"Who is?"

His answer was a shove out the open door of the car. He landed roughly on his back, feeling the gravel's bite against the back of his jacket. Stars burst in his vision and he wondered if he was going to pass out.

Billings didn't give him the chance.

"Stop! Hey! Stop right there you bastards! If you know what's good for you, you'll stop. You hear me? We see you down there!"

The shouts came from men rushing along the side of the tracks. They systematically looked under the cars as they closed in on the men jumping from the train. Woods crowded along either side of the tracks. He recognized some of the men from the train car, as they raced through the trees, spreading out unevenly, like the yoke of a cracked egg.

"Don't stop running, boy!" hissed Billings, his hand gripping Tyler's shoulder.

One of the men running fell face first near the railroad tracks and Tyler watched as two of the uniformed men pounced. They pounded him with fists and night sticks, not relenting despite the man's protests.

"We told you to stop, didn't we? We told you!" shouted one of the uniformed men.

He heard bones snap in the man's hand as they stomped on him. It made him cringe, as Billings continued to shove him through the dark forest. Branches scratched at his face, their bony fingers raking away at his skin, leaves crunching beneath his feet.

A moment later, the report of a rifle sent an icepick through his heart, his breath catching for a moment, his stomach seeming to fall away. His step faltered and he caught his foot on an exposed root, almost tumbling to the ground.

"Did they-?"

"Don't look back and don't stop." Billings held his hand firm against the middle of his back.

Tyler didn't look back, his feet fueled by fear, heart slamming around inside his chest in a frenzy. It was hard to see ahead of them, the darkness only sliced open by the sweeping beams of the flashlights. Tyler could hear the uniformed men calling after them, the night punctuated by the bright reports of the rifles.

The air was like glass every time he inhaled. He couldn't be sure how long they ran, but his legs were barely able to hold him upright when they finally slowed to a walk. Wobbly and weak, he and Billings took in gulps of air, moving carefully between the trees. Both the sounds and flashlights were somewhere in the distance now, as he and Billings caught their breath on the bank of a river. The sound of moving water made him feel even colder.

"Do you know where we are?"

Billings shook his head. "The railroad should still be to our west. Maybe couple-a-three miles or so between us and them. Should do us for a while, but, I don't know what river this is or where the nearest town is. We should rest here."

"How close do you think we are?"

"Kid, I just said I had no idea."

He raised a hand in apology.

"I'm just a little out of my depth here, that's all. I wasn't planning on this little detour. I'm a city mouse not a country mouse."

"Me neither kid. Me neither. I told you I'd get you to the end of the line and I will. I promise, all right? But, for now, you'd better hunker down. We can't cross this river in the dark. It's too dangerous. We have no idea how deep it is or what mess is on the other side. We'll have to find some way across in the morning."

They bedded down, leaning against each other beside the thick trunk of a tree. With upturned collars and their hands in pockets, they rode out the remains of the night with slow dark water passing close by.

* * * *

Tyler didn't sleep much at all. Several times, his heart clutched inside of his chest, as he lurched awake, sure that the railway men had found them. He couldn't be sure, but he thought a few more rifle shots went off during the night. It was terrifying to think they were still searching for them. It was even more frightening to know they were killing the men once they found them.

His stomach was reduced to a muttering mess too, the nerves just too much for him. That was due in part because he was hungry, but mostly because he was just plain scared. He shivered so much, he was shocked that he didn't keep Billings up too, but the old man snored away next to him.

Lucky bastard.

When the gray light of the breaking dawn finally began to filter through the trees around him, lifting the night's curtain, he stood up. Both his knees and back were stiff from trying to sleep between the uncomfortable tree roots. Billings was still snoring as he walked along the shore of the river. It wasn't as wide as he'd thought last night. The water was calm and slow moving, but it looked pretty deep. It made him a little nervous to think about crossing it.

He couldn't swim.

In the distance, a hazy sun tried to peek through the fog. He couldn't wait for it to burn through to kiss his face and warm his bones. Blowing into his hands, he tried rubbing them together, but it didn't help much. He was cold. Stamping his feet, trying to get his circulation going, he noticed something else trying to peek through the haze.

He frowned.

Billings had said the railroad would be to their west, but he was looking due east and he could see the sharp angles of the railroad bridge peeking through the mist.

Why would the old man lie?

He frowned looking back at Billings still slumped at the base of the tree. A lazy finger of doubt stirred his thoughts. The old man had told him that he had ridden the rails a bunch of times. How could he be wrong about where the railroad tracks were?

Tyler suddenly wondered if Billings was telling the truth. Maybe he was full of crap like everybody else he'd met while riding the rails. But, why would he lie? Tyler's nervousness ticked up a few notches and he realized he'd have to keep a closer eye on things.

"Well, look at that," Billings said, making him jump. He turned around as the old man tightened his collar, trying to ward off the chill. He was rubbing his hands together too.

"What?"

"You've teamed up with an old fool's what you did Tyler. I got my head all turned around while we were running in the woods. The damned tracks are east of us."

Tyler nodded, not sure what to say.

"I guess so. You sure you got turned around?"

"Well, why else would the tracks be over there?"

He didn't want to say. If he said what he was thinking that would make things more real than he wanted them to be. Besides, he wasn't sure about anything at the moment. And, more importantly, as much as he doubted the old man right now, he didn't want to travel alone.

"Tyler?"

He looked at Billings and then his feet, stomping on the ground a few more times. "Sorry, my feet are blocks of ice right now. Not really thinking of anything but getting warm."

"Get any sleep?"

"Some. Kept dreaming about those guys chasing us."

Billings ignored his comment.

"We should probably head along the bank to the tracks. Should be an early morning freight we can catch the rest of the way."

"Okay," Tyler said, his eyes following Billings as he walked ahead of him.

The older man held the branches for him as they passed, closing in on the train tracks, pointing out what he claimed to be a water moccasin hole and a squirrel nest high up in the crook of a tree. Maybe he was wrong about Billings.

"We'll cross the bridge and catch the train on the other side. The woods are too close on this side of the river to make a good run at it."

"What do you think happened last night?"

Billings stopped and turned around, his eyes a little dusty. He grabbed Tyler's collar and drew him close. His yellow teeth uneven, his breath holding onto twenty days on the run, he stared hard.

"Son, you really don't know?"

He stayed quiet.

"They killed them. Don't you get that? Weren't you paying attention? Those poor men back there were cut down, plain and simple. They were just trying to get a chance to better themselves. Cut down for nothing. Flat is flat and that is that."

"I don't get it. Why didn't they just arrest them?"

"And, put them where? Nobody can afford food and the jails are over-run with folks just like us. They can't keep us all. More importantly, they can't feed us all. They'd sooner put us down than put us up in a cell."

They didn't say anything else as they walked up the incline to the tracks, the smell of tar from the ties coming to him. Sunlight was burning away even more of the mist, though the tracks still looked like they disappeared into a hazy white nothingness when he looked in either direction.

"Once we're on the other side, we'll have more room to run along the tracks before catching one of the cars. Should be easy peasy lemon squeezy."

Tyler couldn't help but smile.

"What's the smile for?"

He shrugged and said, "Haven't heard that one in a while that's all."

"It's from some old commercial. My pops use to whistle it all the time around the house."

"Mom said may grandma used to sing it around the house while she cleaned."

"Ain't that somethin'."

They didn't talk for a bit, as they made their way to the bridge. The top of the tracks were shiny from wear, the gravel between the ties a cold gray. They began to walk across. He picked up a few stones and tossed them into the water. The ripples tugged downstream each time.

"Isn't much of a current is there?"

Tyler didn't answer. Walking across the bridge, looking at the water moving far below his feet, he felt a little disconnected. He felt a little dizzy and almost lost his footing. Grabbing hold of the railing, Billings turned around.

"You okay, kid?"

He nodded.

"Don't look down. Just keep walking."

Tyler nodded and gave it a try. He looked at the back of Billings' head, tufts of gray waves sticking out from beneath his cap.

He was going to ask how old Billings was, when he felt something beneath his feet. Stepping off the rail, the sensation stopped.

"Billings?"

"Yeah, I felt it too kid. It's all right. Just the freight train I mentioned. It's still more than a few miles off. We got plenty of time to get to the other side."

That didn't keep Tyler from looking over his shoulder, searching for the single eye of the locomotive peering through the fog. He didn't see it, but that didn't stop him from shivering and checking ever few steps. The vibrations were much stronger by the time they made it to the other side.

"Ready?"

"For what?"

"Catching a train running full steam ain't the same as hopping one in the yard like we did back there. You got to be ready. You hearing me, kid?"

"Okay?"

"More than a few guys been tumbled trying to get on."

"Tumbled?"

"Knocked out by jumping at the wrong time, hitting the car with their head or face. Tumbled. Few even been killed, but that only happens when the wheels are hungry."

"When is that exactly?"

"All the time."

The old man suddenly looked thirty years younger, his face taught, his eyes hard, staring into the mist. Tyler could hear the locomotive chugging somewhere in the fog. He could see Billings counting to himself, finding the rhythm of the train, his body rocking to its powerful thrumming.

They both started running as the train broke through the mist. Billings was ahead of him, the old man picking up speed with the locomotive charging past. He could see the open train cars, whipping by them. Just as he was about to grab the handle, a hand reached out and yanked him up.

"Thanks," he said, moments before a fist pummeled him in the chest.

"Watch it kid!" Billings yelled.

A weathered looking man with dingy hair leapt on him, hands moving quickly across his clothing. Fingers in pockets, hands removing shoes, they searched him for any valuables.

"I don't have any money!"

He took a punch in the mouth for that comment.

"Let him up." He heard Billings say.

"Crazy man's got a hog leg," a young man said, knife in hand, eyes looking at the gun Billings was holding.

"Look. We just need a ride. We don't need any trouble from you. But, if you need some, we'll be glad to give it to you."

He was impressed with Billings. The old coot sure could dish it out. Tyler stood up and went over beside him.

"Calm down old man. Calm down."

Tyler took a step back as the man who spoke, walked out from behind the crates. He was enormous, even bigger than the strong man at the carnival. His meaty arms and shoulders looked like stacked stones beneath his clothes.

"We don't have very far to go."

"That so?"

"That it is."

"Name is Tucker," the man said and held out his hand to Billings.

Tyler wasn't sure Billings would shake it, but the old man did. They looked over each other for a few moments, before Tucker motioned for him to sit down on the crates. The train rattled along the tracks unevenly, as the two men sat across from one another.

"How long you been riding these rails old-timer?"

"He doesn't like it when you call him-," Tyler started to say.

"It's all right. It's all right, Tyler. We're just getting acquainted. Name is Billings. I've been on this route more than a few times."

"They say it's not for the weak."

"Ain't one of us weak on this car," Billings said evenly, gun still in his hand.

Tyler didn't know what was happening, though he could feel the tension of the moment. It made it hard to breathe as he watched it unfold. He knew if a fight broke out, they would both be beaten badly and probably thrown off the train. His fingers were suddenly itchy watching the two men square off in front of him.

"That's the truth," Tucker said and almost fell off the crate laughing. Some of the men laughed with him, while others only glared.

The tension slowly seemed to dissipate as Tucker and Billings talked, other men chiming in from time to time. Eventually, he found a place in the hay to bed down for the night. The laughter and talk filled the car. And, just like the previous night, thinking sleep impossible, he was wrong again. This time though, there were no dreams of the railway men or rifle shots.

* * * *

Pain lanced through the back of his leg as he tumbled down roughly, the gravel taking a bite out of his face, as he crashed face first into the ground. The train swirled past in a heated rush of steel and steam. He barely had time to roll over, dirt and dust filling his mouth, before someone landed on top of him in a heap.

The train rumbled down the track as he untangled himself, coughing a few times as dirty crowded into his mouth. Tyler realized it was Billings that had landed on him. The old man wasn't moving.

"Billings?"

He shook him, rolling him over on his back. The knit hat he always wore partially blocked his face. Tyler realized the man's jaw was slack, skin pale. He didn't look good at all.

"Old-timer? Come on now, quit playing games. Billings!"

His hands continued to shake his friend's shoulders, chills moving along his arms.

"Wake up. Please, Billings. Please!" he said, tears first filling his eyes, before racing down his face, washing the dirt away in wet tracks.

He rocked his friend, until the train rushed past, the tail wind, spinning the hat from Billings' face. The man's eyes were the clearest blue, like the color of the sky.

"Son, can I give you a hand?"

As impossible as it was, he half-thought the question came from Billings, until a man nudged him. Tyler looked up. The man had a worn looking hat with a wide brim tipped up and a straw wedged in the corner of his mouth. A few other people started moving down the tracks toward him. That's when he noticed the town sign. He couldn't believe they'd made it.

"Get you some food, son? What about something to drink while we get doc to look at your friend?"

Looking down at Billings, Tyler reached his hands over the man's face to draw his eyes closed. A few minutes later, the doctor showed up with a wagon. He rode in the back as he and Billings were taken into town, a wool blanket covering his friend from head to toe.

Tears still in his eyes, he smiled. Billings was right. This town had promise. Tyler could feel it. He only wished the old-timer had been able to see it.

* * * *

"Mind if I sit here awhile?" asked the old man, handing her a cup of coffee. She didn't even drink coffee, but somehow the warm cup in her hands was comforting. Between the old lady's perfume at the door and the flowers, she was almost overcome by the conflicting smells. Coffee was a welcome alternative.

"Thank you."

"You were his granddaughter?"

She nodded, trying to place the man's face.

"Wendy, right?"

She nodded again recognizing him and said, "We met a few years ago after his stroke."

"That's right, we did."

"My granddad was not a happy man that day."

"No, no, he definitely wasn't." The old man chuckled, the sound comforting, like sun worn leather. "He was a feisty one for sure. Full of spit is what we would've said back in the day."

"I'm sorry for your loss," said someone she didn't even know in passing. She nodded politely.

"Did you know he liked to travel? Years ago, when he was just a kid, I met him on a long train ride. He sure was brave. Left your great uncle and went out looking for work. We both were. That was back when flat was flat and that was that." He put his arm around her shoulders and hugged her gently. She smiled at the gesture. She felt a little better just hearing someone talking about her grandfather.

Standing, they walked past the sign that announced the wake for Tyler Leonard Fitzgerald. Once outside, the winter sunlight bright, she put on her sunglasses.

She smiled at him and asked, "I'm sorry, what was your name again?"

"They call me Billings. I made a promise a long time ago to get your granddad to the end of the line."

"You did?"

He nodded, holding an old knit hat in his hands.

"Did you make good on that promise?"

"You know, it took me awhile, a good long while, but yeah, I finally did," Billings said, winking at her.

He looked back at the funeral parlor for a moment, his face suddenly appearing younger for just a few seconds. She looked at him and realized that his eyes were the color of the sky.

She smiled for the first time in days.

⚡

THE TOAD STOOL PEOPLE
by Chad Hensley

Have fleshy faces of fungi
With two oval eyes of charcoal that twitch and glower malig-
     nantly
Above a triangle-shaped slit nose
And an obscenely elongated, lipless mouth
Filled with what looks like hundreds of rows of barbed fish hooks.

I suppose I should be happy with the view—
Above my head,
A giant mushroom forest
Quivers with hundreds of pink and purple gills,
Each as big as a flapping bed sheet.
Beyond that, a sea of stalactites sparkles
Like thousands of burning candles sputtering in a soft breeze.

A particularly large and muscular mushroom man
Slaps me hard in the face,
Necklace of bleached human baby skulls
Bobbing on his bulbous neck
The chartreuse veins popping out beneath.

Perched upon his cone-like head
A chunky crown hewn from a single monstrous sapphire
Throbs with a cloying, cadaverous incandescence.

The mushroom man hoots like an owl,
Points a puffy finger skyward.
An immense shadow begins to uncoil
From a pitched crevice too far up in the rocky ceiling,

Hands and feet bound with plastic cord to a piece of iron pipe,
I am hoisted upward—
Dozens of huge bat wings beat putrescent winds upon me.
An enormous cuttlefish-like appendage with blinking eyes and
    chewing mouths
Descends with amazing swiftness.
I shut my eyes tightly and clench my teeth,
My body engulfed in a slippery wet silence.

DEATH IS NOT MY MASTER
by Scott Harper

Justain flew above the fray, close to some low-hanging cumulous clouds, as he selected his next target. The night sky, lit by both a full moon and battlefield fires, was textured an unusual mixture of black, gray and orange. The stifling air was saturated with smoke and misery and death.

He dropped down and effortlessly removed a knight from his armored mount, avoiding the thrusts of lances from the other enemy warriors, and soared back toward the moon. The strength granted him by his new existence never ceased to amaze him, as he peeled the metal armor off the terrified man inside like an overripe fruit. His teeth lengthened as he tore into the man's throat, gulping down surge after heart-pumped surge of fear and adrenaline-spiked blood. The warm liquid pushed away the numbing cold that normally saturated his body, filling him with renewed energy. The first meal of the evening always had a similar effect, bringing a semblance of life to his undead form.

He tossed the mangled corpse away with contempt, watching it tumble gracelessly and smash into the enemy forces some fifty feet below, crushing a number of them. Still, hundreds more swept forward relentlessly toward his Master's castle, a virtual sea of men, fighting their way to the gate.

The lust for battle surged through Justain. He dropped into the horde, an odd assortment of dark knights, brigands and putrefied walking dead. He felt the thrusts of their metal lances and swords and long daggers, but took no harm from them. The blades tore his clothing and entered his death-altered flesh, but left no mark, having as much effect as they might on an evening mist. Justain's eyes flared red in the dark as he bared his fangs and roared his disdain for these lesser beings. His arms flooded with strength as he ripped into them like a tornado, smashing skulls and breaking spines. Bodies scattered into the air, like playthings petulantly broken by an upset child. One armored knight managed to strike him in the back of the head with a mace, a blow that would have a shattered a human's skull. Justain absorbed it and struck back, the talons of one hand removing the knight's head in one sweep while those of the other punctured his ribcage and shredded his heart. He fed as he killed, killed as he fed, watching as some of the necromancer Carandini's zombie troops became distracted and began to feed on the corpses of the men he had killed. Still, in spite of all the chaos he had caused, the sheer number of enemy troops was gradually overwhelming the castle's defenses.

The Master had prepared the people of his village as best he could for this night, had called upon his unmatched battle expertise and honed the men and gypsies into a lethal fighting force. Yet such was the nature of a foe like Carandini that an initial advantage could be turned into a liability. The necromancer revived his own dead as they fell, chanting arcane spells and focusing the winds of dark magic, turning the fallen men into living dead shock troops that marched inevitably toward the Master's castle at the center of the village. And Carandini had prepared himself as well, refining his craft over centuries of unnatural life granted to him by his mastery of eldritch energy. He had fashioned giant flesh golems, titans stitched together from dozens of corpses and brought to life through dark rituals and alchemical elixirs, and deployed them with his army. Such creatures were nearly invulnerable to common weapons and possessed the strength of giants. A single such monster was capable of engaging dozens of human fighters at once.

Carandini had, apparently, also found a way to summon hellspawn into this dimension. Justain saw one tearing its way through the battlefield, indifferent as to which side's fighters it slaughtered. The necromancer likely had made the requisite blood sacrifices needed to breach the mystic barriers between worlds, tapping into some backwater side pool dimension and bringing the creature into battle as an added element of chaos. It resembled, in some respects, a giant praying mantis. It was thin but tall, standing nearly nine feet high, its head bulbous and insectoid, the eyes compound and dark green. Its skin was a lighter green and leathery, with splotches of brown hair, now covered in blood and entrails. Its primary weapons were its long, sabre-like arms that it used like swords, impaling and cutting and rending. Justain saw one villager's blade deflect ineffectually off the creature's carapace armor before the demon caved in the man's skull. One of its hind legs shot out at a seemingly impossible angle and skewered a curious zombie through the eye socket, granting it a quick second death.

The demon rounded on Justain with shocking ferocity, reeking of sulfur and brimstone and suffering, one arm slicing deep into his stomach and actually lifting him from the ground. Its dripping maw, filled with dozens of needle teeth, flashed towards his throat. Justain ignored the pain and brought his right fist down on the hellspawn's head, hammering it, pulping it. Viscous pink liquid and brains flowed out of openings that appeared to pass for the creature's ears as it dropped him to the ground. Justain ripped the sabre-arm from his stomach and tore it from the creature's torso. The demon had flopped unceremoniously on its back, twitching spastically. Justain ended its torment, driving the arm through what remained of its head and into the ground. The creature dissolved into a charcoal mist that evaporated into the night, banished from this realm and returning to the netherworld from which it came.

Justain bent over and clutched his stomach as his body's vast regenerative abilities began to heal the huge wound. He returned his attention to the castle and watched as Adam, Carandini's most seasoned golem bodyguard, smashed his massive fists into the castle gate and tore it apart, shredding the metal. The necromancer's troops flooded in to the castle, the villagers and gypsies loyal to his Master fighting bravely but being overwhelmed nonetheless by the sheer number of enemy fighters. Justain reached out his senses, using the unnatural ties of the blood that had connected him to his sire since his mortal death, to locate the Master in the melee.

He found him in the castle courtyard. The Master stood at the center of a pile of fresh enemy corpses, wearing his crimson armor, his preferred vestment for battle, covered in blood and entrails. He waited patiently as Carandini approached. Adam smashed aside any villagers that attempted impede the necromancer's progress.

Justain shrugged off the lingering pain of his wound and seized upon the inherent abilities of his kind, lifting himself again into the sky. He flew above the fray and over the castle walls. He dropped with tremendous force on the mammoth blue-skinned flesh golem, smashing it to the stone floor, which split into spider-web cracks. He knew his time was fleeting. The Master had spent countless hours with Justain documenting and conveying the long history of Carandini's atrocities against mankind, the timeless vendetta he had waged, as well as the immense power he had obtained. Carandini was a Master necromancer, with the ability to control all the dead, including the undead in their various forms. If it came to a one-on-one conflict with such a foe, the Master would be placed at an immediate disadvantage.

Adam recovered and stood. With surprising speed and agility for a creature of such immense size, the flesh golem struck out with his giant fists. The blows landed with the impact of heavy anvils. The first punch shattered Justain's ribcage, while the second whipped his head back. He fell heavily to the ground. The young vampire tried to recover, but was immediately forced back down as the giant pounced on him.

The flesh golem began to throttle Justain. The vampire did not need to breathe to live, but he soon realized that Adam meant to literally pull his head from his body. The vampire's hands shot out, rocking the flesh golem's head with blows that would have punched through iron, but the gargantuan being was not phased. Justain realized he lacked the leverage to inflict the damage necessary to free himself. He panicked, attempting to alter his being into impervious mist, as the Master had shown him, but was unable to harness the mental focus necessary for such a transformation.

The might of the flesh golem's hands forced Justain's head to the side. He saw the Master lying helpless on the ground, controlled like a puppet by Carandini's prodigious willpower, unable to move or shape change as a half dozen of the necromancer's men held him down. He knew that Carandini was controlling the Master mystically and psionically, that even a legion of men would be unable to physically overcome and restrain a vampire of the Master's age and strength. The necromancer had raised high a staff of ash wood, the sharp end bathed in preternatural flames that he had summoned, poised to drive it through the Master's armor and into his heart. Justain struggled with renewed purpose, screaming his Master's name. His claws dug into the unliving flesh of Adam's wrists, tearing them, but drawing no blood. He could not budge the inhuman juggernaut.

An odd look of contentment adorned the Master's face. Justain felt the vertebrae of his neck begin to separate as his world went black and Carandini plunged the stake home…

* * * *

His mind floated fretfully on a dark sea of memories, carried back to a time when air had filled his lungs and blood pulsed through his veins. He had been the king's favored knight, leading his men in defense against barbarian invaders from the south and east, vicious men who pillaged, raped and enslaved. His final human memories were of standing against the human tide, fighting in the twilight before full night, hacking and stabbing but in the end outnumbered. A blade struck home underneath his cuirass, a mortal blow. He staggered but did not fall, reversing his blade and taking the man's head on the backstroke. A dozen villains surrounded him as he fell to one knee, helpless to defend himself as his blood poured out onto the uncaring ground.

Yet, as the barbarians pressed their attack, a monstrous creature emerged from the nearby forest, a hybrid of man and bat and wolf, a blur of talons and teeth. It flowed from one shadow to the next, taking the lives of his enemies seemingly effortlessly. Justain recalled the men's screams as they fell, their swords and daggers useless, their protective clothing no match for the creature's prodigious strength and sharp claws. They died in various fashions, crushed and broken and torn and exsanguinated.

Justain found himself lying on his back, unable to move, staring into the night sky. Ice seemed to have filled his veins. He saw his Master's face for the first time, pale as the moon itself and calm, with a strong jaw and aquiline nose. The sclera of his eyes bled red as the moonlight reflected off a drop of blood on his lips.

The Master spoke to him, not with his mouth but with his mind, a calm inflection that resonated with Justain's dying soul.

"Your fight is not over, warrior. I sense the restlessness of your soul. This will not, cannot be your final battle. I have need of you. You're not going to die now. No, there is something much greater and more interesting for you to see." The Master's teeth were sharp and long and white. They entered Justain's throat like twin daggers of ice. Yet almost as soon as they had entered they were withdrawn—Justain had little blood left to give. The Master opened a wound on his wrist and placed it over Justain's mouth. Justain drank in the thick, rich blood. The vampire's blood began to effect fantastic changes as his body died, burning away all human frailty with a coat of immortal ice. In the meantime his mind and soul were absorbed and cradled by the Master's will, in a bond of indescribable and unbreakable intimacy.

"You will have great power now, and all the time in the world to use it. Things you would never dreamed of achieving are possible now, if you will but learn the discipline required to master them." The Master shielded him from true death, returning his consciousness three days later to the changed flesh of his now immortal frame. And as Justain's hands tore his way from the grave with supernatural strength and ease, it was the Master who stood over the grave watching, waiting for his fledgling to return.

He shared his Master's memories as well as his blood. He saw his Master many centuries before, human at the time, surrounded by rivals and enemies on a field of fading light. They had betrayed him, drawn him away from his loyal retinue, then stabbed and kicked him, knocking him to the ground, where he slipped in the snow and mud and mulch. The Master tried to stand but one traitor shoved a sword through his back, immobilizing him. Justain recognized the traitor as a much younger Carandini. The necromancer flipped the Master over on his back and put a dagger to his throat. The other conspirators came in and seized his arms and feet, holding him down as they hurled jibes and insults, some labeling him a sorcerer.

"I am no sorcerer! I am a warrior! I will not die!" the Master spit defiantly through bloodied lips, unbowed.

"Oh no, not yet you won't, good prince. Not yet, young dragon. There is still much suffering you must endure, many insults committed by your father that need to be addressed." Carandini pierced the Master's cheek with the dagger and cut, disfiguring his mouth.

"No more triumphant smile, good prince. I have taken that away."

"I WILL NOT DIE!" the Master repeated, choking on his own blood.

"If you insist, good prince. And yet I choose to take more than your smile. I choose to take more than your title. I take your tongue now, sorcerer, so that no more spells or curses may pass through your lips. Before you expire I will take your nose, and then your face, so that the recollection of its arrogance is forever removed from my memory. I will only recall you as the shattered, ruined, babbling wreck of a man I now make you!"

Carandini proceeded to remove parts of the Master's face, one bloody piece at a time, but the Master's resolve remained unchanged. His will lived on in that body, an eternal dark presence, even after breath had left it. That same will reanimated the Master's corpse three days later, vengeful rage pushing it to rise from its shallow, hastily-dug grave. The newly undead creature, the first of its kind to ever walk the earth, soon discovered that it needed sustenance to maintain its physical integrity. And the Master learned the significance of a phrase that was old when the oceans drank Atlantis: "Blood is life, and life is blood."

* * * *

Justain fought back from the black and battled with renewed purpose. His eyes blazed with righteous fury as a predatory roar erupted from his throat. He smashed aside Adam's forearms and thrust the talons of his right hand through the underside of the flesh golem's neck, not stopping until they had penetrated through the top of its skull. His mouth latched onto the scarred, stitched neck, his fangs tapping the sluggish, alchemized ichor that passed for blood inside the creature's blue arteries. When he had finished he tossed aside the broken corpse and focused on Carandini.

The old necromancer stood over the Master's body, which was slowly dissolving into the dust that should have claimed it centuries ago. He sought to absorb the original vampire's escaping essence, to convert his powers, yet nothing happened. Justain moved like quicksilver, scattering Carandini's men with powerful sweeps of his arms, breaking them, then snapped the necromancer's neck like a twig. He held the twitching body upright with ease as he whispered feverishly into the old man's ear.

"It was no wizard's spell that created the first of my kind, no thaumaturgy. No, old man, it was the hatred you engendered in the Master—your betrayal. You stoked discontent among his people, treacherously feeding rumor and idle chatter, blaming any misfortunes on him then accusing him of sorcery. In fact, you were the deceitful one consorting with dark magics and robbing graves. Still, the Master's will battled on, even after you had broken his body and slit his throat—his iron will, tested by decades of battle, never left the body. And even now, he lives on in me. His blood is in my veins. And that is the true power of the vampire, a power that will ever elude you—complete mastery over death."

Justain felt the necromancer shudder, drawing upon the last reserves of his unnatural powers in an attempt to restore his shattered body with words of rejuvenation. The young vampire clamped his hand across the old man's mouth, shattering jaw and teeth with the irresistible force of his grip, stopping the spell before it could be formed.

Justain continued. "You think you know death? You merely manipulated it, pretending to be the puppet master but in the end amounting to less than a puppet yourself. We vampires are truly death—molded by it, existing in it. The Master grew tired of his long existence, as was his right. He chose me to succeed him, to protect his people when he was gone. He knew you would continue to hound him, obsessed and envious of his power, to try to destroy him and the model of co-existence he had created with these people. He also knew I would be the one to finally end you."

Justain buried his fangs into the necromancer's neck with serpentine speed, siphoning draught after draught, his eyes blazing crimson. When he had finished and Carandini breathed no more, he shoved the corpse aside. He slowly stretched his arms wide, embracing the light of the full moon, as his encarmined lips peeled back from his wicked fangs.

"Aaaahhh…sublime" he breathed. Justain noted with some satisfaction that the tide of battle had changed. The zombies, bereft of the force of Carandini's will to animate them, slumped gracelessly to the ground and joined the other dead. With Adam and the necromancer dispatched, Carandini's forces crumbled under a relentless counterattack from the Master's men.

Or, rather, my men now, Justain mused. My legacy. As he had inherited the Master's blood and title, he now inherited his lineage as well. He could feel a part of the Master inside him now, rising from within and guiding him. The original vampire could never be truly extinguished. Justain walked over to where the Master had fallen and removed the stake from the remains of the crimson armor, the ash wood burning in his grip.

He began to collect the dust inside. Every minute particle.

THE PROMISE OF A POLIDORI SORE THROAT

Clay F. Johnson

Disembodied screams and surrealist dreams
Is what her unnatural death seemed to bring,
As dark voices—necromantic like serpent-speak—
Whisper moon-strange temptations from her grave:
Silver-carved in jasper-green bloodstone—chaos—
Colored—in honor of Persephone
Symbolizing a rebirth after death—
The same jade-opal greens as the dream-potion
Of witch's brew that she mistakenly drank,
Damning her to everlasting sleep and livid breath

Her pale-purpled bruises will never heal
    The caress of her elf-touched flesh no longer feels real

The spectral glow of dark-emerald green is
Deeply graven on her sleepless phantom,
Haunting the night ever since her eyes closed
Gurgling with demon sounds of her last memories

No c-minor requiem or key-sharped
Séance can silence the demon whispers—
Not even the lucid-sick Romantics
And their half-conscious visions of witchcraft

Nor the nightingale—the midnight composer—
Pining over a subtle-sweet numbness,
Dreaming within the pale glow of ghost candles
That fade like laudanum-maddened forgetfulness

Drawn to the deathly pale luminescence
Of the will-o'-the-wisp flame—the ghost-light—
The nightingale comes not to sing, but to dream

The slow-purpling of twilight-shadowed skies
Was never meant to encourage this hour of lies
Such a beautiful madness turned monstrous,

Elucidating unanswered questions
With the sweet-stung warmth from a poet's potion:
Trembling lips over glass-vialed secrets
Promising a Polidori sore throat

Uninvited and lost in confusions
    Within the shadow I must ask the right questions

Yet the sting soothed cool and touched not like the
Iced heat of absinthe-fire—herbal-sweet but with flame—
Nor scorch the throat or leave it bitter aching

But what it brought was the dark of demon-shadow
And the subtlest of poison-vapored breath—
I inhale their spectral musings like the
Fragrance of vanilla from grave-root blooms of death—
Moon-crystal hued like frosted spider silk
Portending a mildewed and leafless springtime

The sclera-whites now become ruby-flowered,
Twilight-irises fade to pallid grey
While unctuous flesh becomes a gelid opal-silver

I feel the flutter of the nightingale's wing
    A stranger and on my own will my demons come to sing?

Slumping down to a poet-graved coldness
With a heart still wet with dark-scarlet warmth,
It cools to promised possibilities
Without life-spontaneous expression

Yet it is not unchangeable, it grows
Thick and mangled like death-grown graveyard roots,
Twisting like cinnamon-curled witch fingers
That creep and crawl through curdling decay-cream

Enchanted by the pale glow of ghost candles—
A flickering corpse-light of the spectre's beam—
For here—where we grow—comes the nightingale to dream

Precarious of most carious bones
The color of vanilla aches with lust,
Our ruined flesh wrinkles madly in love,
Screaming helpless, but we'll never wake up.

THIS HUNGRY EARTH
by S.L. Edwards

You take the tunnel and venture down,
Into the black, hollow underground,
At the top of the world with heaven close above
Where nothing comes with you, lest even God's love.
There the air is dry, and ruthlessly cold
As you enter the mountain, carved and old.

The smells in entrap you in dark Potosí,
Where ancestors were driven unwillingly
Through chains and worn, broken feet, they were enslaved
Though the Spaniards professed it was their God who saved
The Indians from their sinful ignorance and damnation,
But "salvation" brought naught but endless starvation.

Silver has nearly ceased running through its veins
And yet still the mountain heaves with its pains.
Your ancestors' children became tied to its dirt,
Leaving you to grow up on this sad, hungry earth
While at its mouth, there open wide
Sits the god whose rituals you abide.

Though you take communion during Sunday church
It is not 'Christ' mutter when mine-beams lurch.
When your light dims and a tunnel narrows
When unknown sound and tremble harrows
It is not of the cross that you think
But of El Tío, waiting at death's brink.

At his shrine you lay pig-blood and rum,
For underground it is his will be done.
He looks upon you with stone-blank eyes
And teeth barred, as if he tries
To escape his throne and walk unbound
Through lightless miles underground.

His ears are pointed, smile playful and mean
And with a goat's face, there is a devilish glean
For now in those eyes you once thought empty
There is malevolence, latent, though plenty.

You nod to the god, bow and say your prayers,
Stepping into his domain and the mine-draft air.

You cough in an aching, bloody fit
But you bite down and you grit.
It's been a long time that you've been sick!
Poisoned, no doubt, by the fruits of your pick.
You know your lungs are shriveled, black and ill
But you shallow your bile and force your will.

There is a burning at your chest, under your shirt
A slight, cold-searing pain, a mysterious hurt.
You take a thick-gloved hand and find your cross
You forgot to remove it, but cannot afford its loss.
So you take the burn-pain and just bear,
Descending further into El Tío's Lair.

They've called him a devil, but he does not mind.
Sitting in the dark, he simply bides the time
Between essential offerings of food, rum and blood
Lest he call down a storm to burry offenders in mud.
A devil, perhaps, but beneath there is no dispute
Under the earth he is a god, and a god absolute.

Well beyond forty, you've outlived your brothers,
Those gentle souls, now gone, to meet their mothers.
Your pick his heavier than it was before,
And with youth, your eyes could see more
Into these tunnels' thick, veiling black
But now, you feel something staring back.

A phantom, surely imagined, you old fool!
You take your light, that most sacred tool
And hit it in your palm with force of habit
But when it shines, you make quite a racket
For now before you there sits a new statue
With pointed eyes, it is staring at you.

The statue glistens a jaundiced yellow
As the dark around it yawns and bellows.
Its horns point backward, tall and jagged
And its ornate shirt is now red and ragged.
At its feet lay cigars and colorful paper shreds
Left by miners, perhaps to acknowledge their debts.

You smile, bow, and mutter your greetings
Such encounters, after all, are common meetings.
Erections of new shrines come without warning

Built in the night, and found early morning.
Their makers are quiet and secretive folk
Lest they draw attention, and curiosity invoke.

The pain comes as the cross once again burns,
But your father had saved all that he earned
To give you and heirloom, worthy and divine
So to abandon it would be a monstrous crime.
But you take it off your neck and place it away
Intending to put it back on in the light of day.

You click your light off and again press further,
When in the dark, the earth shifts and murmurs!
Before you can act, a beam above you breaks,
Moving the walls around you with violent shakes!
Dirt and rocks tumble down to seal you in
While vainly from your lips, prayers begin.

Between dust-coughs, your light flickers on,
But its shade is now dim and its glimmer wan.
You collect yourself, but only to see
The statues is not where it used to be.
Now, it stands above you with wrathful grin,
Long, white-ceramic fangs spelling your end.

These are your desperate, final moments
Running madly, screaming for atonement!
But your calls fall unheard on stone ears
While behind you, his heavy footfall nears!
You've offended him, and for this you must pay
And El Tío collects his debts in only one way.

Against your face, his breath is damp and dead,
Rotten with the blasphemers on whom he has fed.
A hard, cold hand grabs you, clenches and lifts
As beyond consciousness, your mind almost drifts.
But nothing saves you from the pain of his bite
As your hungry Tío makes your crime right.

⚡

www.ingramcontent.com/pod-product-compliance
Lightning Source LLC
Chambersburg PA
CBHW020730210626
46807CB00016B/866